LOST ANGELES

Silver Bullets On The Sunset Strip

LOST ANGELES

Silver Bullets On The Sunset Strip

By

Kurt Schlichter
&
Irina Moises

Paperback Edition ISBN: 979-8-9985943-0-4

For J & J

ACKNOWLEDGEMENTS

A bunch of people helped us with *Lost Angeles* and supported previous books. Here is a non-exhaustive list: Larry O'Connor, Drew Matich, @GMFWashington, Matthew Betley, Glenn Reynolds, Hugh Hewitt, and Duane Patterson. Many others have always been supportive. So has our artist, the great Sean "Salty Hollywood" Salter. Check out his *Silence Dogood* series of graphic novels!

Thank you to everyone who got *The Attack* and who read the *People's Republic* series. As always, we appreciate Kurt's *Townhall* supporters and our Twitter and Locals followers. You guys are the best.

Of course, no acknowledgment would be complete without a shout out to Andrew Breitbart. He got this whole thing going in the first place.

KAS & IM, April 2025

PREFACE - IRINA

When Kurt brought up this project, I thought it sounded so fun – a fantasy novel we could collaborate on. That's a dream come true for this sci-fi/fantasy-loving geek. Easy peasy, right? No, not so fast there, mister. When you're married to a remarkable man like I am, who is wicked smart, quick with wit and writing, and has thirteen books already under his belt plus hundreds of columns, it becomes a bit intimidating when you mull it over in your noggin for just a little bit.

Anyway, he was great about how to do this, and how we worked through the plot and storyline has been a great time. It feels like we've had our little fun adventure through Los Angeles. What better city for the backdrop to a 1940s noir novel about gods, demigods, and mortals existing together? I hope you enjoy this fun and fantastic story set in one of my favorite cities in the world as much as I've enjoyed helping bring it to life with Kurt.

Irina

PREFACE - KURT

This book is something a little different, not part of the Kelly Turnbull/*People's Republic* series and not a stand-alone novel like *The Attack*. There's no heavy message here, though anyone except the legally blind is going to see the conservative undercurrent running through it. That was pretty much inevitable. But what it is really meant to be is fun – fun to read and fun to write with the lovely and talented Irina Moises.

Fun is underrated – one of the open secrets of Donald Trump's success has been that his movement is so much fun. He's funny, the associated memes are funny, and the videos where they are eating the dogs, they're eating the cats are funny too. It sure beats the dour misery of the left. They are forever troubled by the notion that we might be enjoying ourselves; it eats at what fragments remain of their souls.

Lost Angeles is meant to be fun, with us playing off some of our favorite genres and themes to create something wholly other. Irina and I decided to write it together since we end up working on the books together anyway – part of the fun was figuring out how to do that. Writing is easy; writing together is a challenge, but we never had any actual conflicts about where the story would go. We both threw in ideas about what would be cool or interesting or fun (of course) and went from there.

The forthcoming books will be back to the usual chaos and mayhem of the conservative novels. In the meantime, we hope you enjoy this one. Life's too short to be miserable!

Kurt

1.

The blood on the wall looked like bad art.

"Hollow point," Jed Dufrasne – he pronounced it "Du-fraz-knee" – observed, as if it wasn't obvious, as if I hadn't seen a hundred stiffs who swallowed a slug after they decided they just couldn't hack life anymore.

Jed was a detective in a hundred-dollar suit, meaning he was bent like a pretzel. I never took a buck while I was on the job, though I was offered plenty. I could have been rich and retired to Florida instead of standing in a shabby one-room flat in Hollywood looking at a day-old dead demigod—and smelling him.

"Silver bullet," Jed said, like it needed to be said. "Just like the ones you pack in that hand cannon of yours. A sawbuck a shot. You private dicks must do okay."

"I want to stop what I shoot," I said, still taking in the scene. "Demigods. Werewolves. Regular issue thugs." Under my left armpit in a cross-draw shoulder holster was my Smith & Wesson Model 27 .357 Magnum with a 4-inch barrel and six cylinders of 158-grain Western Cartridge Company Silver Special hollow points. The 27 was the new kid on the block of wheel guns, coming out five years earlier in 1935. I used to carry a government-issue Colt M1911 .45 automatic, but that brought back too many memories.

"Yeah, Eddie Loud, the gunfighter. How many notches you got on that grip?"

"Enough," I said, but Jed was Jed, and he wasn't letting go. My old partner, Jimmy Duggan, was his lieutenant and probably put him on the case just to bust my chops.

It was working.

"Did himself with a Luger," Jed observed. That was some prime police work right there. The German pistol was lying in the dead demigod's lap.

"You got experience with Lugers, don't ya, war hero?" He leered at me like a dog eying a bone.

Bringing up the war was low, even for him. I considered decking Jed right then and there, but adding his blood and teeth to the mess would have queered the crime scene, and I was always a detective first. I just added him to the Loud List of guys needing some payback. His time would come.

I got back to what I was being paid for.

The dead guy was Alexander Georgiou. He didn't look so good, and not just because m of the back of his head was missing. Most demigods have a shine about them, a kind of glow. Everyone can see it clearly in quarterbreeds or eighths. I'm kind of an expert, and I can see it even in a thirty-second or sixty-fourth. After that, it kind of becomes indistinguishable from being handsome, or in the case of a woman, beautiful.

But as they age, as the decades turn to centuries, the shine fades. There's nothing sadder, particularly when that's all a demi has going for him. From what was left of his face, I could see Alexander was on the long fade. He was losing his shine, and there were even wrinkles. That had to be hard. His hair, where it wasn't matted in scarlet, was too black. The poor son of a bitch was dyeing it, probably with shoe polish.

Imagine that you are part god – not *the* God, but a fractional descendant of one of the Olympians – and after you live a few human lifetimes, you suddenly realize the Grim Reaper is coming for you, too. Georgiou was just 332 years old, according to his Federal Department of Deities papers. I guess that was time enough and he didn't want to waste away. He pulled the trigger while he was still at least a shadow of what he had been during his three centuries of prime.

A lot of normal people hate the demis. They think the demigods have it easy. The looks, the powers, the lifespan. But there is something sad about them, too. I get that. And I still don't trust them.

"Okay, so you got to see the stiff. I've given you your professional courtesy. Now it's your turn to give some back. What do you know about this, Eddie?"

I knew that a rich widow named Cheryl McCleary, former bride of Enos McClearly, the late Southern Californian King of Frozen Chicken, had been out with Georgiou the night before last at Ciro's. I knew it had turned ugly. Cheryl poured a few too many slugs of Taittinger bubbly down her piehole and started getting loud. She started yelling about how Georgiou was getting old, that if she was going to support her own demi gigolo he ought to at least have some lead in his pencil.

The other patrons laughed. That's one thing demis can't take – normals laughing at them. They feed on adoration, but mockery is poison. It is the ugly vengeance of the undivine. Georgiou ran out of the club as they hooted and howled.

I talked to the thick Polish lady who ran the rooming house where we stood before the cops got to her. She was new to America, having got out of the homeland just ahead of Hitler and Stalin's hordes a few months before, but I figured out what she was saying even though her English was like five miles of bad road. Georgiou came home at about one a.m. with a $1 bottle of Wannamaker's Scotch rot gut in his paw – it was standing near empty on the desk by his corpse – and rushed upstairs. She didn't hear the shot. It was muffled by his mouth.

"I got hired to check on him," I told Jed. He grunted.

It was true. A different rich widow had come by my office yesterday, frantic for me to find her missing beau. He had stood her up for their lunch date and he was not answering his phone. It wasn't like him, she explained. Apparently, she did not have much experience with demis. It was exactly like them when dealing with normals.

I could read my client like a book. She had fallen hard for her Adonis, thrilled that an heir of Apollo – no matter how distant – was falling for her. That was one thing demis knew how to do, one thing they could do without breaking the laws against abusing their powers. They could make mortals *feel*. She was pushing fifty and lonely and Romeo had swooped in, with his continental charm and his Apollonian heritage, and taught her how to love again in about two short weeks. I took her case and her $200 a day and looked into it.

My secretary Gladys called around to the clubs to see if he had been in any. I keep good relations with the staff at all the usual places with generous tips, and they are happy to help. In the meantime, I headed to his North Hollywood rooming house from my office on Robertson in Beverly Hills and knocked on his room door. Nothing. I sniffed. Nothing. He hadn't been stewing long enough to stink. I left.

It took Gladys about an hour to establish that he had a rotation of rich, aging widows that he squired through the various nightclubs along the Strip. She passed on the Ciro's tip, and I headed over to Sunset. I spread some dollars around to the busboys. They gave me the Cheryl story. I had a gut feeling this was not going to have a Hollywood ending.

I called asking for Jimmy Duggan at my old haunt, the Los Angeles Police Department's Deity Affairs Division – among ourselves, we called it "the God Squad." Me, Jimmy, and Joe Dale Vance, now the commie head-busting lead detective of the Red Squad, were patrolmen together. We used to talk of us moving on to bigger and better things, and these were apparently our bigger and better things. They were senior detectives and I was sniffing around demi two-timers for money.

When I got a hold of Jimmy, I strongly suggested a welfare check on my demi Romeo. Jimmy sent Jed; the bent detective probably didn't have a payoff to pick up that day and Jimmy thought it would look good for his minion to be seen getting off his ass and doing cop work once in a while.

"He was juggling lonely hearts," I told Jed. "I guess he saw that his prospects were diminishing."

"One of them prospects hired you, right?"

"Yeah," I said. There was no sense in denying it. "I'd like to keep her out of it."

"She should have got herself a cat," Jed said. "Well, you better go before the feds get here."

I didn't like feds, and they didn't like me. I started for the door.

Too late.

A G-man in a black Sears suit had bluffed his way past the rookie patrolmen on sentry duty and walked into the room. He produced his credentials – Special Agent James Randolph Connolly of the Federal Bureau of Investigations, Deities Branch. Probably a jumped-up mick who graduated Fordham and joined the Bureau because carrying a gun and a badge seemed more fun than carrying a briefcase. These guys were always impressed with themselves. I never understood why.

J. Edgar Hoover had made certain his boys got the federal demigod law enforcement portfolio. Word is he found his contacts in the deity world useful for tips and even predictions. Divination is not illegal if you do it for the cops. He no doubt added whatever dirt his boys collected to his famous files on the rich and powerful. He liked dirt, but that was not all he liked. Word was also – confirmed by a sybil I had busted for illegal stock tip soothsaying before Hoover's guys took her out of my hands and disappeared her into federal custody – that J. Edgar liked to hold Georgetown dinner parties where he dressed up like Shirley Temple and sang "Good Ship Lollipop."

"Is that the dead demigod?" Agent Connolly asked, pointing at the stiff.

"No, he went out for coffee and crullers," I said. "That's some other guy."

"You need to show a little respect," he replied. "I'm a federal agent."

"And I'm Ethel Merman," I said.

"Hey, hey, we're all on the same side," Jed said. As usual, he was lying.

"The meat wagon is here to take the stiff," Connolly announced. The federal government always took demigod bodies. They never said what for, but I might imagine why if I wanted to spoil my appetite.

"I'm done here," I told Jed, and I started for the door again. The fed put his hand on my chest to stop me.

"Where do you think you're going?" he said.

"You take your mitt off me or you'll take back a stump," I told him.

"Gentlemen, please," Jed said, intervening. "No need for this. I'll give you feds a complete report. Then I gotta go up into the Hollywood Hills and tell Apollo's mortal majordomo that one of her boss's hundreds of great-great-great grandsons did himself."

Agent Connolly backed off, wisely. I walked past him and out the door and away from the smell of day-old demigod.

"Workers of the world unite!"

There were about a dozen raggedly commies walking through the Miracle Mile along Wilshire at La Brea by the E. Clem Wilson Building, shouting slogans as I drove back to the office after a stop at a bar. They dressed like the unemployed guys during the Depression, except these guys never got jobs after it ended. I never met a communist who worked for a living, except the ones in Hollywood. And all they did was type.

Up ahead was another cluster of knuckleheads dressed in crisp tan slacks and brown shirts with swastika armbands. The two sets of creeps were heading toward each other. I considered pulling over to watch Stalin's flunkies and Hitler's minions have it out – no matter who lost, America won.

But I had work to do, so my entertainment would have to wait. I could only hope that they would rumble, that just one would be left standing, and that the LAPD's Red Squad would knock his teeth out with a truncheon before hauling them all in. When the war came to America, and it was coming sooner or later no matter how often FDR promised not to send our boys overseas again, these idiots were not going to be tolerated. We didn't go fight to come home and turn our country over to Reds or Nazis. But for now, they walked the streets like they owned them.

"Can I get you a drink, Mrs. Darcy?"

She was sitting in a leather chair, her round, red face buried in my handkerchief. It muffled her sobs.

"Gladys, can you get Mrs. Darcy a Dewars with ice?" I figured that if that was not her favorite tipple – and she looked like she had a favorite tipple – then at least it would get the job done and maybe slow or even stop the waterworks. I hate seeing a woman cry.

"But he loved me!" she declared, looking at me for affirmation.

"Of course," I replied. "And maybe he did what he did because he could not be worthy of your love in return."

"You think so?"

"I think if he could not live faithfully, he preferred not to live at all."

She smiled a little. Now she had something to hold onto as a souvenir of her two weeks of aging demigod ecstasy. Gladys handed her a tumbler with two fingers of whiskey and a pair of clinking ice cubes. Mrs. Darcy demurred.

"I take it neat, dear. And top it off if you would."

Gladys smiled wanly, shot me a glance, and walked back to the bar cart. Mrs. Darcy composed herself until Gladys returned and handed her the tumbler. The unmerry widow took a long sip – almost a gulp, but still ladylike.

"He knew Napoleon, you know," she said to me. "Yes, Napolean. He was there in the French Revolution. They were chopping off demigod heads with a silver guillotine. Then Napoleon came and he met him. He was there with him in Egypt when they shot off the Sphinx's nose."

"Fascinating," I said. I was not fascinated. Every demigod had stories, and if you don't stick a sock in their mouth they will tell you them all. You live a couple of centuries and something interesting is bound to happen to you, even if, like most demis, you are mostly concerned with living comfortably off the kindness of mortals.

"It's just such a loss," she said, taking another long sip. "So much history, so much life, cut so tragically short."

"At least he died for the sake of love," Gladys offered.

"Yes," Mrs. Darcy said. "I was lucky to have two great loves in my life. My husband Harold and Alexander."

"The memory of your great romance will be a comfort to you," I said. "Now, I must return to my work. But there is the matter of the remainder of my fee."

Mrs. Darcy nodded. She pulled up her purse and took out another wad of bills.

"The other $500, since you found him so quickly." She handed it over.

As she finished her Dewars, I counted the bills. "Trust but verify" is my motto. I picked it up at The Trocadero one night when I overheard Ronald Reagan saying it to Jane Wyman at the next table.

"You think she'll make it home? She's gotta be soused," Gladys asked after we had closed the door behind Mrs. Darcy.

"Not our problem," I said. "I think I'll punch out early and go home and shower. I smell like dead demigod."

"That's just your lousy cologne," Gladys said. "I keep telling you that you need to stop buying it from your haberdasher and buy it at a department store from a woman or a sissy. Anyway, you have a two o'clock."

"Another lonely hearts caper?"

"Seems like it. Now, hand over the dough."

"It's my dough."

"It's the company's dough and the company's got bills and debts. This office costs a fortune, and you just bought a $100 suit and a $30 fedora."

"I have an image to maintain. My clients are Hollywood stars, Olympians, and the people sucked up into those worlds. They like me classy."

"You can keep $100 and that should do you for a week."

I reluctantly handed the cash to Gladys, but I kept $200. I had a lot of palms to grease – mortal and otherwise – to get the skinny I needed to do my job. Plus, I liked money.

"I am Miss Constance Showers."

She was tall for a woman, and her hat made her taller. A bit of thin black lace draped below the brim of her fascinator, obscuring her face. I could tell it was a fine one, with porcelain skin and sharp features framed by black peek-a-boo hair. Her dress was tight where it needed to be but with all the deniability required of a proper woman.

I brought her in and sat her down where Mrs. Darcy had been an hour before. She declined a drink, and she eschewed pleasantries. She got right to it.

"I am looking for a demigod, Mr. Loud, and I have heard that you are the man to come to for people in that position in Los Angeles."

"In the biz we call it 'Lost Angeles.' Dealing with the demis is my job, Miss Showers. Who is he, and does he want to be found?"

"You assume it's a he."

"I think it's a safe assumption."

"It is. His name – his current name, because he has used many during his long life – is Charles Gaultier. And I expect he is desperate to be found."

"I've heard the name."

"He is a halfbreed."

"Now that's impressive. Fifty percent deity. Who was his father?"

"Again, you assume a male."

"It's always a male," I replied. That was not technically true. In the olden days you would get female deities mating with humans, including some of the Divine Dozen – before they became the Enduring Eleven. But, as a practical matter after the major Olympians were forbidden by law from breeding, only the males could jump the fence undetected. And now, the problem for them was holding off eager women who wished to bear a half-demigod child.

"It is a male," she said. "Our own Apollo, right up there in his mansion in the Hollywood Hills."

"Did he send you?"

"Suspicious. I like that. It probably serves you well in your profession. No, Apollo did not send me. As you no doubt know, Apollo is notorious for his, shall we say, lack of interest in his progeny."

"I assume because there are so many," I replied. Perhaps half of the demis out there traced their lineage to Apollo, and in America there were over 36,000 registered demis – people with greater than or equal to 1/64th divine blood. And maybe several million with less, but they did not really count. Apollo was one busy and turgid demigod back in the day.

"Why do you want to find him?" I asked.

"I have my reasons."

"Romantic ones?"

She paused, a look of disapproval spreading across her face beneath that peek-a-boo hair.

"I ask because it will help me find him if I know all the facts. I do not make any judgments about divine/mortal relationships."

This was untrue. I disliked them both as a practical and a moral matter.

"No, we are not lovers if that is what you are getting at. Mr. Gaultier is currently unmarried and unattached. He has had a dozen or so wives and I expect he is tired of burying them. He focuses on work and charity. He is a successful businessman and has been for nearly a thousand years. I am, for lack of a better word, his majordomo. I assist him, and have for several years. Moreover, Mr. Gaultier has many partners in his various endeavors, and they are likewise worried that some foul play has befallen him."

"What kind of foul play?"

"I do not know. Mr. Gualtier is an exceptionally moral and upright man. He is a devout Catholic and he tithes to his parish. Obviously, he rejects any attempts at worship."

Now that was unusual. Most demis lapped it up on the sly.

"Lots of people have secrets," I said.

"Not him. He is a man of integrity. He achieves not through illegal powers but with talent and hard work. And now he is gone. We do not know why."

"I can try to help. And we have one advantage as we start our search."

"Which is?"

"We know he's not dead."

This was true. A halfbreed who inherited immortality – not all did, but Gaultier clearly had – cannot die. The original twelve Olympians – Zeus, Hera, Poseidon, Demeter, Athena, Apollo, Artemis, Hephaestus, Aphrodite, Hermes, Dionysus, and the unfortunate Ares – were all immortal. They could neither grow old and die nor be killed by disease or violence. Their children with mortals who inherited the gift were likewise immune from misadventure – you could blow holes in them with pure silver bullets and it would only make them mad, while silver slugs could kill the quarters and down. You get to the 1/64ths and a few lead slugs would put them away. Whether a non-mortal halfbreed might ever grow old was unknown – none had in recorded history. Perhaps in a thousand years they would. Even some quarters were still going after an eon.

"That's a comforting thought, though not entirely," Miss Showers replied. "Of course, we know of Ares's fate, which was far worse than death."

The Doom of Ares kept the Olympians in check, keeping them from freely exercising the full scope of their powers. Even an Olympian was limited in power by nature. He could change form, call down curses, have lightning strike, sometimes tell the future, things like that. They were never omnipotent, but they could – if they sought to – use their powers to openly change human history. This was intolerable, and the punishment Ares suffered when he tried to was so horrible that the Olympians had refrained from doing so ever since.

In 1462, Romanian prince Vlad Tepes – known forever as Vlad the Drowner, Vlad the Vampire or, sometimes, Vlad the Impaler – was defending his nation against the invading Ottoman Turks under Mehmed II. He retreated ahead of the force, scorching the Earth before the invaders. But the Turkish potentate had a plan, one common to rulers in the Balkans. He would enlist an Olympian to aid his army. Of course, an Olympian was not omnipotent; they were not like the real God. They became tired quickly exercising their powers; they could not destroy a whole army, but an Olympian could do great damage. Mehmed II would set Ares upon the enemy monarch; with Vlad dead, his army would shatter.

Ares agreed, wooed by the promise of a million worshippers and likely by the chance to practice his art, war.

Yet Vlad was cunning. He knew that nothing, not even silver, could kill an immortal. But silver could neutralize one. He gathered all the silver in his kingdom and made his plan. With great stealth, his men infiltrated the field palace of Ares while he lay drunk on ambrosia and bound him in silver chains. The demigod was then whisked in front of Vlad, who mocked Ares before sealing him inside a silver box shaped like a coffin. He then ordered his men to sail to the middle of the Black Sea and dump it overboard.

Somewhere, nearly a mile below the surface, lies Ares in his silver tomb, trapped, cursed to struggle and scream for eternity in the frigid depths. Even if Poseidon was inclined to look for him – and he was not – he would never have found him. The silver coffin would hide its captive forever.

The remaining eleven demigods, already pressed by Christianity and losing worshippers, reevaluated their relationship with the mortals. A demigod could easily destroy a hundred knights; he could destroy a second hundred knights, but that would exhaust him. But a third hundred knights would come with their silver chains and seize the demigod and sink him into black horror. And men understood this too.

Both immortal and mortal understood the calculus had changed. For the next six hundred years, they had behaved, for the most part. Though immensely powerful, they would no longer seek to rule over men or directly control their affairs.

"We know Mr. Gaultier is not dead," Miss Showers agreed. "Though I am not sure he would not take death if offered. Immortality is a burden we mortals cannot understand or appreciate."

Not dying did not seem so bad to me after the Argonne Forest. I changed the subject to something more pleasant.

"There is the matter of my fee."

She answered before I could tell her.

"Two hundred a day, plus expenses. And a thousand upon locating him."

I liked that answer. She would have my undivided efforts.

"You really do want him back."

"I do. But I also realize that there may be...competitors."

"Competitors?"

"I am not the only one looking for Mr. Gaultier."

"That could complicate things."

"You are being well paid to deal with the complications. Where will you begin?"

"At the beginning. Take me to his house."

2.

I drove since Miss Showers had come by cab. We headed out along Olympic Boulevard in my black 1939 Buick Century. Ladies liked its style; I liked the 320-cubic-inch straight-eight engine that gave me 141 horsepower to get out of trouble as fast as I got into it.

My office was on the 600 block of Robertson, just south of Santa Monica Boulevard in Beverly Hills. We were heading northeast to Los Feliz. We would pass under the new Cahuenga Pass Freeway, which would open in a month and connect Hollywood to Burbank and the Valley.

I had the window down. According to the sign on a Crocker Bank branch, it was 72 degrees.

"Mr. Loud," Miss Showers said to break the silence. "Is that a German name?"

"Scot, I think. I'm cheap and long for the moors."

She smiled wanly beneath her lace.

"His house is up the hill on Glendower Avenue."

"Just under the Griffith Park Observatory?"

"Nearby. It's a rather exclusive area."

"He is the son of a demigod."

"Mr. Gaultier always tried to put that aside. He prefers to be known for what he does rather than who he is."

"In my experience spoiled demi kids never have to work or struggle, and so they do nothing except enjoy themselves and exploit mortals."

"Not Mr. Gaultier. He loved mortals. He was a philanthropist. He understood his rare status and tried to use it for good."

"You are using the past tense, Miss Showers."

The house was remarkable, less a mansion than a Mayan temple planted on a Los Angeles hillside. I pulled up on Glendower in front of it and just took it in. Sure, I had seen it before, but now it really struck me.

It was a huge, squat structure that took up half a block. It perched on the hillside overlooking downtown. Its façade consisted of tan and grey cement blocks, some blank and some decorated with geometric designs.

"It's called the Ennis House. Frank Lloyd Wright was the architect," Miss Showers said as I pulled up to the black wrought iron gate. An attendant rushed out, squinted, and being satisfied it was Miss Showers, pulled it open. I drove inside and parked. The gate clanged shut behind us.

The inside was dark and cold, with all right angles and straight edges. The walls were the same as outside – concrete blocks, perhaps? We continued through the hallway and the servants nodded but left us be.

"He went missing the night before last," Miss Showers said. "He was last seen by his butler at nine in the evening when he was brought his nightly glass of ambrosia in the study."

"Ambrosia is illegal," I noted. It was the only thing that truly got near-pure-blood demigods drunk, and you do not want one of them drunk.

Miss Showers smiled. "A harmless indulgence. He never drank to excess,"

"Maybe the butler did it," I suggested as we continued through the mansion.

"Wellington is nearing eighty and has been serving Mr. Gaultier for a half-century. He is beside himself with concern."

"Can I talk to him?"

"Certainly, if you wish, but we have already established that he neither saw nor heard anything. It was Wellington who discovered that his master was missing when he brought Mr. Gaultier's morning coffee to his bedroom."

"I will talk with him," I said, but we had just walked into the main living room. I was taken aback first by the stunning late-afternoon view of the city framed by two ornate rectangular columns. Then my eyes were drawn to the decorations. It was a tribute to Mr. Gaultier, who had always been a handsome and fit specimen. I could tell by the dozens of art pieces—paintings, drawings, statuary, and even photos depicting him.

"A tapestry?" I exclaimed. There was one hanging on the wall, obviously very old, showing the adventures of a young knight slaying what appeared to be Englishmen and a dragon.

"It's from Brittany, where he was born and raised. Apparently, Apollo seduced a minor princess while traveling the lands, and so he began. You understand that for minor nobility, allowing a daughter to be taken with child by an Olympian, even outside the bounds of Christian marriage, was quite prestigious."

"Just how old is Mr. Gaultier?"

"He celebrated his thousand-year birthday five years ago."

"I'm no art expert, but those look to my untrained eye like Renaissance art."

She pointed to one where Gaultier posed with a cuirass and long sword.

"Michelangelo," she said. "Priceless, of course. If you meet him – when you meet him – ask him about watching the painting of the Sistine Chapel."

"I'll make a note. Did anyone see any sign of struggle? Actually, let me go back a step. Is there a car missing?"

"Mr. Gaultier had many skills, but driving was not one of them. His car is in the garage and his driver was home with his family. The neighbors confirmed it."

"You did some of your own investigation."

"And reached a dead end. As for your question about a struggle, there was no sign of one in his bedroom or the study where he took his ambrosia."

"Take me to the study," I said.

The study was impressive in its own way. The shelves, rich, dark mahogany, were loaded with ancient books. It was clear they were not well cared for. The room smelled like mildew and money.

It was bright, though, with an angular iron chandelier whose six bulbs cast off a great deal of light. You would need it for reading.

An ornate dark wood desk, maybe maple, was to one side. There was a fireplace with a marble mantle that was clearly an add-on since it clashed with the modernist style of the rest of the building. Above it hung a crucifix.

"Devout," I muttered to myself.

There was a reading chair as well, overstuffed and low, with a marble-topped side table adjacent to it. The furniture did not quite fit, at least, I did not think so. But what the hell do I know?

The side table bothered me. It took me a moment, but then it hit me. It was not quite next to the comfy chair.

"You said there was no sign of a struggle, right?" I asked.

"Correct," Miss Showers answered.

"Can you go get the butler?"

"Wellington?"

"Sure, whatever his name is. Can you bring him here?"

Miss Showers exited as I continued to look over the scene.

She returned in a couple of minutes with Wellington, who looked every bit his age. His mouth hung open a little as if he was beyond caring about his own aesthetics.

"You're the butler?"

He blinked a couple of times. "What?" he asked.

"You are the butler?" I repeated, only louder.

"You want butter?"

"Wellington is a little hard of hearing," Miss Showers added superfluously.

This time, I illustrated my deposition by pointing at him and nearly shouting.

"You are the butler."

"Yes."

"Was there anyone else on the household staff here that night?"

"No," he replied.

"You brought Mr. Gaultier ambrosia about nine?"

"Ambrosia, yes," Wellington wheezed.

"What did you do then?"

"He released me for the evening, so I went to my room downstairs and went to bed."

I did not need to ask if he heard nothing. He clearly heard nothing.

"Was there a mess in the study in the morning?"

"A mess?"

"Was it out of order in here?"

Wellington shook his head. "Oh no. Everything was in order."

"And you took his empty glass back to the kitchen in the morning, right?"

"His glass?"

"The ambrosia."

Wellington furrowed his brow. "I suppose so."

"You suppose, or you did?"

"I must have because I brought him a glass that night."

I looked over to Miss Showers, who seemed to savvy what I was getting at.

"Thank you, Wellington. You've been a great help."

"Please bring the master home," he implored me.

"We will do our best," Miss Showers assured him. He turned and shuffled out the door, but I was already on my hands and knees next to the side table, running my hands over the reddish-brown hardwood floor.

"Ouch," I said, keeping my language clean in the presence of a lady. I lifted up my paw, and there was a scarlet trickle of blood going down my palm.

"Glass," I said. "Someone cleaned up, but quickly."

I moved closer to the bookshelves behind the chair and the table, glancing back and forth, calculating the angles. I then moved closer to the shelves, trying not to block the light cast from the chandelier. It took me a few seconds, but I found it.

"Blood," I said.

"Yours?"

"Your friend's. Come here. There's not a lot, and they must have missed it when they cleaned up. Dried splatter, from the chair."

Miss Showers knelt and squinted where I was pointing.

"Blood."

"He got hit, probably in the head, while in the chair and fell over the table. The glass broke, so they did a quick clean-up and put the table back upright, but not exactly where it should be."

"But how do you make a halfbreed bleed?"

"A silver blackjack across the noggin. Enough to cut and stun him. They had to work fast."

"Work fast?"

"To bind him in silver to take him."

"They would need a lot of silver."

"Yeah," I replied. A lot of illegal silver.

"You think that's what happened?" Miss Showers asked.

"I do. And one more thing. Whoever came in here to get Mr. Gaultier knew there was only one servant and that he was deaf as a post."

"Meaning?"

"Meaning, as we used to say in the Army, someone did his reconnaissance, or you have a traitor in your organization."

I left Miss Showers at the Ennis House and began my drive not to Beverly Hills but to Santa Monica. There was a guy I needed to talk to. It was nearly six, but the June sun was still high over the Pacific. I flipped on the radio. The Pirates were just finishing up beating the Braves back at Forbes Field in

Pittsburgh 14-2. Not my cities, not my teams – when the hell was LA going to get a pro club of its own?

The news came on. It was bad – the Germans were continuing their blitzkrieg across France and the Brits were reeling. Their new prime minister, Winston Churchill, was announcing that they had managed to take most of the beleaguered British Army off the beaches at Dunkirk. My mind flashed back to France, to the muddy holes and rat-infested trenches.

It was 72 degrees under the palm trees lining the streets and I still shivered. But that was old war – this was new war, a lightning war, all fast movement by planes and tanks. My gut told me that we Yanks would be back in the thick of Europe's blood feuds soon enough.

Winnie went on:

> *Even though large tracts of Europe and many old and famous States have fallen or may fall into the grip of the Gestapo and all the odious apparatus of Nazi rule, we shall not flag or fail. Together, mortal and divine, We shall go on to the end, we shall fight in France, we shall fight on the seas and oceans, we shall fight with growing confidence and growing strength in the air, we shall defend our Island, whatever the cost may be, mortal and divine, we shall fight on the beaches, we shall fight on the landing grounds, we shall fight in the fields and in the streets, we shall fight in the hills; we shall never surrender, and even if, which I do not for a moment believe, this Island or a large part of it were subjugated and starving, then our Empire beyond the seas, armed and guarded by the British Fleet, would carry on the struggle, until, in God's good time, the New World, with all its power and might, steps forth to the rescue and the liberation of the old.*

I have to say that Old Winston got me right here. I knew the Hun from personal experience, in my sights and at the sharp end of a bayonet, and from my experience with the Nazi variety, I despised them even more then than I had even when I was fighting them. America would be fighting them again soon, and I resolved that we damn well better finish it this time.

3.

I was making good time heading west on Wilshire toward Santa Monica and the beach when I saw it behind me, candy apple red and top down. I knew the ride, a 1939 Alfa Romeo 6C 2500 Super Sport. There were only a few in car-crazed Los Angeles, mostly driven by dizzy starlets and gifted by their producer beaus. Love always comes with a price tag in sunny Lost Angeles.

But there was one that belonged to someone else, someone who meant trouble with a capital "T."

I hoped it wasn't her.

After a few blocks, the scarlet sports car peeled off to the left up San Vicente toward Brentwood. I confess that I sighed in relief. I had plenty of trouble heaped on my plate already, and there was no room for another helping.

There was some traffic going west toward the Pacific, but I was in no real hurry. The guy I was looking for did not keep banker's hours.

Goldman Jewelers was on Third Street with a big neon diamond on the sign out front. Stan Goldman catered to everyone. You got picked up by a smiling salesman when you walked in the front door and walked to where you needed to be. Sailors and their girls who just met, got soused and decided to get hitched were walked to the left, where they picked among the $200 and $300 wedding rings. Their salesman, dressed in a crisp suit for that classy look, was only too happy to help prepare the Department of the War allotment form to take out the $10 a month to pay for it. With interest, that $200 band could be paid off in 50 months.

Look like you had a few bucks in your pocket and you got walked to the right. Once there, they felt you out and decided what they could wring out of you. Movie stars were always welcome; they usually came from nothing and thought nothing about spending their latest check on whatever was shiny and got them the girl.

And then there was the third category that Goldman catered to. I was one of those, the folks on the fuzzy edge of the law.

"How can I help you?" inquired an oily fellow who looked like he should be tying an ingenue to the train tracks in a Roy Roger oater.

"Tell Stan that Eddie Loud's here," I told him. He frowned.

"Mr. Goldman," he said emphatically, "is with a customer. Perhaps you might wish to wait."

I was about to object when an eager-looking GI with private stripes on his brown Class A sleeves bounded in, his giddy fiancé in tow.

"I'm shipping to Camp Roberts in the morning!" he blurted out. "We gotta get married!"

"Take a hike, private," I said. "Or you'll be paying on that ring long after she's run off with Jody."

He looked crestfallen; the salesman looked worse.

"Kid, I was killing Jerries before you were an itch in your daddy's dungarees. Take it from an old lieutenant who's seen too many times how this movie ends. You kids run along now."

The kid and his girl backed out of the store. I hope they had fun and that he ended up giving her a few good memories but no alimony.

"Now, I'm going to stand here and greet every single customer who walks in your door until you get Stan Goldman's backside out here. You read me?"

The salesman stifled his urge to mouth off, probably figuring that was a bad idea, did an about-face, and marched off into the back room. I took out a Lucky Strike and my Zippo. Another couple came in, a smug fellow and his haughty girl, and they looked at me like I was stealing their oxygen even though I hadn't lit up yet.

"You came to the right place. They'll take good care of you," I assured them as another oily salesman hustled them away to first-class stock on the right.

Stan Goldman emerged from the back, scowling. The salesman was nowhere to be seen, but he had his shaved ape Louie with him. It occurred to me that Louie might be a golem, but I didn't check under his tongue for the slip of paper with the scripture that animated him. It didn't really matter. Louie was a rock, but he was useful for collecting from customers who stopped paying. Louie was a necessity because Stan had a sideline that brought in some questionable characters, even more questionable than me.

Golem or meathead, Louie could pound me into next week given the order and the opportunity. I kept an eye on him.

"Eddie Loud," Stan proclaimed, spitting out my name like it was a curse word. He did not extend a hand. Louie just stood there, looming a good six inches and fifty pounds over me, breathing through his open mouth, waiting for instructions. Louie was not the self-starter type.

"Hi, Stan," I said, ignoring the slight. "We gotta talk."

"Then talk," he said. "But make it quick. I got business to do and no time to waste on some gumshoe with questions."

Stan's last name may have been "Goldman," but he was a man known – to those in the know – for something else.

Silver.

"I need to know if you've had any big buyers lately. Not little odds and ends you sell at 300 percent markup to boys who want to impress their girlfriends. Big buyers. Like a few pounds."

"No idea what you're talking about."

I sighed. So he was going to play dumb.

"Silver, Stan. Element Ag. Shine. Demikiller."

I saw his eyes twitch, and I knew. He got his composure back.

"Selling silver is illegal without a license. Roosevelt collected it all up and stuck it in Fort Knox. National security, right? Now, Joe Citizen can only get it for approved purposes from an approved dealer. And I ain't approved."

"Hence the 300 percent markup you put on it before you push it out the back door. Cut the crap, Stan. I know somebody was buying and you're the go-to for illegal silver on the Westside. So let's stop doing the foxtrot and you tell me who it was and I go away."

"I got a better idea," Stan said. "How about Louie makes you go away right now? For good."

I looked at Louie, and he looked at me, mouth open to facilitate breathing. I could see his tongue in there, like a pink slug.

Back in the Meuse-Argonne, when we were crouching in a trench surrounded by the jerries, my commander – Captain Nathan Holderman, who later got the Medal of Honor – told me, "When in doubt, go over the top." So, we did, and the Huns were so shocked by the sight of a hundred screaming Americans with M1917 bayonets stuck to the end of their M1903 Springfields rising out of the ground that they turned and ran.

Best man I ever knew. He came home and, instead of cashing in on his war hero fame, he went to work running the California State Veterans Home. Every month, Nathan Holderman got a check from Eddie Loud to help him do it, a fat one when I was flush and a fat one when I wasn't.

So, what would Captain Holderman do in my predicament? I knew.

I went over the top.

My hand slid under my jacket and grabbed the handle of my .357. I was fast, but damned if that lummox wasn't faster. I got my piece out, and one of those meaty paws slapped it out of my hand, sending it bouncing around the foyer.

I took my best shot. I swung hard at the golem's jaw, connecting with four knuckles. I know how to punch – I used to push leather a little bit in the Army – and when I hit a man, it hurts. But Louie was not a man. He was maybe three men. I might as well have slugged an oak tree.

"Damn," I spat as I realized my hand hurt a hell of a lot more than my opponent's face did.

Now, it was Louie's turn. He sure was fast for someone so big. That fist came out of nowhere and next thing I knew I was slamming into the wall and sliding down it. When you get hit, you sometimes see stars. I saw a galaxy.

The swell and his dame came out of the right side room and looked at the tableau, eyes bulging.

"We're closed. Get out," Stan said, and the couple beat feet out the front door. Their salesman vanished into the back.

Stan was queering a big sale. This was serious.

"Break him in two, put him in his trunk, and drive the pieces out to a hole in the desert," Stan told his minion.

"Murder, huh?" I said, looking around for my gat – the bad news it was ten feet away. "I guess I guessed right about the silver."

"Good-bye, Eddie," Stan said. Louie, his face still the same, took a step in my direction.

"You boys finished with your fun and games?"

It was a woman's voice, sweet like honey but with some habanero pepper mixed in. I had a feeling about who it was, and I looked over, and I was right.

She had dark black hair like Veronica Lake and a grey coat over a blue skirt. There was a red scarf wrapped around her neck. But it was her skin that you noticed. She had a glow, a shine you usually only see in a demi. I knew she wasn't one, but you could be fooled into thinking so.

In her delicate left hand, she held a Star Model CO automatic, tiny, chrome, and engraved. It was little, but that bee could sting. An elegant gun for an elegant lady.

"Who the hell are you?" Stan demanded.

"That, gentleman," I said, dragging myself up to my feet, "is Miss Gamble."

"Trixie Gamble," my savior elaborated. "Hello, Eddie."

"I thought that was you following me in the red coupe," I said, now fully upright. The stars were largely gone.

"Why don't you turn around, little lady, and let the men do their business," Stan said.

"Now it's my business, too," she said, smiling a little, in that honey and habanero voice.

"You think that pea shooter is going to stop Louie here?"

"Mr. Goldman, I once shot a fat boy in the liver with a .25, and he folded like a house of cards."

"I don't need Louie to handle some dame," Stan said.

She paused for a moment. Her eyes went wide and left us, then came right back. Stan was too fascinated to take advantage of the moment, and Louie was Louie.

"Oh, Mr. Goldman, if you do what you are thinking you'll regret it. So, don't."

But he did. And it was like Trixie knew how he was going to come at her and was sidestepping him before she even started stepping. She dropped the barrel and crack! She put one of those pea-sized slugs right in the side of his left knee.

Stan screamed like a little girl as he fell. Louie was taking it all in, face blank, and that took the attention off me. I dived for my piece and scooped it up.

Stan was rolling on the ground, shrieking, and Louie finally decided to follow his last order and stepped toward me. The big barrel came up on him.

"Stan, call off your gorilla because this .357 will *remove* his liver."

"I think you should listen to the man, Stan," Trixie added. The .25 was now pointed at something higher up than his knee, at the kind of jewels Stan didn't sell.

"Hold on, hold on, Louie!" Stan yelled, and then he groaned. "You shot me! You shot me!"

"I told you not to do it, and you didn't listen," Trixie said sadly, more sad than you would have expected. "They never listen."

"Stan," I said, waving the barrel of my black piece toward the right side room, why don't you send King Kong here away. He makes me nervous. I think he thinks I'm a banana."

Stan nodded at his golem and Louie stepped out. That let me relax a little. I wasn't sure if six silver hollow points were enough to stop him.

"Now, I think you two were talking before things got out of hand, am I right?" Trixie asked sweetly.

"Yeah," I said. "Stan here was about to tell me about a big silver buyer he had recently."

"Now, why would someone want a lot of silver?" Trixie asked, but I expect she already suspected the answer. What the hell was she doing there anyway?

"I don't ask and they don't tell," Stan said, still holding that knee. A thin red trickle of blood was oozing out between his fingers and pooling underneath on the linoleum.

"We've established there was somebody," I said. "Now, I want a name."

"I can't!"

"You do have another knee," Trixie observed.

"The lady's right. You're already going to be on crutches. Don't make it a wheelchair."

"I said I can't tell you!"

"I pinky swear I won't give you up to whoever it was when I find him. Your secret is safe."

"I don't care about them," Stan said. "My family, my temple."

"I don't understand. They would go after your family?"

"It's Nazis, damn it! I sold the silver, ten pounds, to some damn Nazis. Now, do you see? My reputation if it got out I did business with those bastards – ruined!"

"How did you know they were Nazis?"

"They told me. They said it sickened them to do business with a Jew."

"Yet you did it?"

"It was a lot of money."

Trixie paused again, her eyes far away.

"You have family in Germany still. Tell them to leave. Tell them tonight by telegram," she said.

"What?" Stan said. "I don't understand."

"Just listen to me. Please."

I had no idea what this was, so I ignored it and got back to the matter at hand.

"Which Nazis?"

"Names? I don't know their names. Jimmy, Joe, Horst, Fritz? Who knows?"

"Wait, were they American Nazis or German Nazis."

"Both. A couple Americans, a couple Germans."

"Did they say what they wanted it for?"

"They did not tell and I did not ask. I can't believe this dame shot me!"

I looked over at Trixie.

"That's all he knows," she said. "We should go."

I pushed the door open for her, but she stopped and turned back to the man on the floor.

"You should do what I said," she said, but the habanero in the honey was now sadness.

Stan ignored her and went back to moaning as he rocked, holding his knee.

"He won't listen. They never listen," she said and went out the door.

We had two martinis, so dry that the bartender just whispered "Vermouth" over top of the gin.

Trixie Gamble sat cross-legged on the barstool next to me, a classy lady in a not-so-classy joint. Every man who walked in looked her over and calculated his odds. Most calculated them as zero and kept their distance. One, having already gotten a load on before stumbling in, made a play. She told him to go home to his wife, kids, and box of smut magazines that he kept hidden out in his garage. That was the last we saw of Romeo.

"Thanks for pulling me out of the fire," I said.

"Professional courtesy," she replied. "From one private eye to another."

I figured I owed her a drink. She accepted. Now, maybe I could get some answers from her because I had a boatload of questions.

But first, we drank. She had a Marlboro smoldering in a chrome holder that she held in her left hand. This was before men discovered the brand and it was still for the ladies. I had a Lucky Strike teetering on the edge of our ashtray.

"So, how did you come to be following me?"

"A little bird told me you were looking into the disappearance of Charles Gaultier. And I figured that was my way out of the dead-end in my case."

"Your case?"

"Have you ever heard of Reynaldo del Lopez Fortuna?"

"Yeah, sure. When I was on the God Squad, we had some run-ins. A bit shady. Nothing too bad – mostly scams. Old women love him."

"Loved. He's dead."

"That's impossible, Trixie. He was a half-demi. A child of Zeus, if I remember right. Some halfs are mortal if they get it from their mortal parent, but this one was not. He had immortality."

"And he's dead."

"Like I said, impossible. If he's dead then he was never an immortal half."

"He was over a thousand years old. The records prove it."

"They have to be wrong. Something has to be wrong. The half-demis can't be killed, not if they don't get mortality from their mortal parent. Maybe quarters. But not halfs."

"The feds sure think he died. They took his body."

"What's your stake?"

"I got hired by a lover to get answers."

"Lot of that going around."

"Fortuna disappeared, just like your Charles Gaultier. I thought he ran off with someone else. They are always running off with someone else. But when I dug into it, people got very tight-lipped. Turns out the cops tried to pull over a Buick on Pacific Coast Highway under Santa Monica three weeks ago. Four guys in the car came out blasting. The cops shot back, and the four ran off. In the trunk was Fortuna. When they figured out the stiff was a demi, the FBI shut everything down. Put a gag on everyone. And took the body."

"Yeah, I think they would be very interested in an immortal dying. So, how did he die?"

"I don't know. I'm not sure that even the government does."

"And you think my case is related to yours?"

"What do you think?"

"I think that if we were smart we would finish these drinks and cigarettes then go quit our cases and forget any of this ever happened. I almost got killed today, and I have a feeling it won't be the last time if I keep on this trail."

Trixie lifted the glass to her ruby lips and paused. Her eyes went away again, and in a moment, she was back. She took a longer sip than I expected from her.

"Yes, we really should quit, but we won't."

"How do you know that?"

"I know things sometimes. I can't control it."

I scoffed and picked up my cig. The smoke danced off the tip in the low light.

"I don't believe in that stuff. Premonitions. Prophecies. Magic."

"Eddie, do you remember Cassandra?"

"I was a bad student. I was thinking about baseball when I should have been paying attention in Pantheon class."

"She was Hector's sister in Troy. Apollo wanted her – another old story – and gave her the power of prophecy. But she turned him down when he got handsy, so he cursed her. She would see the future, and no one would ever believe her."

"How's that relate to you?"

"My family says we're descended from her. The women always have a sense of what will happen, and our men always ignore it."

"Sounds like a bunch of hooey to me."

"See," she said. That honey and habanero voice was back. She was not mad; more like resigned.

I found the whole idea silly. Lots of people claimed some tenuous connection to the demis. Most rich families claimed some kinship to some demi or another or maybe a hero or heroine. If you didn't have one lurking on a branch of the family tree, you were just ordinary, and that wouldn't do. Sure, she was smart, and gorgeous, but neither of those were exclusive to the Olympians or their associates.

"Where do you think we should try next?" I asked. I had an idea, but I wanted to see what she had to say.

"I think we need to find ourselves a silversmith."

Strange, but that was exactly what I was thinking.

4.

Illegal silversmiths weren't my beat. I got my silver bullets nice and legal through a fancy gun dealer in Beverly Hills, a guy who had a government license for dealing in Ag and who carefully noted down each pricy .357 hollow point I purchased in his ledger. There was no way a reputable dealer was going to risk his business doing side jobs working illegal shine. Whoever bought the metal from Goldman the jeweler took it to a crook, and nobody knows crooks better than cops.

It made sense for us to ride together. Trixie offered to give me a ride in her little red convertible. I told her that if anybody saw me sitting in the passenger seat, they would think I was a swish. She got that faraway look in her eyes and said that someday most men wouldn't mind that. I laughed. She was always saying crazy things. I guess it was part of her charm. Anyway, I drove.

It was quite a hike across the city to the downtown headquarters of the LAPD. That was where the God Squad hung their hats, and my pal Jimmy Duggan would know who I should talk to about my silversmith.

It was a full moon, and all the freaks were out. It had been a while since there had been a werewolf problem in the Southland, but there were plenty of other kinds of low-lifes on display in the cop shop. Hookers, junkies, hobos, and petty thieves all milled about, usually in handcuffs, waiting to get processed. The lobby was loud and smelly, but if the foul language bothered Trixie, she didn't show it. I had to push and shove through the unwashed masses. She glided through there like an angel, and all the scumbags, including the cops, made a hole and let her pass.

I dealt with human debris for years as a cop, and I had no illusions. Over the years, all of my sympathy had spilled out in red on sidewalks, liquor store linoleum, and crappy flophouse floors. I had been a janitor for this city for nearly two decades, cleaning up the filth and the blood, and I guess I wasn't much on the forgiveness that Sister Mary Immaculata had tried to teach me about as a kid at Loyola High School. Maybe the war had hardened me.

No, the war *had* hardened me. I looked on them all as garbage, something I would scrape off the bottom of my shoes. But not Trixie. She didn't judge. She just accepted them as they were. Oh, she had no tolerance for their crimes nor any illusions about who they were. She just wasn't jaded like I was. I wondered how that could be. For all the sunshine and palm trees, Lust Angeles can rot your soul. Maybe, when she was seeing the things that she always saw, she also saw hope.

I worked my way through the crowd, finally getting up to the head of the queue after skipping the line of the degenerates waiting to be processed. They protested that we were cutting in front of them, like they were in a rush to get to a holding cell. I ignored them. The watch commander overseeing the circus was a pal of mine. We had knocked back more than a few shots of Jameson's after a hard day of breaking heads and snapping cuffs. He was too busy to shoot the breeze with me, so he just buzzed us back. We left the chaos behind us and went through to the elevator.

The car door opened to let off a couple of young detectives at the fifth floor, which was the Robbery-Homicide Division. I did my time there, wheeling out the corpses and making a few of my own along the way. We were straight-up gunslingers, most of us veterans of the Great War who had already taken lives over there and didn't hesitate to do it again back home. The mob from back east had been trying to move in on the West Coast rackets and we weren't having any of it. The gangsters owned most of the cops in Chicago, New York, and so forth. They didn't own us. They left on their own, or they left on a slab. But they left. Nowadays, Bugsy Siegel and his lieutenant Mickey Cohen were digging into the city like ticks, and were just as hard to dislodge.

After a few years there, I got moved. It was supposed to be a promotion. I didn't think so. But then, I didn't get asked what I thought. The chief spoke, and I got transferred.

The God Squad was on the sixth floor. I spent years there, dealing with the deities. They would get into fraud, steal things, and scam mortals, but one thing we rarely had to deal with was homicide, and then only among the lesser deities. It was almost never murder – most of the dead demigods we dealt with did themselves in. It always struck me as odd when guys who could live nearly forever chose to flip the off switch.

The Demigod Affairs Division was a plum assignment for most guys, and it was reflected in the decor. There was some. Instead of a wild hodgepodge of mismatched furniture, overflowing file cabinets, and tattered carpet with stained linoleum peeking through, the office was actually a classy joint. But, then, we dealt with a classy crowd. Most demis were well-off. If you live long enough, you usually figure out how to make a few bucks. Not all of them, of course. Some were born to peasant girls, or of peasant boys, and never rose out of their peasant mindset even if they lived 500 years. But on the God Squad, you were usually dealing with the upper crust of society, and if you had to bring them downtown, you couldn't bring them to a pigsty. So, the desks and chairs matched, the carpets were clean, and the secretAres were pretty – most of them. And the detectives got an extra $10 a month to dress just a little better.

We also got issued 24 silver bullets for our department issue .38s. Of course, I couldn't go with the flow. As soon as it came out, I got a Smith & Wesson .357 just to be contrary. But silver bullets aren't really silver bullets, if you know what I'm saying. They do a number on some of the lesser demis, but we all knew they wouldn't stop the greater ones. Of course, no one on the force had ever had to shoot a greater one.

Trixie stepped out of the elevator car first and all eyes went to her, which I noticed happened all the time. She didn't seem to notice at all. We stepped on through and Betsy, the senior secretary – not one of the pretty ones – looked at me like I was a bad omen. We didn't get along real well even when I was on the job, and now that I was off, she didn't have to pretend to tolerate me.

"Where's Jimmy?" I asked her, forgoing the pleasantries.

"Detective Duggan is in his office," she told me, "and he's currently engaged."

"Does his wife know?" I asked as I walked past her and towards his closed door. On a plaque, it said "James Monahan Duggan, Lieutenant of Detectives, Division Chief."

I barged in. I had earned the right to barge in on my former partner the hard way. Once, I was driving us back from bracing some great-grandson of Dionysus, who was passing counterfeit twenties through all the bars and bookie joints in Westwood when we saw a couple of squad cars parked outside a warehouse on Pico. The officers were nowhere to be seen, and we looked at each other and thought we might as well provide some backup. We were climbing out of the car when the desperados burst out the front door. They had just shot down those uniforms, leaving three of them dead and one crippled back on the warehouse floor.

Jimmy, stepping out on the passenger side, took a slug in the thigh before he could even get his .38 out of his holster. He tumbled to the ground spurting blood like a geyser. And suddenly, it was me against a quartet of bad guys. I was always fast, and when it's him or me, I don't hesitate. It's him. That saved my life in the Argonne, and it saved my life that night, too. I had my heater out and blasted the first one in the belly before he saw me. His buddy made the mistake of looking at his groaning pal, not the enemy in front of them. I shot him through the heart. The third one got off a blast with his double barrel hog leg. It blew out my windshield, and I got a few shards of glass on my cheek. He got a slug through his.

The last guy had a .45 automatic and was about to finish Jimmy off. He was a big guy named Roscoe, and I found out later Roscoe had spent 25 of his 40 years behind bars. He didn't care whether he lived in a cage or died. He just wanted to kill some cops. He died doing what he loved. I shot him once through the chest and he didn't drop. I shot him again in the solar plexus, and he didn't drop. I raised the blade at the end of my barrel up a little and shot again. He may have been a dummy, but his brain was still a vital organ, and most of it was splattered against the warehouse wall.

Jimmy owed me. And when I barged into his office past his closed door, he knew better than to give me any grief. But I didn't mean he was happy to see me.

"Eddie," he said, like he just stepped on something on the sidewalk. He had been engaged in reading the paper, smoking a stogie, and knocking back a tumbler of Jim Beam.

I walked up to his oak desk, and Trixie followed me inside, pulling the door closed behind her.

"I know you," Jimmy said. "You're Trixie Gamble. What are you doing with this guy?"

"Well, detective, we're just a couple of working folks trying to earn an honest dollar doing our jobs," she said sweetly.

"Eddie Loud and an honest dollar," Jimmy said. "That'll be the day. What do you want this time, Eddie?"

"That any way to talk to a guy who saved your life?"

"You know, Eddie, you keep going to the well on that, and eventually, you're gonna find that well has dried up."

I smiled.

"Jimmy, I need you to point me in the direction of the big-time bent silversmith of choice."

"I thought you got your silver bullets at Bonfilio's Gun Store in Beverly Hills like every decent person."

"It's for a case, not for me. We're looking for somebody who could process a few pounds of silver."

"Processing it into what?" He was eyeing me hard now. Jimmy was no fool.

"Chains," Trixie said. I wished she hadn't. Jimmy Duggan may have been a little slow on the draw, but he was a good detective. He was like a bulldog when he gets on a case. He didn't like to let go. That's why we worked so well together when we were partners.

"Now, why would somebody want a chain made of silver?" he asked, but I knew he knew the answer, and he knew that I knew he knew the answer.

"Somebody took my client's demigod boss," I said.

"He must be a pretty major demigod if he needs a silver chain to hold him," Duggan said. "Why is this the first time I'm hearing of it?"

"I think the client wants to be discreet," Trixie said.

"Maybe it's internal demigod stuff," I added, leaving out the part about the Nazis that Goldman the jeweler had spilled to us. "We mortals can't ever really understand it."

"Eddie, I better not have to clean up another of your messes."

"Like you had to help clean up those four dead guys I kept from finishing you off?"

"Like I said, Eddie, that well's gonna run dry someday."

"But today is not that day," Trixie said. She had that faraway look like she was hearing it in her head and repeating it.

"Who do I talk to, Jimmy?"

Duggan considered it for a moment. I thought for a second that he might just toss us out on our asses, but he came through. He sighed, defeated, and reached for the intercom, hitting the red button.

"Betsy, tell Jed Dufrasne to get in here right now."

"They had no right to do that, to burst in there like that, Detective Dugan!"

"Betsy, just find Dufrasne!" He slammed the intercom button again. "She's worse than my wife."

"Your wife is a nice lady. She puts up with you."

"Can I ask you a question?" Trixie interjected.

"Why the hell not?"

She looked at him closely, staring into his eyes.

"Have you heard anything about the discovery of a dead demigod?"

Duggan swallowed. I watched Trixie as she watched him. Her eyes locked into his.

"Well, there was the one who blew his brains out the other day, but you're running buddy here was there."

"Not him. And not the other day. Someone dead who shouldn't be dead, who *couldn't* be dead."

Jimmy licked his lips. Trixie kept staring. I swear I saw the glint of sweat on his forehead. And in all the years I've known Jimmy, I'd never known him to sweat when he lied. He was Irish. He had the gift of blarney. And he was a cop. They're almost as good liars as lawyers are.

"Thank you anyway, detective." Trixie broke the stare and smiled. Duggan swallowed, relieved.

The intercom buzzed. It was Betsy. Jed Dufrasne was here. Jimmy told us we could go talk in one of the interrogation rooms. I told him to give my best to his wife. I could see he was glad to see the backs of us.

As we walked through the door, Trixie whispered, "You know he was lying to us?"

"Through his teeth," I whispered back.

The three of us stepped into an interrogation room, the only one I had ever seen with rich Corinthian leather chairs and an oak table. There was a framed print of Vincent van Gogh's "Starry Night" on the wall, and I had no clue why. I lit up a cig.

"So, how can I be of service to the legendary Eddie Loud and the notorious Trixie Gamble?" Jed asked, leering. He was wearing a different hundred-dollar suit from the one he wore inside the other day in the stiff's room. It made sense Jed would be the guy on the God Squad who handled the scutwork – middlemen selling illegal relics, fences handling stolen goods, and those in demi-adjacent businesses. Unlicensed silversmithing was one of those.

I was tired and sore from where that golem slugged me, and I was about to tell him to cough up some names or I'd pound his skull into that oak table when Trixie spoke.

"Well, Jed – I can call you Jed?" she asked. I swear her eyelashes fluttered.

"Honey, you can call me anything you want, as long as you call me."

I bit down on the burning butt in my mouth as Trixie smiled at his naughty talk.

"Jed, we're looking for someone, and everyone says you're the fellow in the know, the guy to ask."

He stood up a little straighter. It wasn't every day that Jed Dufrasne got something like a compliment, and never from a woman like Trixie Gamble.

"That right," he said. "I know the score. What do you need to know?"

"Silversmiths," she said.

He swallowed just a little. I inhaled a blast of tobacco.

"Why do you want to know about silversmiths?"

"A case. Nothing big. Just enough to keep a girl's lights on in her apartment."

"What's with him?" He meant me.

"Kind of working together. What do the wrestlers call it?"

"A tag team?"

"Yes, that's right. A tag team. Now, if I had a lot of silver and needed it worked, who would I talk to?"

"Worked into what?" Most illegal silver was worked into something the owner could show off – utensils, sculptures, things like that. Nothing was more impressive to some of the

Hollywood swells than to have the help circulating around their parties serving *hors d'œuvres* on a silver platter that doubled as a felony.

But what we were looking for was very different.

"How about a chain?" I asked. Might as well ask a clear question and just maybe get a clear answer.

Jed Dufrasne stared for a moment, thinking that through. I could almost hear the clicking in his head.

"Why would somebody want a silver chain?" he asked, leery.

"You're a smart guy, Jed," Trixie said. "You're not like everyone says."

"Gotta be for a demi. Who would want to chain a demi?" he demanded. "Are you thinking someone is going to try to pull an Ares on another demigod?"

"No," I said. "It would take more silver than we're thinking, and after Ares do you think any of them are ever going to get tricked into getting wrapped up in silver chains and dropped in the ocean again?"

"Probably not," Jed conceded. "So, who are you two looking at, and why?"

"It's not police business. It's our business, and don't worry – we take care of friends who help us with our business," I told him.

"Consider this a deposit in the favor bank," Trixie purred. "And someday, when you need it, you can come to one of us for a withdrawal."

He was suspicious now, wary, but not bright enough to be subtle about it. He hadn't risen to the middle and stalled out as a detective by being smart. More like by just continuing to show up.

"There's a few in town who could do something like that," he said. "It would take a lot of silver though."

I exhaled a cloud of smoke. "Someone bought a lot of silver. We want to know who they took it to."

"In East LA, Manny Rivera. Has a foundry and does silver work as a sideline. Mostly religious stuff, though. Crosses, bowls, that sort of thing. The Mexicans are all Catholics, you know."

"See, you're the man with the answers. Who else?" asked Trixie.

"There's Lionel Washington down in Crenshaw. The dark side of town. He's a fence mostly, but does silver work as a sideline."

I glanced over at Trixie and saw she was thinking what I was thinking. She leaned in close to me.

"The Nazis probably had to swallow hard to deal with a Jew. A black man would be a bridge too far," she whispered.

I must have raised an eyebrow at what she said about the bridge – I'd never heard that turn of phrase.

"It just came to me when I thought of the krauts," she told me, shrugging.

Dufrasne was visibly annoyed at being left out of our side chat; he was straining to hear. Trixie turned back to him and smiled.

"Who else, Jed?"

"Well, there's Mickey Sixx down on La Brea by Pico. He has a metals plant. International Metal Works or something like that. Does silversmithing on the QT as a...uh..."

"Sideline?" Trixie said, finishing his sentence.

"Yeah, a sideline."

"This Mickey Sixx, is he mobbed up?"

Jed shrugged. "I don't know about that, but I do know he's a pain in the ass."

"You've been a big help, Jed. I'll remember," Trixie promised. Jed smiled.

"See you around, Jed," I said. Jed looked at me like I kicked his puppy.

I opened the interrogation room door and Trixie glided past me into the hall. We headed down it and out of the God Squad's suite. We were quiet until we got to the elevator.

"You get the feeling Jed knows more than he let on?" she asked me as we stepped into the car.

"What Jed Dufrasne knows wouldn't fill a Baptist's shot glass," I answered as the doors slid shut.

5.

It was too late to go follow up on our silversmith lead that night. Mickey Sixx would have to wait until the morning. I drove home alone to my apartment building and rode up to my sixth-floor flat overlooking Wilshire Boulevard. Inside, I collapsed into my leather chair after I poured myself a tumbler of Johnny Walker and lit a Lucky Strike. There was honking from the street down below. Out the window, I had a pretty good view of the hills. Right there, near the crest and brightly lit, was Elysium, Apollo's mansion. The party was in full swing tonight. It was in full swing every night.

Knocking back the belt, I decided I needed another. I was on edge, and the booze did nothing to sand it off. Something seemed off, and besides, my jaw hurt from where Goldman's pseudo-golem had smacked me.

I hit the sheets and lay on my back wide awake. That was unusual. I usually sleep like a baby. I could sleep on a roller coaster. I could sleep on the Fourth of July. I could sleep under the *thud thud thuds* of the Hun Big Bertha trench mortars back in the Argonne. But tonight, lying in my bed, with the window cracked open a bit, all I could do was stare at the ceiling. There was a brown water stain in the corner. It was the first time I'd noticed it, and it had obviously been there a while. I paid for a quality flop and the ceiling was stained. That rubbed me the wrong way.

But that was not what was wrong. The stain was not keeping me up. What was eating at me? I couldn't quite place it. It was just a gut feeling, and I trust my gut. My gut has gotten me out of a lot of bad situations. That and my gun. Right then, I had my .357 on the nightstand beside me, right by my whiskey. And I was afraid that it wasn't enough.

I got through the night and showered and shaved in the daylight. Then it was off to Max's Diner for the usual – a couple of runny eggs over easy and some dry strips of bacon. I washed it all down with three cups of tarry coffee and a couple of cigarettes. The waitresses always got taken care of, so they were just how I liked them – quick on the refills and light on the conversation.

Breakfast was my time to catch up on current events. The front page of the *Los Angeles Times* was the usual collection of crime, war, and a celebrity story or two. Some starlet I had never heard of was getting divorced down at the courthouse. Apparently, she got her roles the old-fashioned way, and her husband didn't appreciate it. There was a bank robbery in Long Beach that went very sideways when a car outside backfired and one of the mugs started blasting. And across the pond in Europe, enjoying marching over the same dirt that my buddies and I had bled over twenty-some-odd years ago. I'd wonder what it was all for if I wondered about things like that. In my line of work, wondering makes your mind wander, and if your mind wanders, you're likely to catch a slug.

It occurred to me that I read the *Times* every morning but had seen nothing about the shootout on PCH with LA's finest that had Trixie mentioned. You had to be pretty strong to pull enough strings to make that kind of happening unhappen.

I finished the eggs, drained my last cup dry, and left a dollar tip. Time to go to work.

You couldn't miss Trixie Gamble standing outside her apartment building off Hollywood Boulevard. She looked elegant and practical all at once, like a lady who had work to do but knew how to look good doing it. Her ruby-red lipstick made an impression. The regular Joes walking by all ventured a glance, but none of them dared talk her up. Rarely had I seen a woman so attractive so not attracting anyone. Her would-be suitors were probably afraid of her, and they were probably right to be.

I went to get out to let her in the passenger side, but she walked around the car and let herself in before I had a chance. I guess it was her way of reminding me that this was all business. That was fine with me. Normally, I'd be interested in a dame who looked like her, but she wasn't a regular skirt. I'd already seen her in action and I didn't want to be on her bad side.

When it came to romance, I always ended up on their bad side.

We headed down to La Brea. It was 10:30 in the morning and the roads were a couple hours clear of the battalions of Johnny Lunchpails and Sally Secretarys heading into work. They were regular folks living regular lives. I didn't get it. Punching in, punching out, sitting at a desk – it didn't appeal to me. In fact, it terrified me. I grew up with guys like that and fought beside them, too. They were alive once, as alive as they could ever be, and then they came home from the trenches and died a little every time they headed out the door to go to work. Me? I was free. I did what I wanted, when I wanted, for who I wanted, and for how much I wanted. I wasn't rich, but I was comfortable. My wallet was full and I was above-ground, and that's more than I had any right to be. I wasn't changing the world, but I wasn't making it any worse either.

We started the ride off quiet. Maybe she hadn't slept either, though you couldn't tell from looking at her. The only thing keeping me going was the Folgers I'd guzzled. I focused on the road. The sun was up and bright. It was in the seventies. There were palm trees. And there was a billboard from the local

Baptist Church depicting an angry minister holding a Bible and urging the faithful to "Reject the Abominations!" I took that personally. There was only one real man upstairs, and I never thought the Olympians were anything sacred or holy like the real God. Primitive men in the past, and some in the present, saw their powers and leapt to that conclusion. Of course, formal demi worship was illegal and had been for centuries, not that the law stopped all of them. There were always a few willing to kneel on the sly, and the demis lapped it up. Still, those abominations were my meal ticket.

Finally, she broke the silence.

"So, what's the plan for Mickey Sixx?" Trixie asked after coming back from wherever her mind had drifted off to. She lit up a Marlboro and turned to look at me. I kept my eyes on the road. There was a Happy Cow Dairy truck ahead of me that was swerving back and forth across the two lanes like the milkman had already hit the sauce.

"I'd be happy with the names of his customers. Since it's ten years in Alcatraz, I'm not sure he'll be too happy to talk. I may have to get a little rough with him."

"I could try to charm it out of him."

"Sure, or I could put my .357 against his appendix and count to three. Either way is good to go for me. You just let me know how you wanna play it, Trixie."

"You always start with the rough stuff?"

"No, but I always seem to finish with the rough stuff."

"You do have a reputation for leaving people in heaps on the ground, Eddie."

"Well, maybe Mickey Sixx has heard of me and my reputation will save us all a lot of trouble."

Mickey Sixx ran something called International Metal Processing, an ugly tan building back off of La Brea near Pico. This was a real, legit metal works with the silversmithing being an illicit addition to his cash flow. Even over the traffic running north and south, you could hear the machinery inside at work, clanging and grinding. There was a smokestack with black fumes belching out, adding to the perpetual smog that smothered the city.

A few grimy metalworkers loitered out front, smoking cigarettes and drinking out of brown paper bags. I'd probably need a belt or two at break time to work in there all day, every day. I parked on the street between a Ford and another Buick, and the workers gave me the once-over as we stepped out. Trixie got the twice-over.

They gave me that look like I was a cop, a look I got a lot even after I stopped being one. They didn't know what to make of Trixie. Her kind didn't mingle with their kind.

We walked up the four steps to the double door, past the gauntlet of sour machinists. Trixie smiled at them.

"Gentlemen," she said.

Stirred to chivalry, the ones sitting stood up and the ones standing doffed their hats. I heard a couple murmur "Ma'ams" as I pulled open the door for her. The sounds of industry got even louder. It was a wonder any of those guys could hear anything at all.

The lobby turned right towards the factory floor with no wall separating it, and went left towards some offices. I figured Mickey would be in there and went over to the door that said, "Keep Out." I was in no mind to be kept out and opened it up. Inside there was a secretary at her desk, probably 200 years old with an ashtray heaped with butts. A low cloud of gray smoke hung over the room. If smoking was really as bad for you as some people said it was, it was a wonder she was still alive.

She had a little Hephaestus totem on her desk, not unexpected in a foundry. Most people worshipped the real God if they worshipped anyone, but some people hedged their bets with the occasional nod to the applicable Olympian even though that was a mortal sin. You shall have no other gods before me, He commanded, but if everyone followed the Ten Commandments, the Bible would be a lot shorter and a lot less dramatic.

"We're looking for Mickey Sixx," I announced.

"You cops?" she replied, then thought better of it. "No, you ain't cops. She's definitely not a cop, but you do look like one. Course, if you were a cop, you'd flash a badge and ya didn't, so you ain't welcome."

"What is it with you and secretAres, Eddie?" Trixie asked.

"No, we aren't cops," I told the ancient receptionist. "But if your boss would rather talk to the cops, I can make that happen."

The old bag thought it over and decided we should be her boss's problem. There was a door across the way. She got up and walked over to it, staring back at me over her shoulder with a scowl. She rapped on the wood three times with her ancient fist, and somebody shouted from inside, "What the hell do you want?"

She opened the door, leaned in, and said, "You better talk to these two." Then she walked back to her chair, still glaring, plopped herself down, and lit another cigarette.

Mickey Sixx wore a white dress shirt with the sleeves rolled up and no tie. He was a short, red-faced man with a shiny bald spot and a face like an angry rat.

"Well?" he demanded as a way of introduction as he stepped up to the office threshold. "You two cops?"

"Do we look like cops?" I asked. I knew I did, but if Trixie looked like a cop everyone would be looking to get arrested.

I walked over to his office, and Trixie followed. I told him our names and told him we'd talk in his office. He grumbled something, but I didn't care. He did an about-face and returned to his desk. Another Hephaestus idol rose above the piles of papers. Trixie came inside next, and I closed the door behind her.

I decided to start with "rough."

"Word is you've been making silver chains," I said, laying my cards on the table. "And you're telling me all about it."

"I don't know who you're talking to, but whoever told you that doesn't know what the hell he's talking about."

"Oh, come now, Mr. Sixx. I can see you're lying," Trixie whispered sweetly.

"How the hell do you know if I'm lying?"

"Because, darling, your tongue is wagging," she said pleasantly. "My friend Eddie here has a short fuse so maybe you should avoid lighting it. Just tell us who you made the chain for and we'll be on our way. We don't care about you. We don't care about your little side business. We just need to find somebody. We just need a name."

"What the hell is this silver chain you're going on about and what's it have to do with me?"

"We're looking for somebody they wrapped up in that chain," I said. "And if you don't cooperate, you're going down as an accessory if something bad happens to him."

"Or not," Trixie observed. "I mean, if you cooperate."

"We're private eyes. We don't get paid by the conviction. We don't want the police involved either. Now spill it."

Mickey looked particularly rodential, his beady eyes darting back and forth between us. I could see he was sizing us up, trying to figure out if there was a way to nick the cheese out of this trap without the bar flipping down and snapping his neck.

"What the hell does it matter if I do some silver work on the side? It don't hurt nobody. A victimless crime."

"What about the guy tied up in those silver chains, Mickey?" I asked. "Wouldn't he be a victim?"

"A victim? You sure?" he replied, leering obscenely. "Some people like that sort of thing."

"Mr. Sixx, I assure you that this is not that sort of situation," Trixie explained with her trademark patience, even as I was losing mine. I picked up a monogramed letter opener off his cluttered desk.

"I'm getting tired of dancing around with you, Sixx. Start singing now, or you'll sing your next song soprano."

He thought about it for a moment, and I let him stew over my threat. He made his decision.

"Some fellow came to me to make some chains. Brought their own silver, of course. I didn't ask questions. I didn't ask who they were or where they got the glitter. They offered me a sack of money and I did the work after hours all by my lonesome a few weeks ago. They never said what they were gonna do with the chains, and I didn't ask."

"Tell us about the men. What were they like? Americans or foreigners?"

"Some were American, some foreigners. I didn't spend a lot of time conversating with them."

"What kind of foreigners?"

"What the hell am I, the *National Geographic*?"

"No, you don't seem like a big reader, but I bet you love the pictures."

"Maybe Germans?" suggested Trixie.

"Maybe. They all sound the same to me. Krauts, pollocks, frogs."

I looked at Trixie to see what she thought, and she looked pale—not her normal pale, but more pale than usual.

"There's something wrong," she said. "We need to go, Eddie. Right now."

I didn't see why. I certainly wasn't afraid of Mickey. Plus, I had some more questions for this two-legged rat man.

"Do you have a phone number or an address?"

"Hell no. I wasn't making friends. I was making money. That's all I know, so get the hell out."

Trixie stood up.

"Let's go," she insisted.

"Yeah, you listen to the broad. Get the hell out."

I stood, but I wasn't ready to leave yet. I was ready to walk over and knock the smart out of his mouth. But Trixie grabbed me by the shoulder.

"Now," she said. "It's important."

I didn't believe her. I thought she was overreacting, maybe even hysterical. But Mickey Sixx seemed to have told me everything he had to tell, so I decided we could leave. Trixie couldn't get to the door fast enough. I moved slow.

We walked out through the smoke-filled secretarial foyer, with Mickey Sixx following behind us. I guess seeing us leave got his courage up, and he started shouting some things that could have earned him a shot to the nose that would knock him all the way into next week. He would've got one, too, if Trixie hadn't pulled me outside through the front door and down the steps past the machinists on break.

"He can't talk to us like that."

"It doesn't matter. We're in danger."

"*He's* in danger." I wanted to take him apart.

Mickey Sixx was at the front door, still yelling at us as we walked to my car. I finally got fed up and turned back to face him. That's when I heard the shots. The spray of lead came over our heads and passed us loud and fast. I knew that sound. I had shot a Tommy gun before. I saw three big bloody holes erupt across his shirt, and the .45-caliber slugs tossed him back into the building.

His last words were, "Oh hell!"

The workers scattered, and I acted on instinct. I grabbed Trixie and pulled her to the ground beside me, all while reaching for my heater and looking up.

The two shooters were inside a Mercury coupe, with the barrel of the submachine gun hanging out the front passenger window. It had a stick magazine and there was no foregrip – this was an M1928A1 military model, not one of the M1921s Bonnie and Clyde had used a few years before.

Lucky for us, it was still spitting fire too fast to be aimed accurately, and that probably saved us. The shooter did not pause the fusillade, instead pinning the trigger back and dropping the barrel to aim in our general direction. The bullets dug into the concrete around us, showering us with cement chips and dust.

A round hit five feet out, another four feet out, and another three feet out, each one closer than the next, walking in right at us. I figured three more shots and he would be zeroed in on us and we would be done for. Then it stopped.

That's the thing about submachine guns. They fire fast, but they also run out of bullets fast. If he had had a drum magazine instead of a column mag, we would have been Swiss cheese.

He scrambled to reload and that gave me the moment I needed. I went over the top, like I always do when in doubt, getting to my knee and drawing a bead on the passenger door.

No car door was going to stop one of my .357 slugs.

I squeezed off two shots, loud enough that I could hear them over the ringing in my ears, blasting pits into the sheet metal right beneath the window. That did the trick. The Tommy gun went akimbo as the gunman caught the pair of slugs in the chest.

The car did nothing for a moment but keep on idling, and then the driver realized he was wearing a good chunk of his buddy's innards splattered across his suit. He threw the Mercury into gear and hit the gas, spinning the tires. The white smoke formed a cloud by the rear wheels, but not enough to stop me from doing what needed done.

By then, I was up on my feet, and my blood was up, too. I took aim through the back window and fired off four slugs. I couldn't exactly see where I hit, but glass shattered in a rain of shards. For a moment, I thought maybe I had missed, but I hadn't. The Mercury stopped accelerating and wheeled off to the left, hopping the curb and knocking over a yellow fire hydrant. A geyser of water erupted underneath, spraying white foam in all directions.

Trixie was on her feet next to me. We both stared for a moment.

"They're going to call that a 'drive-by' someday," she said to me.

"A what?" I asked, confused.

"A drive-by shooting. I think that that's what they're going to call it. It's going to happen a lot in Los Angeles."

"Where do you get this stuff?" I asked, marveling. She always said the craziest things.

"I got it right that something bad was going to happen," Trixie said.

"I think you got lucky. And then we both got lucky that Machine Gun Kelly doesn't know how to shoot. I mean didn't."

"They never listen to me," she said to herself.

I didn't realize that I had instinctively swung out the chamber of my magnum, dropped the shell casings to the street, and was reloading fresh rounds. Instinct, I guess.

"You and your feelings."

"It just comes to me," she said. "I can't help it, and I don't even want it."

I snapped the cylinder shut on my Smith & Wesson and slid it back under my shoulder. A crowd was gathering, and some passersby were peeking in at the mess inside the drenched Mercury. Nobody was coming out of the wreck, which told me that nobody was going to come out except on a stretcher.

And then it hit me. It hit me hard.

"That was six silver slugs," I said. "Those dumb bastards just cost me $30."

6.

My old pal Special Agent James Randolph Connolly of the Federal Bureau of Investigations, Deities Branch, was first on the scene with one of his cronies.

"Eddie Loud," he sneered, surveying the waterlogged sedan. "I might have known."

"That the same Sears suit you were wearing the other night? J. Edgar needs to give you a raise."

"You have a smart mouth, gumshoe. And some explaining to do."

"Right after you explain why the FBI was right around the corner when those two stiffs decided to start spraying lead."

"That's government business, Loud. Above your pay grade."

"I don't have a pay grade. I'm not a government flunky," I told Connolly. He didn't take it very well. He seemed a little sensitive about it.

"Fidelity, bravery, integrity," he sputtered at me, his finger pointing at my chest. "You don't know anything about those things. But that's what I do for a living."

"Really? I thought you were in the FBI."

His partner had to grab him because he was making like he was going to come at me. That would've been a mistake on both our parts. I would've ended up in a cell, and he would have ended up in a dentist's chair.

"You really screwed this one up, Loud! You and me aren't finished," Connolly raged as his partner dragged him away. I laughed. I never thought much of the FBI. They were always way too impressed with themselves, and I could never figure out why.

I considered suggesting to Special Agent Connolly that if he got himself a nice frilly dress, he could join his boss J. Edgar for a tea party. No, that would just escalate things, and I had work to do. I looked around. I was alone.

While the G-man and I were facing off, Trixie had slipped away to the wreak. One of the workers had come out with a big lug wrench and shut off the hydrant. She could get close without getting drenched, and she looked inside. All that water couldn't wash away all of the mess.

"I think these two have probably looked better," she observed as I walked over to her. She was by the driver's door, shaking her head.

That was an understatement. The driver and the shooter looked like a couple of ripe watermelons that somebody had taken a Louisville Slugger to. My .357 hit hard.

I reached in through the driver's window and flipped off the ignition. Then I felt around inside the driver's sopping suit jacket. No wallet, no papers.

"I'm betting their boss didn't want anyone to know who they were if this went south," Trixie said.

"So, who's their boss?"

Trixie shrugged. I guess she didn't know everything.

I opened up the back door, reached in, and patted down the shooter in the backseat. His Thompson was on the floorboards in an inch of filthy water.

"Nothing on this one either," I said.

"I got something," Trixie replied, still at the driver's door. I stepped back and saw that she had pushed up the driver's coat sleeve. There was a tattoo etched onto his forearm, and I knew it well.

"An iron cross," I said.

"You know any Americans with one of those?"

"Nope. This guy is a German. Nobody else would paint on one of those."

"Maybe he liked heavy metal," Trixie replied. I looked at her funny, and she kind of shrugged at me. Then she went on.

"Goldman said some were German, some were American. Looks like a couple of Nazis just tried to blitzkrieg us, Eddie."

"I'm feeling like Belgium right about now."

"We need to look out for the rest of the Reich."

"I hate Nazis," I said, shaking my head.

"Especially California Nazis," Trixie added.

"The question is who tipped them off we were on the case. Dufrasne?"

"Maybe Goldman," Trixie said. "He should have listened to me. But regardless, we're on the Nazis' radar now."

"Their what?" I asked, baffled.

"I don't know what that means," Trixie said, confused. But she had no chance to elaborate.

"Get the hell away from there, that's a crime scene!" Connolly shouted as he advanced on us. He had slipped out of his partner's warm embrace, and now he was foaming at the mouth even more than usual.

"Maybe the FBI can make something out of this," I told him innocently. "These two don't have any ID and they're not going to be doing any talking." I felt no obligation to share Trixie's tattoo insight with Hoover's boys.

"You better both clear out of here before I take you in on a federal beef!"

"You don't want our statements?" Trixie asked, fluttering her lashes a little bit, working hard to act dumb.

"A couple guys just tried to machine gun us and killed a guy," I said. "But you feds seem to be taking it pretty much in stride."

"Get out of here while you still can," Connolly growled. The firemen were pulling up, along with an LAPD prowler and a couple more unmarked cars with what were clearly G-men. Yeah, it was time to go.

We went back to our sedan, got in, and got out of there before somebody changed their mind about taking us into custody as material witnesses or worse. I was heading north on La Brea, drumming my fingers on the steering wheel, when Trixie broke the silence.

"What's it tell you that the FBI doesn't seem interested in taking a report?" Trixie asked me. I don't think she needed any special powers to know what I was going to say.

"It tells me that there isn't going to be any report. That this whole incident, including two dead Nazis and one dead illegal silversmith, is going to get covered up just like that shootout on PCH."

"The feds are in this deep. Here's what I'm wondering, Eddie," Trixie said. "Why was Connolly so angry?"

"Dead-end job? Ugly wife? Maybe because he's Irish and it was almost noon and he hadn't had a whiskey yet."

"I'm serious, Eddie."

"You think I'm not? You don't know many Irish cops."

"He said that 'you really screwed this one up,' remember? What did you screw up, Eddie?"

She had me there. I had done everything right, including defending myself when we almost got turned into Swiss cheese by Machine Gun Adolf.

"I didn't screw up anything."

"Not for yourself. You screwed it up for *him*."

I laughed. Of course.

"He was watching us because he thought the Nazis would be coming after us, and he wanted to follow the Nazis," I declared.

"After they put holes in us and left us on the sidewalk."

"I think Connolly would consider that a fringe benefit."

"So, what do we do now, Eddie?"

"I think we ought to do what Connolly couldn't – figure out where those Nazis would've gone home to. And when we do, I bet you we will find us a demigod tied up in silver chains."

It was about one in the afternoon, but I'd already been machine-gunned once that day so I figured that it counted as five o'clock. I took a slug of Jameson's. Trixie sat across from me with a slender flute of champagne. I didn't catch the brand.

We were at the Hollywood Brown Derby restaurant, the one on North Vine. We were sitting under a wall of movie star caricatures. Vivien Leigh's pic was staring down from the wall into my tomato bisque. Across the way, the genuine article was nibbling on a lobster salad when she wasn't berating her fiancé, Laurence Olivier, about something. The tabloids were calling her a homewrecker for stealing him away from his wife.

"She doesn't seem to care much about the scandal," I observed to Trixie.

"You don't have to when you just won Best Actress," Trixie replied. Leigh had picked up a little naked gold man for *Gone With the Wind*.

"Hooray for Hollywood," I said and slurped a spoonful of soup.

Trixie got that strange, far-away look again.

"Someday, a man will be nominated for Best Actress. He might even win."

I about spit out my mouth full.

"You know Trixie, I'm going to have what you're drinking because it's making this Jameson's look like iced tea."

She shook her head, like she was shaking off something, and got back to business.

"Nazis," she said. "Where do we find Nazis?"

"Sewers. Loitering around elementary schools and playgrounds. Bus station men's rooms."

"Be serious."

"I am serious. They're not just creeps. Word on the street is that they prefer the Hitler Youth. You remember the Night of the Long Knives when Hitler cleaned house? One of the places they went in and did the cleaning was an all-Aryan boy orgy."

Trixie rolled her eyes in disgust.

"I'm guessing you know somebody who knows his way around the world of degenerates. After all, you were a cop," she said.

I sighed.

"Yeah, I have an idea who we can ask." I didn't want to go there, but I didn't see a lot of options.

She upended her flute and drained the rest of the champagne.

"So, who are we going to see?"

"Sit back down and get a refill because it's going to be a few hours. He won't be available until after sundown."

She sat and looked at me expectantly.

"Well, when you want a lowlife," I said. "You go find yourself a vampire."

"I always imagined you vampires as classy, cultured creatures," Trixie said, grimacing as she pushed aside the moist, threadbare drawers drying over a rope strung across the one-room apartment. It was past sundown, but construction paper was taped over the windows, and the only light was from a bare bulb hanging from the yellowed, peeling ceiling.

Ted Hockney frowned, but you could still see the tip of one of his long, pointy canines peeking out. He was in a bathrobe sitting at his two-seat kitchen table, smoke from a butt twisting up above the ashtray and adding to the haze hanging in the air of the seedy tenement.

"I'm not a full vampire. I'm a vampyr, not a master. I'm pretty much human, I just like a little blood along with regular food, I stay out of the sun, and I'm not diurnal."

"Diurnal. That's a big word, Ted," I said. Actually, I was a little impressed by his vocabulary, if not his habitation. It looked like he slept on a stained sofa under a bunch of covers instead of in a coffin like a proper bloodsucker.

"It means I am not active in the daytime."

"Yeah, I know what it means. It means you can't get a regular job. It means you can't be around decent folk, not just because decent folk are diurnal but because nobody decent wants to be around a vampire, or vampyr, or whatever. It means you spend all night out doing whatever you do, mingling with whoever you mingle with."

Hockney frowned at me again.

"And it means you can't make vampires of your own, that you can't turn into a bat, and that a stakedriver doesn't have to go through all the rigamarole of killing a real vampire to kill you."

"I didn't ask for this."

"How did you get turned, Ted?" Trixie asked kindly.

"It was a misunderstanding," the vampyr replied sullenly.

"And I'm sure it's a tale that's both fascinating and tragic, but we're not here to get our heartstrings tugged, Ted. We just need a little bit of information, some rumors off the street, and I'll give you a nice, crisp sawbuck. You can go out on the town tonight, live it up, and top it off with a nice fresh glass of blood. My buddies on the vamp detail once told me that AB negative is the – Trixie, what's a fancy champagne?"

"Dom Perignon?"

"Yeah, the Dom Perignon of blood. That so?"

"What do you wanna know?" he growled.

"Nazis."

"Nazis?"

Trixie leaned in, which was brave. I could catch the scent of his bad blood breath from five feet away.

"Nazis," she said. "Hitler's own goosestepping, French-beating, *seig heiling* Nazis."

"I don't know any Nazis. I do know some communists. Are you interested in them? They tried to organize us. They said vampyrs were oppressed, that we need unity because we're part of the proletariat."

"Save the commie gobbledygook," Trixie said. "We just need to know where you go if you want to find some Nazis."

"Why would I wanna find them? They are bad news. And they're weird. I mean really weird. Scary weird."

"We get it, Ted," I said. "You don't like Nazis."

"They say they're into black magic and worse."

"Just tell me where they're at."

"Murphy Ranch," he said. "That's the rumor."

"Murphy Ranch?" I asked.

"It's in a canyon up by Pacific Palisades. Very remote," Trixie said. "Last I heard, it was an artist colony."

"Last I heard," Ted said, "the artists were out, and the Nazis were in. And that's all I know."

I looked at him, and he seemed straight to me, but I looked over at Trixie because she was better about this sort of thing. She nodded. I reached into my pocket, pulled out my money clip, and handed him a ten-spot.

"Drink up," I told him.

7.

We got what we needed from the vampyr. Now, we needed to figure out what to do next.

Tully's saloon was down the street. It wasn't the kind of place I take a lady, usually, but Trixie Gamble wasn't my usual kind of lady. We went in, and the drinkers looked us over and went back to their business. It was that kind of place, a place where you could hover over a shot of whiskey, lost in your own thoughts, confident that no one was going try to chat you up. We grabbed a booth in the back and sat down. The waiter, with a curled lip and a cauliflower ear, took our drink order. A glass of Lucky Lager for me, some champagne I couldn't pronounce for the lady.

"We have champale," he growled.

"Two Lucky's," she said, smiling and fluttering her eyelashes. The waiter walked away.

"I guess I'm going to Murphy Ranch," I said.

"I guess we are," Trixie replied.

"I don't think Adolf's boys are going to just give up their prize, and you are not exactly dressed for a gunfight."

"I don't intend to get in one," Trixie said. "Maybe we need to think our way through this instead of shooting our way through this if we can. But first, we need to figure out the answer to the big question."

"What's the big question?"

"Why would a bunch of Nazis kidnap a demigod?"

That was a good question, and I had no idea. And at the moment, I didn't really care. They had him, and my job was to get him back. The whys weren't part of that equation. Eddie Loud did not have much, but he had a code.

I shrugged.

I needed to call the office, so I went over to the phone booth. I dropped my dime, picked up the receiver, and waited for the operator, casually perusing the graffiti. If I needed a good time, I could call Vivian. I guess it was good to have that in my pocket if I ever got desperate. The operator came up with that nasal Southern California Telephone Company operator voice all of them seem to have.

"Connecticut 7-2265," I said.

"Connecting."

There were clicks and whirs, and Gladys picked up on the other end. She sounded a continent away.

"Edward Loud, private investigator. May I help you?"

"It's Eddie. I'm following up on a lead. Any messages?"

"Miss Showers called several times. I think she wants an update."

"Give me the number."

"You got a pen, Eddie?"

I instinctively patted my jacket, and then a hand with a pen came into view. Trixie was at the other end of the arm.

"How did you...," I began, but she just smiled and walked off back to the table.

I took down Constance Showers's number, got off, and dropped another dime. She picked up on the first ring.

"Mr. Loud?" she asked. She wanted it to be me.

"That's right. I got your message. And I've got some news."

"What have you found? I'm terribly frightened for Mr. Gaultier."

She was right to be. I had to be diplomatic.

"I think we have a line on who took him."

"We?"

"I'm working with another PI. Related case."

"Where is he, Mr. Loud?" She seemed eager, which was understandable.

"I think he's up at Murphy Ranch. That's far back in a canyon up in the Palisades. We're gonna go get him."

"Who took him, Mr. Loud, and why?"

"I think a bunch of Nazis," I said "And I still don't know why. Maybe I'll ask around after the fireworks. If there's anybody left to ask."

"And you don't think we should involve the authorities?"

"I made a promise to bring him back to you, and I think the authorities might just complicate matters."

"When are you going?"

"Tonight, later. Let them get complacent and comfortable."

"That was Murphy Ranch, correct, Mr. Loud?"

"I hope you don't have any ideas about showing up there yourself, Miss Showers," I said, regretting that I had spilled too much to her. Sometimes clients didn't understand that they were also paying me *not* to tell them things.

"Of course not, Mr. Loud. I will be here at the house, waiting for your call to let me know that Mr. Gaultier is safe."

I got back to the table, and Trixie was halfway through a Marlboro. Our empty glasses sat along with the bottles of Lucky. Our waiter at least popped the tops. I picked up one of the bottle caps and flipped it. They always have these little puzzles on the underside – a rebus. I stared at it. There was a picture of a stovepipe hat, the letter "K," an eyeball, and a trombone. I had no idea what it meant. I poured my beer as Trixie poured hers.

"How was Miss Showers?"

"Nervous. She wanted to know who had him."

"Did she want to know why?"

"I think she's as clueless as we are. But I told her I'd ask around. You sure you're up to this?"

"Sure," she said, taking a long swig of suds.

Trixie drove up the eucalyptus-lined road toward Murphy Ranch. It was a gentle, but long, grade; we were ascending. I stayed low in the passenger seat, my .357 out and ready just in case things got interesting. The krauts and their kraut-adjacent American collaborators would buy a beautiful woman getting lost in the backroads and tell her to turn around. They would probably open up on me again, and I'd cheated death once already that day.

It was after ten and there was a lot of illumination from the moon. Thankfully, it wasn't full – you don't want to be out in the boonies in a full moon even with a cylinder full of silver slugs if you can help it.

"It's deep back in these canyons," Trixie observed. She was driving my sedan maybe twenty-five miles per hour because the road was narrow and twisty. We got off the main drag a while back, and the houses to the side were thinning out, becoming fewer and farther between.

"Nazis like their privacy, I guess," I observed. Half the time they were on the down low, half the time they were strutting around town in their toy soldier uniforms. Same with the damn communists.

"This place is a fire trap," Trixie said. "I see fire. Fire all through here. And a communist mayor and governor with magnificent hair who can't stop it."

"Where does this stuff come from?" I asked.

"I don't know," she said. "But the future is very confusing."

"Well, stop looking at the future and watch the road."

"Car," Trixie declared.

"You see a car in the future?"

"No, there's a car up ahead."

I peeked over the dash. To our front, a pair of headlights swung back and forth across the road, like the driver was either in a hurry or had had a couple of belts before hopping behind the wheel.

"Two cars," Trixie said. "Moving fast."

I didn't like it, not a bit.

"That driveway on the right, take it," I told Trixie. There was no room for coming and going traffic without slowing and working around each other, and the two sedans did not seem inclined to do that. Best we look like some locals coming home from a late dinner.

She made the turn smoothly and went up a dirt track to her right. At the top, somewhere in the trees, were some lights, no doubt a house. Behind us, the two black cars – Fords, I think, and a couple years old – roared past the driveway and down the hill, out of the canyon. I caught a glimpse of the driver and front passenger in the first car. It was the same guy – twins? The second car was full of mugs, too.

"Give them a minute," I said. Was it our boys clearing out their prisoner? Or something else?

Trixie gave them sixty seconds, then put the car into reverse and eased my car back onto the road. She shifted into first, and we started climbing again.

It was another mile to Murphy Ranch. I ducked down as soon as I saw the gate, so it was Trixie who alerted me to the situation.

"The gate's wide open," she said, slowing the car. "You need to take a look at this."

I lifted my noggin up over the dash. The headlights illuminated the wrought iron gate that barred the driveway and maybe fifty yards beyond. It was wide open inwards. There was a low brick building to the left, probably a guardhouse. And there were shapes on the ground.

Human shapes, two of them.

"Slow," I said as I rolled down my window and my thumb drew back the hammer on my magnum. The air was colder than I expected and slapped me in the face.

The first stiff was lying face down on the driveway on my side. Trixie pulled up, and I gave him the once-over. He wore black pants and a brown shirt, and, sure enough, there was one of those red, white, and black swastika armbands wrapped tight above his right elbow. A scarlet stream flowed from under his chest into the culvert.

"Nazi," I said. "DOA."

She pulled forward – the other one was on her side. She paused and looked out the window at him.

"Looks like he tried to fight. There's a .38 on the ground next to him."

"Whoever was in those cars raided this place. You think they got what they were after?"

"I don't know," Trixie said. "I'm not feeling anything about this, not seeing anything."

"I think we go further on foot," I said. "Pull the car off the road, and let's point it downhill in case we need to get out of here fast."

"Like if there's a zombie apocalypse?" she asked.

"What?" I asked. She shrugged.

Trixie backed the car in behind the guardhouse, so it was out of sight. If somebody else came along, no sense in advertising that we were on the premises.

We got out and I motioned for her to wait. I listened. It was an old Army trick. Before you moved, you stood there and listened. You wanted to get the sounds down so if there was something off, you would know it.

We waited, still and silent, for a couple minutes. Nothing except the caw of some bird lower in the canyon.

"You might want to take the dead guy's .38," I suggested. "Just in case."

"No," Trixie replied. "It's unlucky."

We started up the driveway, climbing into the darkness. My magnum was in my paw, hammer back, ready in case something came down that driveway out of the woods. I felt naked, exposed, out in the middle of the asphalt, but I could not very well take Trixie and her heels into the woods to flank the big house up ahead. She seemed unconcerned by the potential threat, so I swallowed and kept going.

The big house was really a mansion, a baroque thing built by some occultist for his coven and then passed from fringie buyer to fringie buyer until it came into the possession of the Nazis. That was part of the charm of Lost Angeles – weirdos and strange-os. Most were a lot less sinister and a lot more harmless than Hitler's fan club.

It was three stories, with turrets, garrets, and windows across the front. Light poured out of some of them, but there was no movement. It was as quiet as a tomb.

We approached cautiously. If there were survivors, I expected they would be trigger-happy, and I did not want to be trigger-sad.

There was a wide porch out front. In the center was a large double door that was the main entrance; it was wide open, just like the gate below. And just like at the gate, there were stiffs. A couple of dead Nazis with shotguns were lying on the grass out front, peppered with shots. Whoever was doing the shooting made up for the lack of accuracy – they were hit from toes to temples with no rhyme or reason – with volume. At least one of the krauts had got off a couple blasts with his trench gun; two empty shells were lying on the turf.

"Must have been quite the battle," Trixie opined.

"And we're so deep in the canyon no one outside of here heard a thing."

I went first up the steps to the porch, the barrel of my hand cannon leading the way. The open doors were pocked with bullet holes, as was another Nazi lying on his back in the foyer. The sight of the dead fascists had me torn; they were in the optimal condition for Nazis, but I had questions, and none of the ones we had come across as yet had been in any condition to chat.

We went inside, and I saw Trixie had her .25 out. We worked our way through the first floor. It was empty, except for the odd dead Nazi. Then we went through the upper floors quickly. This was where they slept. There was a large dorm-style room with multiple cots for *der flunkies*. It was littered with girly mags, beer bottles, and there was a target board on the wall with a dozen darts stuck through a picture of Winston Churchill.

"Guess they don't appreciate old Winnie spoiling their dreams of victory," I said to Trixie.

"Someday, how you feel about him will be an IQ test," she said, in that haze of hers when she got to prognosticating. "If you hate him, you fail."

There were also some quite nice rooms for the bosses. No vulgar pilsner bottles littering their digs. They seemed to enjoy champagne. We found some dead flunkies, but the bosses were absent in body, if not image.

"Look at that," Trixie said, pointing up.

There was a painting of a gentleman in full Nazi regalia over the fireplace, chin jutting like Mussolini, and an American flag on his brown shirt.

"Ulysses Jameson Merz," Trixie read from the plaque below the edge of the frame. "I've seen him around. He's the local *Fuhrer*. He tries to wrap himself in the red, white, and blue. A rich heir to a concrete fortune back east."

"Daddy must be so proud," I said. "But apparently, he's not so popular with the visitors from earlier tonight." A line of bullet holes ran from top to bottom of the portrait.

"Somebody took the time to do that," Trixie said.

"Somebody sure hates Nazis," I observed. "I guess you can't paint anyone all black."

"So, we have a house full of dead wannabe Adolphs and nothing else. What next?"

"Well," I asked. "Where would you be if you were a prisoner?"

Trixie paused, then smiled.

"Basement."

We searched the first floor for a few minutes but came up with nothing.

"There has to be a door," I said.

"It's going to be a secret one," Trixie said. "Goes with the motif."

"Where would I be if I were a door?" I said aloud. I looked around. We were in the main room under the glare of Herr Merz. Besides a dead Nazi who someone had finished off with a round to the temple, there was some furniture, a sofa, and a bookcase on the wall.

Of course. The dead Nazi had probably spilled the beans before they finished him.

I walked to the bookcase and started feeling along the edges. It took me a minute until I found the button and pushed it. The bookcase detached from the wall and swung out.

"How did you know?" Trixie asked.

"I watch a lot of movies," I said. "And Nazis are too dumb to read."

There were wooden stairs descending into the basement, which was lit with bare light bulbs. I listened for a few seconds and slowly walked downward, satisfied it was safe. There was a creak, very loud, and I paused for a moment before continuing.

The basement was enormous and was probably the site of bizarre rituals long before the Nazis got it and converted it. It was now a laboratory, or had been. There were large workbenches in the center. Most of the tubes, beakers, and burners were shattered and broken. There were file cabinets, and the records were tossed, with some probably taken.

"What is this place?" Trixie asked.

I scanned the racks on the walls. It was a storehouse of ingredients. Some of the jars were gone, while others were still there. Eye of newt. Wolfsbane. Belladonna. Satyr essence – I grimaced at the thought of having to collect that.

"Look," Trixie said, pointing to a chair by the wall, a wall with rings bolted into it. Something shiny was on the cement floor. I knelt down and picked it up.

"Silver fragment," I said. "Like someone used a bolt cutter on a silver chain."

"But they didn't free him," Trixie said. "Why not?"

"Because they wanted him and whatever else was being made here.

"What do you make out of a demigod?" Trixie asked.

"I don't know, but someone else was not here voluntarily either." I pointed to some more cuttings, these steel and not silver. On the wall was another bolt, and a steel chain hung from it. It had been snipped off after about four feet.

"They had someone else chained up here," Trixie observed.

"This is a lab. I bet it was the chemist," I said. "Their involuntary chemist."

"But what was he making?" asked Trixie.

The voice came out of nowhere, weak and throaty.

"Heil Hitler!"

I wheeled around, and there was a wide-eyed young man, probably early-twenties, in a bloodied brown shirt swaying unsteadily. He must have come from one of the corners, overlooked as dead. He certainly was not far from his reward, and he swayed unsteadily, his eyes unable to focus.

"Herr *oberst*, we tried to stop them!" he blurted out. A trickle of blood coiled down from his lower lip. He had clearly been shot. He stood expectantly.

"He means you," Trixie said, adding, "Herr *oberst*." It meant "colonel." I guess I looked like one of his bosses when you had a bullet in your belly.

"Uh, *heil* Hitler," I said for lack of anything else to start the conversation with.

"We tried to stop them. There were too many, but we fought like Aryan tigers!"

"Great work," I said. "The Fatherland is proud. Now, who did this?"

He looked at me, confused.

"The communists."

"The communists?"

"And probably the Jews, but definitely the communists. They defiled the portrait of Herr Merz!"

He staggered forward, and I caught him before he fell.

"They," he said. "They took the doctor. They took the prisoner! You must tell Herr Merz!"

"Isn't he here?"

"No," the young stormtrooper said, looking at me as if I was the stupid one. "Ciro's."

"Ciro's?"

"Ciro's. You must tell him! All our work will be for nothing!" he gasped and coughed up a plug of blood, which I narrowly dodged.

"*Heil*," he began, then groaned and went limp. I let him fall to the floor. He hit like a sack of mashed potatoes.

"The communists have Gaultier?" Trixie said. "Even I did not see that coming."

"Time to go," I said. We headed upstairs, through the first floor, and out the front door.

There were headlights coming up the road. Four identical cars tore up the road past the guardhouse and toward the big house.

"Those look like feds," Trixie said.

"I've had enough of Connolly for one day. Into the woods," I said. Trixie would have to do the best she could in her footwear.

We moved surprisingly fast – say what you will about the Nazis, but they sure kept their forest clean as a fire precaution.

We got to my car, and I drove, rolling out in neutral to the road and not cranking the ignition or turning on the headlights until I was well past the open gate and down the street.

"Now what?" I asked.

"I think that's obvious, Eddie," Trixie said. "Ciro's. Time to go nightclubbing."

8.

The Sunset Strip was the beating heart of Lost Angeles, not the downtown – almost no one went downtown, at least not at night. The Strip ran across the northern edge of the city, from Hollywood west out to Beverly Hills, skirting the foot of the hills. It was a festival of neon and searchlights, much swankier than Hollywood itself. This is where you came to do LA properly.

It was bright enough on Sunset to be daylight as we headed east. Up ahead, there was a billboard for Chesterton's with little Shirly Temple taking a puff – "Healthy tobacco for growing boys and girls!" it admonished. Another, for some overpriced Scotch whisky, featured Basil Rathbone, Sherlock Holmes himself, in full evening dress, informing us that a pop before bed was elementary.

The sidewalks were crowded with a mix of gawking yokels and local gawkees, all parading along the sidewalks, slipping in and out of the bars and clubs and theaters. You could actually meet your heroes here, getting close enough for them to maybe stop being your heroes. I was down by The Purple Owl one night where a nice corn-fed couple from Iowa, probably, ran into a bleary-eyed Mickey Rooney and asked for his John Hancock to show the folks back home. I guess they confused Movie Mickey with the real deal. They caught him on the tail end of a bender and got his Crab Louie splashed all over themselves. At least it was more memorable than another scribble in their autograph book.

The Strip was crowded with the glamorous and the envious, and they seemed not to have a care in the world regardless of what was going on across the pond. I figured we would be part of that mess soon enough – no one ever listened to George Washington's warning about foreign entanglements – so I did not begrudge people the chance to celebrate while they still had something to celebrate. The curtain was coming down on the good times, and once it fell, it would be a long time before it rose again.

Ciro's was one of LA's primo night spots, situated on the Western edge of the Strip on the north side of the street. It was a squat, sprawling building that pushed up against a rough-hewn cliff where someone had clawed out the hillside to fit it in. The east side was where the valets, clad in red uniforms with fezzes for some reason, parked the cars. But only the nice ones – if you were some schmoe with a jalopy, you could go find a spot off one of the side streets. Caddies, Duesenbergs, Mercuries – the gawkers were gawking at the lineup of premium Detroit steel almost as hard as they gawked at the ladies and gentlemen dressed to the nines who were flowing in and out of the club.

Trixie, of course, was a perfect fit for the glamourous crowd. Me, that was a different story. I was looking rough after my day, and my car was nice but not that nice. If I were anyone else, the valet captain would have shaken his head sadly, apologized for the full lot, and waved me off. But I was Eddie Loud, and Eddie Loud was everybody's best buddy. I cultivated the parkers, the bellhops, the maître 'ds, and everyone else who made this town tick. Yeah, it's nice to pal around with the demis and the stars – I'd done my share – but it was some young Betty just off the bus from Terre Haute who spent her days auditioning – that is, fighting off handsy producers – and her nights at the front of the club who could get you and your honey a two-top up front by Henny Youngman or way in the back in Siberia next to the swinging kitchen doors.

She got a buck from Eddie Loud when he came calling and her boss got a five spot. The guy parking my car got a buck, and that was just for bringing it back without any dents. Toss in a little good information – who was going home with who, who wasn't going home with who – and there was another five on top. I laid it on thick, and tonight was the kind of night all that generosity paid off.

"Eddie!" Vic, the valet captain, said, cutting off his boy as he stepped to get my door himself. His accent was vaguely Italian. He came from somewhere but had been here a while. On the opposite side, one of the other lot boys was helping Trixie out. She looked like royalty, and I could see the kid was impressed.

My hand went out to the captain; Vic took it, and the fiver tucked inside my hand, as I stood up.

"Who's here tonight?" I asked.

"Big night," he said. "All Tinseltown, it seems. You taking your lady out on the town?" He seemed impressed that Eddie Loud could draw that kind of quality dame.

"I'm taking *him*, honey," Trixie said as she sashayed over. Vic grinned.

"Eddie, you dog," he said. A lot boy slid behind my wheel – I had left the keys in the ignition – and rolled my ride away to park.

"Say Vic, I'm wondering if you got anybody here who might be, you know, a little sketchy."

"There are some guys I wouldn't borrow money from, if that's what you mean." The mob guys loved to hit the clubs.

"Not gangsters, Vic," I said. "Something else."

"Like?"

"Nazis."

Vic's smile faded fast; I had struck a nerve.

"Yeah, those sons of bitches are in tonight. As bad as the damn commies, though at least the Hitler set tips."

I could imagine Vic wasn't thrilled. Like him, lots of the help at Ciro's and many other places had come over from Europe, some a few steps ahead of the Gestapo. The clubs loved to hire them because they understood service. Their continental style really impressed the stars – most of whom were themselves five or ten years off a farm or out of a tenement and didn't know any better.

"Frenchie working tonight?" I asked. Frenchie was the general manager. He may have been called "Frenchie," but he ran that club like a German, with exacting standards and no slack. That's why Ciro's was Ciro's, the top of the heap.

Frenchie got a ten.

"Yeah, he's here tonight," Vic answered. I took Trixie by the arm and we started to the front of the line. I knew the two big guys at the front and they shepherded us in, right past the queue of waiting customers. One of them seemed to be someone I recognized.

"Bela Lugosi," Trixie told me, though I had not asked. Stars usually didn't have to wait, but he was probably in the doghouse for not paying his bar tab. I had heard that with his movie career winding down, he was making extra money at private parties thrown by rich vampires who impressed their bloodsucking buddies by hiring the Tinseltown archetype to show up in a cape and lurk around for their amusement.

Lost Angeles used you up and spit you out.

Trixie and I had both been to Ciro's many times; it was relatively new, yet it seemed like Ciro's would be an institution forever. But not to Trixie.

"Someday this will be a comedy store," she said. "But I don't know what that means. Maybe they will sell jokes. I can hear lots of complaining about airline food."

"If you can afford to eat on an airplane, you have no business complaining," I sniffed. "Comedy store? You sure are an odd duck."

"I never asked to be."

We went inside, and it was ten degrees hotter. The ballroom was packed, positively busting at the seams. It was all talk and laughs – the bandstand was empty, with the musicians on a break. Everyone was dressed in their finest, and most sat either at intimate two-tops or four-tops with their cronies. The champagne was flowing, the money was rolling in.

And Frenchy was at the front, right by the coat check, berating a busboy for some minor misstep. He liked things perfect; that's what kept the swells (and their money) coming back night after night.

When he saw me approaching, he dismissed the busboy, then smiled and greeted me as if I were his long-lost brother.

"Eddie!" he said as if my appearance was one of the nine wonders of the world. "And Miss Gamble! Together! What's the occasion?"

"Frenchy, sorry to say that it's just business tonight," Trixie said. She batted her lashes.

"But Miss Gamble, we have Ethel Merman coming in later," he said, pausing for a reaction and repeating it for effect when none was forthcoming. "Ethel Merman? And Sir Julio, the funniest demigod of them all!"

I liked Ethel, but Sir Julio's act was old two centuries ago.

"Ciro's is where the stars truly shine," Trixie said. "We're looking for someone, Frenchie."

"Everyone comes to Ciro's."

"How about Ulysses Jameson Merz?"

The light went out in his eyes, and his fake smile faltered.

"He and his friends are here," Frenchie said flatly. "They seem to enjoy it."

I assumed Frenchy didn't.

"Their money spends like everyone else's," Frenchie said by way of explanation. "We strictly leave politics outside on the sidewalk."

"We're not here to make trouble," Trixie said, smiling warmly. "We just have a case and some questions, and we'll be on our way."

"Like I said, politics stay outside."

Trixie nodded.

"Eddie, thank the man."

I handed Frenchy a ten, and we went into the main room.

I had seen many of the faces around before. Some of them I saw on the big screen, like Jimmie Stewart, who was knocking back champagne in a corner with Katherine Hepburn and her lady friend. Others I saw on the job.

Joseph Onassis was there with an older mortal woman who was swooning over him. He claimed to be the grandson of Aphrodite, but he was an eighth or sixteenthbreed at best. Old Joe was pushing four hundred but still didn't look much older than sixty, and he still had that glow about him as well, a certain sad tiredness. He was always scamming some local dowager. I had had to run him off marks at the behest of their mortified families more times than I could count.

He saw me and stayed smooth as silk.

"Eddie Loud, always a pleasure."

"Got yourself a new friend, Mr. Onassis?"

"A *charming* new friend," he replied, turning to stare deeply into his latest companion's eyes. I did not know if *she* was charming, but he had sure charmed her.

"You kids behave," I said. His date giggled. She hadn't been a kid in about fifty years.

We moved through the crowd, looking for our quarry. Busboys scampered to clear tables as waiters and waitresses hurried to take and deliver drink orders. I saw Edith, a young singer just in from Paris making ends meet at the club. She gave me a warm smile as she carried a bottle of Maker's Mark over to an angry John Garfield. He sure knew how to put away the sauce; word was that he was also a secret commie.

That was Hollywood, all right. A lot of them fell in with the Reds, mostly because a lot of them never had much common sense to begin with. Acting wasn't about brains. It was about looks, luck, and, once in a blue moon, talent. Being a Red was in fashion in some circles, so they did it. But all the kissing Stalin's feet never meant a thing when it came to business – even the most dedicated Tinseltown pinko made Henry Ford look like Clara Barton where the subject was money. Workers of the world unite, and where the hell is my check?

"The movie stars are out tonight," Trixie observed. She nodded ahead to where an obviously smitten Humphrey Bogart sat with the luminous Carole Lombard. He was dressed in a white coat with black tie, and even the jaded denizens of Ciro's were impressed.

"Poor thing," Trixie whispered.

"Why do you say that?" I asked.

"I don't really know," Trixie replied sadly.

Bogart began talking to Dooley Wilson, a black musician who stopped by the table as the band slowly emerged back into the bandstand. Bogie had a glass of something brown in his right hand and one of his ever-present cigarettes in the other.

"That's going to be the death of him," Trixie whispered.

"You sure know how to spoil an evening," I replied.

"Speaking of a spoiled evening," Trixie said. "There's the Fatherland crew."

The Nazis were seated at a large, round table headed by Ulysses Merz, celebrating like they had just blitzkrieged one of the Low Countries. They did not wear armbands, of course – no politics across the threshold at Ciro's – and they were not wearing their formal uniforms, but their suits had a distinct Bavarian *putsch* quality, with a military cut and epaulets. Just enough to make their presence known without provoking too much of a reaction.

There were empty champagne bottles scattered across the tabletop – French vintages, just to rub it in. It was obvious that they had not yet heard the news from back at the ranch. Everyone was laughing and having a fine time, except one ramrod straight Prussian with a thin mustache and what was probably a student dueling scar across his right cheek. I smelled Gestapo right away. He seemed offended at seeing others enjoying themselves and was probably dreaming of a world where people practiced the goosestep instead of the foxtrot.

We started in their direction. We had no real plan, but I was looking forward to seeing Merz's expression when I delivered the bad news about Murphy Ranch.

Edith, the waitress, gave the ungrateful Garfield his bottle, and she took his growl with a smile even though she knew there was no tip at the end of this night from the proletarian hero. Then she swallowed hard and walked over to the Nazis. We were right behind her.

"Is that a French accent?" Merz inquired with mocking innocence.

"It is," Edith replied with cold formality.

"Ah, you should go home. Paris is much more efficient now under German management!" The table convulsed with laughter at Merz's jest.

I tapped Edith's shoulder, and she turned.

"Frenchie is asking for you," I said. She looked relieved and grateful.

"Excuse me," she said and turned and left us. I stood there with Trixie, looking down at the six fascists.

"Well, I guess you'll be taking our orders!" Merz said jovially. The Nazis howled, finding this hilarious. "Get out your pad and pencil!"

"You know," I said, smiling. "I pinned the last Hun-lover who mouthed off to me to a French oak tree with an M1917 bayonet."

They went dead silent.

"I'm Eddie Loud. The Eddie Loud you missed ventilating earlier today. Sorry about your boys. And for ruining your evening. Guess I'm like Winston Churchill, always spoiling your plans."

"You are playing a dangerous game, Mr. Loud," Merz said. "We won't miss twice."

"We're both playing a dangerous game, Herr Merz."

"Eddie," cautioned Trixie.

"You should listen to your woman, Eddie," Merz said, standing up. It was meant to be threatening.

"I was going to tell him to sock you in the head instead of a vital organ," Trixie explained.

Merz looked daggers at her. She smiled. He moved in her direction.

I got ready to act – the only question was head or gut.

This was going to be fun. Except the Prussian ruined it. He grabbed Merz's sleeve.

"*Nein*," he said, glaring at me. "Not now, not here."

"You should listen to Gestapo Fritz here, Merz," I taunted.

Merz froze for a moment and then began laughing. His comrades – less the Prussian – paused momentarily, then joined in. Within a few seconds, they were roaring. Had they gone mad right in front of me?

"Eddie, Eddie, we can't let mere politics spoil our evening! Why, tonight is about comradeship and drinking and singing! Yes, singing, that's it! Before the band settles back in, why don't we make our own music? Get up, up!"

His fellow Nazis stood, pushing back their chairs.

"A song, gentlemen, a song to unite us and the world!"

Where was this going?

They began to sing, loudly:

Lieb Vaterland
Du hast nach bösen Stunden
Aus dunkler Tiefe einen neuen Weg gefunden

"*Die Wacht am Rhein*" – "The Watch on the Rhine," a Nazi anthem playing here in my country. I balled my fist.

They were just getting wound up.

Ich liebe dich
Das heißt, ich hab' dich gern
Wie einen würdevollen, etwas müden, alten Herrn

The place went dead quiet except for that damned song. Every eye in the place was on the Nazis, and the brownshirts were loving the attention. They held the whole room in their hands, tormenting it, and especially those who had escaped their clutches.

Trixie was not having it. She turned to Edith, who had come back with a bottle of champagne for a nearby table.

"Do you sing?" she asked.

"*Oui*," Edith replied.

"Then sing," Trixie told her. "*La Marseillaise*. Sing it!"

Edith took a deep breath and sang loudly and clearly:

Allons enfants de la Patrie,
Le jour de gloire est arrivé!
Contre nous de la tyrannie!

Edith only soloed for a moment. Then, all around the room, the waiters and waitresses, along with many of the customers, stopped, stood, and joined in.

L'étendard sanglant est levé (bis)
Entendez-vous dans nos campagnes
Mugir ces féroces soldats?
Ils viennent jusque dans vos bras
Egorger vos fils, vos compagnes!

The Nazis were shocked. They tried to out-sing the response, but Trixie turned to the bandstand and yelled, "Play it!"

The band swung into action, roaring out the music. Around the room, everyone was now standing. Joseph Onassis sang along, and obviously knew the words; he had probably been there when *La Marseillaise* was written.

I joined in too, though I did not know the lyrics: "Da da da da da da da daaaa da duh da de da dah dah, da da!"

I turned, and even Frenchy, tears welling in his eyes, was bellowing out the refrain:

Aux armes citoyens,
Formez vos bataillons
Marchons, marchons
Qu'un sang impur
Abreuve nos sillons

The Nazis fell silent, broken and beaten. Only the Prussian's face was redder than Merz's.

The band hit the final note, and the crowd went wild, cheering and howling.

"*Vive la France!*" shouted Edith. "*Vive la libertie!*"

The beaten Nazis fell back to their table to gather up their jackets. I moved in.

"You think this ridiculous display makes any difference?" Merz asked, eyes flashing. "You think a song will keep Major Strasser here and the Fuhrer's armies from marching across this degenerate country?"

"You're pretty sure of yourself, Merz," I said. "We aren't Czechoslovakia. Behind every oak tree will be an American just dying to take down a kraut with his deer rifle."

"Oh, I am sure of the future. The future is America, and the world, all under the swastika! You have no idea what power you are dealing with!"

"Be silent!" Major Strasser shouted at his putative master, and Merz obeyed. That clarified the chain of command for me. The German was in charge.

I ignored the ridiculous American traitor and stared into his Prussian master's eyes.

"The best part of tonight wasn't watching you be made fools of, though that was nice," I said. "The best part is going to be watching your face when I deliver the news."

"What are you talking about?" the Gestapo officer demanded.

"Guess you haven't heard. While you were out on the town, somebody hit Murphy Ranch."

"Hit?"

"Yeah, like a ton of bricks. All the little stormtroopers you left behind are pushing up Aryan daisies. Seems like the commies got the drop on them. They found your lab. They took your demigod. And they took your chemist."

"They took the doctor?" Merz blurted out.

"The doctor is out," I said, smirking.

Strasser went pale, probably thinking that his boss back in Berlin would be very displeased. Merz just stood there, his jaw twitching. They knew exactly what this meant.

"So, let me ask you, why did you goosestepping punks have a demigod chained up in a lab?"

"We must go," Strasser said to his companions. "Now! *Raus!*"

"Yeah, you should *raus* right over there, but there's not much left except stiffs and feds."

Strasser stepped forward and attempted to push around me. I put my hand on his chest.

"This is America, Fritz. You need to pay your tab."

He glared at me with pure hate, then looked at Merz. Crestfallen, Merz reached inside his jacket and pulled out a billfold, leaving his cash on the table.

Strasser moved forward.

"Goodbye," I said, adding, "*Auf Wiedersehen.*"

"That means 'until we meet again,'" Strasser hissed. "And, believe me, we will."

"Looking forward to it," I replied. I was.

"You have lovely singing voices," Trixie added as the stormtroopers trooped past, with the crowd laughing and jeering as they went.

"I was hoping for more information from them," Trixie said. "But that had its charms."

"I think they will be looking for their lost demigod."

"And their lost doctor. He said 'doctor.'" She caught onto nuances like that.

"We start looking again tomorrow," I said. We began walking to the door past the tables of movie stars.

"Did you see that? The song?" Bogart was telling Dooley Wilson. "That was great stuff! Sensational. It will fit right into my next movie. Say, Dooley, you should be in it! There's a part for a pianist. It's going to be called *Casablanca*!"

9.

I got back to my flat after dropping Trixie off at her place. It had been a hell of a day, and I poured myself two fingers of Jameson's to help take the edge off. Sitting at my rear window, I looked up into the hills. There was Apollo's house, Elysium, brightly lit, no doubt shaking with the party that never seemed to end. Down here, I took a sip from my tumbler. It was good. Just what the doctor ordered.

I pulled Constance Showers's number out of my pocket and grabbed the phone. The operator connected me, and it was a couple of rings before my client picked up.

"Yes?" she said. I was starting to know that voice.

"It's Eddie Loud," I said. "We didn't get him."

Sometimes, it's best not to sugarcoat it.

"Oh," she replied. She didn't sound surprised. Maybe she was getting used to bad news, though I wasn't getting used to delivering it. This gig wasn't turning out the way my jobs usually do. I usually get results, but now I felt like I was just getting deeper and deeper into something I didn't understand.

I didn't like it.

"We went up there to Murphy Ranch, but somebody else got there first," I reported. "The Nazis had Charles Gaultier, all right. He was chained down in the basement in what looked to me like a laboratory. By the time we got there, he was gone, and the guys holding him prisoner were gone too, except they were gone to hell."

"All the Nazis are dead?" she asked.

"No, unfortunately, just the flunkies who were watching him. The bigwigs were out partying at Ciro's when the shooting started. I went down there to deliver the news to them. They weren't happy to hear it, but I didn't get much more out of them."

"Merz is alive?" she exclaimed, sounding distressed.

"You know him?"

"Everyone in the city knows him, strutting around in his ridiculous uniform with his mob. A disgusting little man. Did he say anything?"

"He did a little singing, but that worked out poorly," I said. "He wasn't feeling very chatty after I told him his Red rivals had liberated his prize and that his junior stormtroopers were shot to ribbons.

"Red?"

"It looks like the people who took him were the communists."

Again, she didn't seem surprised.

"Of course, the feds are on it too," I added. "Have you talked to them?"

"No," she said.

"The feds have jurisdiction over kidnappings. Do you remember the Lindbergh baby? Are you sure they're not involved on your end?"

"Mr. Loud, I would know if I talked to the FBI."

"Just making sure there are no secrets between us, Miss Showers, because I came very close to becoming an ex-private eye today. I don't like getting shot. It's bad for my suits."

There was silence at the other end of the phone. I could hear her breathing softly.

"What now?" she asked.

"It was the Nazis who had him, and it looks like the communists have him now," I said.

I was aware of how ridiculous that sounded. Why would the Nazis want a demigod? And why would the communists? Hell, the official Communist Party line on demigods was that they were part of the capitalist oppressor class. Most of the Russian demis had fled after Lenin got sent back and had his little Bolshevik revolution a couple of decades ago. The ones the Russians couldn't kill outright they sent off to Siberia somewhere. I didn't want to think about what they were going through, but it probably made Ares's sojourn underwater in a silver box seem like a tropical vacation.

I got why the Nazis would be interested in the Olympians. They have that whole *ubermensch*/superman thing. But the Reds? And J. Edgar Hoover's boys? What the hell did they all want with Charles Gaultier?

I asked what she thought.

"I wouldn't know," Miss Showers insisted.

"Maybe give it some thought because I'm running out of ideas."

There was a cold silence on the phone for a moment. Then she spoke again.

"Can you find him?"

Could I find him? The hell if I knew. But I was getting to be sure of one thing. I wasn't going to be able to figure out the "where" until I figured out the "why."

"Maybe," I said. "I don't know. Whatever this is, it is going a lot deeper than it looked like when I started. Why does everyone want him?"

"I can't help you there," she whispered.

"No idea at all why they took him?"

"I don't know. I truly don't. I've worked with him for a couple of years. He was a nice man, a kind man, a good man. He doesn't deserve this."

"I'm not sure anyone deserves this," I said. "We found where they kept him. It was in a basement, chained up with silver. It was like a laboratory in there, test tubes, beakers, and so forth. Lots of ingredients, not normal medicine but demi medicine.

Was there something about him, something special, maybe in his blood? Maybe something they wanted from him?"

"I can't think of anything. He rarely went to a doctor, a demigod doctor, that is. They can get sick, too, in their own fashion, but not usually Charles. He is so pure blood and all."

"But when he did, where did he go? Who was his doctor?"

She paused for a moment. Even demis get sick sometimes, but not the same way we do. We get sick and die. They get sick and get miserable, at least the ones with the stronger immortal blood. The ones with only a touch of immortal blood have it worst. They caught the Olympian ailments and the human ones, too. There is nothing sadder than somebody whose great-great-great-grandmother was Athena coughing his lungs out with tuberculosis even as his mind is fading away with deity dementia.

But there were doctors with that specialty. It was a vaguely disreputable specialty. For the most part, demis can't use the medicine we do. You're not going to hand a demi two aspirins and tell him to call you in the morning. They can get depressed or break a bone, and then they have to go to somebody special, somebody who knows how to treat them. Those jars I had found in the basement, the wolfsbane, the eye of newt, that sort of thing – were the kind of things that you gave to a demi when he was feeling down.

Of course, there were a lot of quacks out there, frauds who took advantage of somebody who was a sixteenth demi and for whom mortal medicine just didn't have the answer. Most doctors would have nothing to do with them. It was a sideline, kind of unsavory, but then it was still science. There were a few with class, as opposed to hacks operating out of back rooms off dark alleys. My money was on Charles Gaulthier, on those rare occasions he was feeling down, going to a top-shelf demigod sawbones.

"I don't really know," Miss Showers said. "He didn't share that part of his life with me." That struck me as odd. Constance

Showers was Charles Gautier's majordomo, the woman who ran all aspects of his life. Now, she was telling me she didn't know who his demigod doctor was? That seemed far-fetched. Maybe he was ashamed. Maybe he was covering something up. Maybe it was one of those problems where he wasn't cutting it in the manhood department and didn't want her to know. If you think that's bad news for a mortal man, imagine you're a demigod who can no longer pull off the Casanova act.

"How about his driver?" I asked.

"No, he wouldn't know that," Miss Showers said emphatically. "Look, I just need you to find him. If the communists really have him, you locate him and tell me where he is. I need to know."

I thought it over for a minute. I considered quitting, just walking away, but now it was gnawing at me. I didn't like starting something and not finishing it. Plus, even if I pulled out, there was no guarantee Trixie Gamble wouldn't keep at it. I hadn't known for very long, but what I did know of her was that she didn't seem to be the type who just gave up. And it wouldn't be right to let her go it alone, not just against the Nazis but against the damn communists, too.

"I'll find him," I said.

"You tell me as soon as you think you know where he is," Miss Showers instructed. "But no more rescue missions. I'll pay his ransom. If they are communists, they'll want money."

I never met anybody greedier than a Red, but there was something bothering me about all of this.

"I don't think this is about money," I said.

"No, Mr. Loud, it is always about money. The only people who will tell you that it's not about the money are the people who don't have any money."

My breakfast at the diner was a Lucky Strike and a cup of black coffee. I also had a side dish, a plate of sunny-side-up eggs. I just picked at them. Trixie watched me, the smoke curling out of the end of her Marlboro. She took a puff and elegantly exhaled, considering my report about the previous evening's phone conversation with my client.

"I don't trust this Constance Showers," she declared.

"I don't trust anybody," I replied. I took another drag. It was hot and good. At my last physical, my doctor had warned me I wasn't smoking enough. Nicotine keeps the lungs clean, he told me. Kills all those bacteria that make you sick. I was doing my best to stay healthy.

"The thing that's been bothering me about this isn't the who, it's the why," Trixie said. "Why would Nazis want this guy? Why would the communists want this guy? And does it seem like the feds want this guy? What's so special about Charles Gaulthier?"

"He's rich," I said.

"That doesn't make him special, not here in Los Angeles. Lots of people are rich. And lots of people who aren't rich are faking it."

"He's lived through a lot of history," I suggested. "Maybe he knows something about the past. Something important."

"Maybe," Trixie said thoughtfully. "But do Merz and his pals strike you as history buffs? The communists are all about the end of history. And that fed Connolly probably thinks history started the day J. Edgar Hoover got out of diapers."

"And into a sleek little cocktail dress," I added, not that I was much for gossip. I just preferred the juicy facts.

"That'll make him an icon someday," Trixie said, looking a little confused.

"What?"

"Hoover dressing up like a dame."

"Trixie, maybe you should hop on a ship over to Europe to talk to that Sigmund Freud guy because I frankly think you're crazy. No one would ever believe a man pretending to be a woman would be anything but a nutcase."

"I'm just telling you what I see. I don't understand it."

"Okay, enough of your wacky prognostications. Where were we?"

"What else is special about Charles Gaulthier that makes everybody want him chained up in the corner of their basement?"

I thought about it for a minute, and then it came to me.

"He's immortal," I said.

"As far as we know," Trixie replied. "He might die of old age in a couple of thousand years."

"I don't know if he'll still be around in a couple of thousand years, but I know enough about these near-full blood immortal demis to know that you can't put them down. I could unload six cylinders of silver hollow point slugs into his forehead, and he'd come out with a bad headache and a worse attitude, but he would still be breathing. You can't kill the guy. He can't die. Maybe that's the thing."

"They had a laboratory there. They had all sorts of demi medicine. And they had a doctor chained up, probably the guy doing whatever lab work was being done."

"Do you think they were experimenting on him? Taking his blood or something? Trying to make some immortality potion?"

"Could be," Trixie said. "But then, it's not like that hasn't been done before. It's not like mad scientists haven't done all sorts of experiments on demis, trying to capture their essence. Mankind has always tried to figure out a way to live forever, and they've always thought that demi blood might be the key."

"That sort of thing is a mortal sin in the church, and it's against federal law big time. No experimentation on demis. No trying to make regular people into demi gods."

"Which explains why they're doing it on the down low."

I took another drag off my cig.

"I get the Nazis. They want to make a master race and maybe they think demigod blood or whatever is going to do it. I can see that. But the communists? That's not their style. The workers of the world want to unite to lose their chains, not to be workers for eternity. Hell, when you're living as one of Stalin's slaves, death is the only thing you've got to look forward to."

"Maybe they're not doing it for the regular folk. Maybe it's for the bigwigs," Trixie suggested.

"But why *here*? Why in Los Angeles? Why not in Moscow? The Russians have a bunch of demis rotting away out in Siberia somewhere. Why don't they experiment on them?"

"Maybe the talent is here," Trixie said.

"The doctor?" I said.

"A demi doctor. But a real one. Not some quack."

"Now, where would we find a top-flight demi medical doctor?" I asked.

"Someday, this medical center is going to be named after Ronald Reagan," Trixie announced.

I looked at her sitting in the passenger seat as we drove onto the campus of the University of California, Los Angeles and shook my head. I knew Ronald Reagan from around town. Nice enough guy. A Midwestern guy. Straightforward, honest, liked horses, hated commies. A good guy, but I didn't think they would be naming a cul-de-sac after him, much less a hospital.

"What is he going to do? Discover the cure for the common cold?" I laughed.

"No, I think he's going to overthrow the Soviet Union," Trixie said. She seemed almost as confused as I was.

"Are you sure you haven't been hitting the sauce when I wasn't looking?"

"I just tell you what I see. I don't pretend to understand it."

"And we're all gonna have those little Dick Tracy wristwatches where you can talk to people and watch movies on them, right?"

"Uh-huh. And every book in the world will be inside them."

"Trixie, do you ever get tired of being related to Cassandra?"

"I get tired of the part of the curse where no one listens to me."

"Well, you know, maybe there was a reason no one listened to Cassandra. Maybe she was crazy, too."

"You should park over there," Trixie said.

I pulled into one of the guest spaces. The medical school was housed in an imposing Spanish-style building with a red adobe roof next to the hospital. The students, young men in suits and ties, wandered in and out. They seemed impressed by Trixie Gamble and her high stiletto heels. They didn't seem to notice me at all. I was getting used to that.

We went through the front door, and it was evidently between classes because the hallways were packed with students carrying their books from seminar to seminar. I looked around for a directory on the wall but didn't see one. Instead, there was an information desk with a mousy young lady sitting there, head buried in a paperback potboiler called *Love's Savage Fury*. She is probably a student at the undergraduate campus who took the job in hopes of lassoing a future doctor.

We stepped to the counter and she looked up, a little confused. We weren't her usual clients.

"Hi, honey," Trixie said, sweet as molasses. "Maybe you can help us. We're looking for the right professor to talk to about a very particular medical issue."

"Do you have an appointment?"

"Oh, we're not sick. We have some specialized questions that maybe he could help us out with, but we're not sure who to talk to."

"Oh, well, what's your question?"

"It has to do with unusual medical problems. Medical problems related to demigods."

The girl seemed taken aback, and I got the distinct impression that the demigod doctors were the redheaded stepchildren of the medical school.

"You could go up to Dr. Florence's office," she suggested. "He's the head of the department... ever since..."

"Ever since what, honey?"

"Well, ever since Dr. Hollister, you know."

"What do we know, dear?"

"Since he disappeared," the girl whispered as if she was repeating a terrible secret.

"When was that?" I asked.

"Maybe a month or so ago. It's been a while since the detectives were last here."

"The detectives looked into it?"

"They were from the FBI," she whispered, in awe. Obviously, she did not know many agents.

We went to the far end of the building, nearly empty and well off the beaten path, and waited endlessly for the ancient elevator car to finally drop down to us. Our objective was two floors above.

"We should have just walked up the stairs," I muttered.

The car finally came, and I was sure it would stall out and strand us between floors, but it finally stopped and the door creaked open.

We proceeded down the dingy, empty hallway. We were definitely on the wrong side of the medical school tracks.

We found what we were looking for and went in. Trixie took the lead with our subject.

"We appreciate you taking the time to see us, Dr. Florence," Trixie said to the young professor. She had turned on her maximum molasses act, but he seemed suspicious and shook our hands as if he worried he might catch something. His office was in the far corner of the building, past a closed door marked "Dr. Xavier Hollister." It was dusty, like no one had used it for a while. Dr. Eugene Florence was now the entire demigod medical department at UCLA.

"I've told the police everything I know," he insisted.

"No doubt," I replied. "But we have our own case and think it might peripherally involve Dr. Hollister. We'd love to help solve that mystery, too."

"You have some information on where he might be?"

"We're putting the pieces together," said Trixie. "So, what happened? How did he disappear?"

"He was working late. He often did that. He would see his private patients all day and then do research alone here at night. He has a small laboratory in his office. The janitor last saw him at about eleven. His car never left the parking lot, but he was not here in the morning. That was about a month ago."

"What was his area of specialty?"

"Doing medical research into demigods. It's not a popular subject. You have to walk a fine line to make sure you're not breaking any laws, and, of course, he never did. He was very scrupulous and very serious. Demis are fascinating creatures, so like us but also unlike us. The traditional medical community looks down on what we do, though we have the potential for making breakthroughs that traditional doctors can't even imagine."

"Like involving immortality?" I asked.

Dr. Florence's eyes flashed at me.

"Absolutely not. That's highly illegal, as well as immoral. No, Dr. Hollister wasn't looking into how demis can live forever. Quite the opposite. He was looking into how they can die."

I did not see that twist coming.

"Why?" Trixie asked.

"Because he is a scientist," Dr. Florence said.

"May I look in his office?" I asked.

"Absolutely not, it's private. No one can go in there."

Trixie glanced in my direction, and our eyes met. I knew what she had in mind.

"Dr. Florence," she purred. "I'm very impressed by your courage in swimming upstream against the establishment to study what you believe in."

Dr. Florence's eyes locked onto hers. She fluttered her eyelashes. Even I felt it, the feminine energy. She circled him like a cat, walking to the window on the other side of the room. He followed her.

"I'm trying to help humanity," he said grandly.

"I so admire that," she cooed, hovering over him on her stiletto heels.

That was my cue.

"I'm going to find the little boys' room," I announced. Dr. Florence ignored me, if he even heard me at all. Trixie was telling him how impressed she was with his work as I slipped out the door. And last I saw, he was lapping it up like a kitty at a bowl of warm milk.

I walked over to Dr. Hollister's dusty door and checked up and down the hallway. Nothing – no one seemed to come out here unless they had to.

It had an old-time mortise lock, battered with age. I slipped my paw into my jacket pocket and pulled out my pick set. It took me less than a minute of jiggling until I heard the satisfying "click." That was the thing about most office locks – they were designed to keep honest people out. They couldn't stop a thief or a private dick from getting in.

I went through and closed the door behind me quietly. The lights were out and the blinds were drawn, but enough of the warm California sun streamed through the seams that I could see just fine. It was surprisingly large, with a desk up front and an exam table. Further back was another door. No desk for a secretary, though – they really exiled these demigod professors. He probably did all his administrative work and saw patients in here, too.

There were shelves on the walls with a lot of dusty volumes, some with titles in Latin or what I bet was Greek. I made out a few titles in English: *Biologies of the Immortals, Bacterial Load Ratios in Demigod Patients*, and *Apollonian Cell Structures*. Real page-turners.

He had his diplomas and certificates on the wall – Harvard Medical, a residence at the Mayo Clinic. He was something of a prodigy, I gathered. Awards, honors, but most of it was from the teens or twenties. I did not see any accolades after about 1930.

Maybe that was when he got off the traditional medicine path and started trifling with demigod medicine. His peers must have blackballed him, and the only reason they kept him around UCLA was tenure.

There were file cabinets, but they had been gone through. The locks had been busted off. Maybe the cops had tossed the place while looking for the missing sawbones, or maybe it was someone else.

I went to the second drawer down, which was marked "F-L." It was full of files with the last name, followed by the first name, written on the folder tabs. I looked at the "G" section, and I was not the first. No surprise – no Gaultier. If he had been a patient, someone had taken his medical records. The "G" files had been pulled out right where "Gaultier" would have fit in. That seemed to me more than just a coincidence.

I skimmed over the other names. The doctor sure had a healthy practice of unhealthy demis. I recognized some of the names from my time on the God Squad and my own cases. I took the opportunity to flip through some of them—why not? Did you know that a demi can get the clap? I didn't, not until then.

Apparently, there was a whole other world of medicine for the Olympians. About half the files I skimmed through had a common problem called "Minoan Ear." Apparently, you treated it with a mixture of vinegar, lilacs, and the blood of a sacrificed dove. Other ailments included "Sisyphus Heart," which required more esoteric remedies, including chimera venom.

I was learning a lot here. I knew they could get sick, especially the ones with thinner divine blood. I did not realize there were so many ways for them to do it. But the thing was that these ailments did not kill them, at least not the fuller-blooded ones. They just made them miserable, on and on and on, unless someone could find a magic potion to cure them.

And there were some surprises. I knew some people kept their demi blood on the down low. There are a lot of reasons why you might do that, and I was keeping more than a few secrets for people around LA. But the one at the back of the "L" section got me.

Hedy Lamarr? Yeah, I guess that made sense. She was gorgeous – I saw her walk into Ciro's once and the band stopped playing – but rumor had it she was a genius, too. A real super-brain. I heard it had something to do with radio waves or the like – top-secret stuff for the government. Looked like Dr. Hollister was her personal physician. I didn't dig through her records like I had for some of the sketchy characters I had met before; that seemed like an intrusion.

Closing the drawer, I looked around. Dr. Hollister had a corkboard mounted above his desk with lots of newspaper clippings from *The Times* pinned on with silver thumbtacks. Some of it was innocuous, with some stories about various gods and goddesses in or passing through town. Athena had come through town again and had been honored at the opera house a couple years ago. There were a few gossip items about others as well, but most of the clippings were about Apollo. Of course, he locked himself away behind the gates of Elysium up in the Hollywood Hills. His life was a never-ending party. Dr. Hollister seemed very interested in him.

A patient?

I went back to the drawers and checked the "A" files. There were no medical records for Apollo. But then, the good doctor might not have committed that kind of sensitive information to writing.

So far, I had not accomplished much except to confirm that Gaultier had likely been one of Dr. Hollister's patients and that Hedy Lamarr was full of even more surprises than anyone thought. Being a secret Olympian topped her swimming around in the altogether in that *Ecstasy* movie that everyone went to see because it was an artistic statement, but really because they just wanted to see a movie star in her birthday suit.

What next? I stood in the middle of the room, tapping my feet cogitating over what to do next, when my eye caught sight of a clipping tacked to the cork that I had overlooked before.

"Medusa At The Museum." The headline was circled in red. A petrified Gorgon from Greece was being shown in the Los Angeles County Natural History Museum. Some people had a problem with that; after all, it was a corpse, and Medusa had gotten a pretty rough deal simply for comparing her beauty to Athena. Some suffragettes, not satisfied with getting the vote, had put up quite a stink about it.

It struck me because a couple of weeks ago, over my breakfast, I had read that the museum curators had come out one day and found that one of the snake heads growing out of her skull had been broken off and stolen. The suffragettes denied it, and the mystery had faded. Now, there was a velvet rope around her at the Museum to keep back anyone looking for a keepsake.

So, why did Dr. Hollister care about Medusa, and was the vandalism of a dead monster a coincidence?

There was no other clue on the corkboard to give it some context. I looked around the room. It was time to check the closet.

I opened it up, and it was not a closet. It was a doorway to Dr. Hollister's laboratory.

There were no windows, so I had to turn on the lights. It was not particularly big, but it was well-used, and the equipment was all old. It looked to me like it was all secondhand like he scavenged what he could from the traditional medicine labs here in the building to create his own workplace.

Whoever tossed the place had been in here. There were no notebooks or papers. They took all that. There were racks on the wall, though, that reminded me of what we had found in the lab at Murphy Ranch, except the ingredients were gone. It looked like someone had come in and taken everything. I saw one broken jar on the floor and reached down to check it. The label read "Hemlock." It probably broke as whoever cleared the place was shoving everything into boxes.

Maybe it was the school cleaning up after its most embarrassing professor. Maybe it was the cops gathering evidence, though I doubted that – it seemed like a lot of work, and most of the force was allergic to effort.

Or someone was bringing along Dr. Hollister's supplies so he could continue his work in captivity. That was my guess.

But what was he working on?

What had Dr. Florence said? How demigods can die?

They could be a pain in the tail, sure, but why would anyone – much less Nazis and now communists – want to expend that much effort on beings that had mostly withdrawn from society and were loath to use their powers to influence it lest they find themselves on the frigid seafloor in their own pitch black, silver box that made Hades look like Bora-Bora?

I figured that I had seen enough, that if I stayed any longer, I was going to have another dozen questions come up and I'd want to beat my head into the wall. I went back out into the office and to the door, carefully turning the ancient knob and pulling it back so I could check out the hall.

Empty. Just some muffled noises of Trixie and Dr. Florence flirting in his office.

I slipped out into the hallway and carefully clicked the door shut behind me again, then returned to Dr. Florence's office. Trixie was sitting on his settee, still smiling, and so was the professor, though he seemed less than thrilled to see me return. He gave me an odd look, and I realized I had been gone for a long time.

"Had a ham sandwich last night that just didn't agree with me," I said by way of explanation. As I hoped, he did not push me for details.

"Well, I have to say that I do not believe I have ever had a more stimulating conversation," Trixie said. "Eddie, you would not believe the accomplishments of Dr. Florence. He found the cure for Corinthian Heat Rash. It was a terrible scourge of our demi friends. What did you say the ingredient was that tied your remedy together?"

"It was dryad tears," he said.

"Dryad tears," Trixie repeated triumphantly.

"For Olympians, they seem to react to a combination of both esoteric materials and supernatural elements."

"Fascinating," I said. "I'm sorry I was otherwise occupied and missed the conversation."

"He kept me very entertained," Trixie said, standing up and hoisting her leather purse's strap around her shoulder.

"You know, doctor," I said. "I was wondering. What kind of parts of Olympian creatures are effective in your work?"

"Lots of them," he said suspiciously.

"I remember a few weeks ago when someone broke a snake head off Medusa at the museum, and I wondered whether that might be something you might use in demi medicine?"

Dr. Florence eyed me suspiciously. The goodwill Trixie's flirting had earned us was fading fast.

"Something like that would not be medicine. It would be extremely dangerous," he said.

"Well, I hope the authorities track it down. Anyway, thank you for your time."

"I am absolutely charmed," Trixie said, holding out her hand. Dr. Florence shook it tentatively, but he was still giving me the stink eye.

I guess I struck a nerve.

Dr. Florence walked us to the door and shut it firmly behind us as we stepped into the hallway.

"Someone stole one of Medusa's snake heads?" Trixie said.

"Yeah, from the museum. Dr. Hollister seemed to think it was important. Had a clipping of the story about the Medusa showing tacked up on his wall."

"I always felt bad for Medusa," Trixie said. "My family knows what it's like to get on the wrong side of one of the demigods."

"Did you get anything out of your loverboy?"

"No, he was definitely playing second fiddle to Dr. Hollister. He's sad the old man is gone, but he sure likes being the department head in his absence."

"You think he was in on the disappearance?"

"No," Trixie said. "I think he respected Dr. Hollister, but Dr. Hollister had some secrets."

"Well, I'm pretty sure Gaultier was his patient. His records were gone, but the ones around it alphabetically had been pulled out."

"You saw his records?"

"Yeah, Dr. Hollister's patient list was a who's-who of LA's most famous and infamous demis. And a few secret ones, too."

"Like?"

"Hedy Lamarr."

"That's Hedley."

"What?"

"I don't know where that came from," Trixie said.

"Maybe Dr. Florence can cure you and take off the curse," I suggested, half in jest. Trixie's odd tangents always baffled me.

The dial on the elevator said that the car was on the first floor. There was no sense in waiting for it when we could walk down two flights faster. I figured she could make it down the steps in those white stiletto heels of hers.

"No," she said, taking my arm. "Let's wait for the elevator."

"We have things to do, Trixie," I said. I was not going to cool my jets waiting for the ancient lift a second time. Plus, it seemed to me like a rickety brass and walnut coffin.

I headed down the stairs, and behind me, Trixie sighed and followed.

I got to the midway landing and turned the corner. In front of me were a half-dozen young men, scowling, in affected worker's garb. They were all in their late-teens or early-twenties, clearly students, clearly thinking this was a good idea. Only college students could be that dumb.

One had a hammer and sickle pin on his shirt, and another had what I believe was a fraternity pledge pin. Communist cadres found fertile ground on college campuses—no one was quite as foolish as a sophomore who thought he knew everything.

"Well, look at this," I said. "You know, you boys are in my and the lady's way. So step aside."

"We don't step aside for fascists!" said the biggest and dumbest looking of the bunch, which was saying something.

"Gentleman, I don't know who sent you here, but he is not doing you any favors. Step aside."

"We're going to teach you not to interfere with the Revolution," another one announced. He pounded a fist into his palm.

"The only revolution I care about was in 1776. And it had nothing to do with teenage commie punks."

Once again, I had gone over the top.

"Get him!" the big one shouted. They were excited to be doing their part for Uncle Joe and the workers' struggle. That didn't last.

They had more enthusiasm than street smarts. If they were brighter, they would have let us get into the hallway foyer, where they could come at us from multiple directions. On the stairs, they were stuck coming at me at a time, which evened the odds considerably.

The first one came at me too fast, too eagerly, so focused on getting in close to toss a shot at my snoot that he didn't expect me to pound my fist into his face before he even pulled back his arm. I felt the nasal cartilage give way and warm blood gush out as he stood there, stunned. I grabbed him by the shoulders and threw him over the rails down to the floor below, then pushed forward.

The next guy was caught between me coming down and his buddies pushing up from behind. I grabbed him and slammed his face into the wall so hard the plaster cracked, and a couple of yellowed photos of ancient, mustachioed professors from long ago were jolted off the wall. His head was jiggling like a jack-in-the-box, and I pulled him behind me.

The next guy managed to get off a punch, but he did not have any wind-up and he was throwing it upwards besides. I'd taken harder hits from angry Girl Scouts. I caught his fist in my right and threw a vicious uppercut with my left, catching him right under the jaw. There was cracking, either jawbone or teeth or both, and he dropped straight down.

The next guy tripped over his predecessor, falling to his knees on the stairs at my feet. I grabbed him by his hair and pulled his face up so he was looking into my eyes, and then I slammed my fist into the side of his face and sent him spinning.

I stood there for a moment, catching my breath, as the last one in line scrambled backward.

Behind me, I heard Trixie's voice, sweet and innocent, talking to the fellow I had introduced to the wall.

"You wouldn't hit a lady," she said kindly.

Apparently, he had to think about that for a moment, and that was a big mistake. Those stiletto heels of hers were not just for show. She kicked, and I heard a scream I would have thought came from an eleven-year-old little girl. But to tell you the truth, I probably would have screamed, too.

Trixie kicked him in the worst possible place with that stiletto heel and it went deep. He staggered back, and I saw the red stain right in the target area on the face of his slacks. He grabbed himself and fell backward down the stairs on top of his buddies.

I exhaled, breathing hard. The wounded and broken were moaning but not making any effort to get back in the ring. Wise move. The one student commie left at the bottom of the steps figured that it was all up to him to save the Revolution because he reached into his jacket and pulled something out.

Click.

A switchblade.

"You're dead," he announced.

I sighed, drew out my .357 magnum, and aimed it at his face.

"Didn't they teach you in college not to bring a knife to a gunfight?" I asked. My thumb pulled back the hammer, and his face danced in my sight.

Now a second guy had a stain at the front of his chinos, only this one was not red.

"Tell your commie pals that the next time they cross me, they better make sure their affairs are in order. Now run!"

He did, dropping the switchblade and turning tail down the hall.

"I should have listened to you about taking the elevator," I said to Trixie as I slid my hand cannon back into my shoulder holster.

"They never listen," she said. She was perfectly calm, not even breathing hard. Around us, the junior Bolsheviks were busy groaning and bleeding on the stairs and down below on the floor.

I knelt down and picked up the nearest punk, who seemed somewhat intact, if a little loopy.

"Okay, who sent you?"

He said something I could not quite make out.

"You want another kiss, kid? Because I've still got some punches left if I don't get some answers. Talk."

"Our cadre. Said to make sure you stopped sticking your nose in Party business."

I scoffed.

"The Nazis tried to machine gun me. The damn commies sent the Cub Scouts. I don't know if I should be insulted or what."

I threw him back down the steps.

"Let's go," I told Trixie. We started down the steps. She paused at the one who had tried to take a swing at her.

"I want you to think of me every time you sit to tickle," she said.

Ouch. Even I felt that.

"Who told the Reds about us?" I wondered to Trixie as we descended.

"Could have been lots of people."

"Yeah," I grunted. "Lots of people."

We got to the bottom of the steps and we walked down the empty hallway like nothing had happened.

10.

"You know, the next time they're not gonna send a bunch of schoolboys after us," Trixie said. She was sitting in the passenger seat of my Buick as we headed east on Wilshire.

Yeah, I kind of figured that.

"I'm not sure if that was designed to take us out of the picture or just to send us a message. But now they know that we know about them, and we probably ought to watch our backs."

"Is there anybody in this town *not* trying to get us?" she asked.

"You mean besides the bartenders? At least they still love us." I had to admit it was all getting a little uncomfortable. Our enemies were adding up. Time to do something about it, or at least to be prepared for the next time they tried to kill us.

We got into Beverly Hills and I took the turn onto Rodeo Drive. That's where the swells swell. The men were dressed to the nines, the ladies to the tens.

"You buying me some jewelry, Eddie?" Trixie asked coyly.

"We're here for precious metals, but not the wearing kind. Sorry."

"No bling for me."

"No what?"

"I don't know. Sometimes nonsense words from the future just pop into my head."

"I'll say," I said.

We pulled into Bonfilio's Gun Store, this town's high-end purveyor of weapons and accessories. I got my .357 magnum there right after the Smith & Wesson Model 27 came on the market. Mr. Bonfilio always had the latest products, and he sold everything a growing boy needed if he wanted to spit some lead.

Of course, I wasn't there for lead.

We stepped up to the counter. There were lots of chrome-plated automatics and revolvers in the display cases. If you were a star, you wanted something shiny. Me, I preferred something dark and intimidating. Mr. Bonfilio curated quite a selection. The walls were covered by long guns, including dozens of very fancy shotguns for the sporting clays and duck hunting sets. If you loved things that went "bang," this was heaven.

"Good to see you, Eddie. One of my best customers!" the old man at the counter exclaimed.

"Always good to see you, Mr. Bonfilio." That wasn't quite true. I liked him well enough, but I usually came to see him when I was on the verge of getting into trouble.

Then again, my clients felt the same way about me.

"Who's the gorgeous lady, Eddie?"

This is Miss Trixie Gamble. We're working together on a case."

"How do you do?"

"I do fine," Trixie said sweetly.

"Let me get a box of two dozen .357 hollow points," I told Mr. Bonfilio.

"Silver?"

"Of course," I sighed. I had Scottish blood and the price tag hurt. But then again, it would hurt a lot more if I tried to put bullets into something that lead won't stop. And that was a real possibility in my line of work.

"Hard to believe you've already run out of the ones I sold you last time."

"You know how it is, Mr. Bonfilio," I explained. "We had a problem the other day, but your bullets solved it."

"Well, that's good to hear. Not that you had a problem to solve." The old man handed over a box of 158-grain Western Cartridge Company Silver Special hollow points. I opened it up and looked at the slugs.

Just what I needed.

"Let me get some speed loaders, too," I said.

"Why, do you plan on starting another world war, Eddie?"

"It's coming whether I start it or not."

"I'm afraid you're right about that," he said sadly.

He handed over four speed loaders, and I took a look at them. They were bulky, but it beat carrying a handful of clinking shells in my suit pocket. I started loading them.

"Of course, silver is a federally monitored strategic mineral. I've got to keep a record of it."

I didn't much care for the federal government knowing what kind of ammunition I was buying, but the feds were very sensitive about silver. One had to have a good reason to buy it. Luckily, I had one – not getting myself killed.

The proprietor filled out some paperwork in triplicate on a clipboard and slid it over to me. I skimmed it. It was all in order, and I added my John Hancock and the date to the bottom, then passed it back. Mr. Bonfilio pulled the yellow sheet off the bottom and handed it to me. He kept the other two pages. The pink one would go off to the federal government and probably end up in a warehouse somewhere.

I finished slipping the shells and the speed loaders into my jacket. I already had three sitting in my pocket, so that made seven. That meant forty-two shots plus what I had in the chamber already. I hoped it was enough.

"Anything else I can help you with?"

I turned to Trixie.

"You have silver slugs for that little pea shooter of yours?"

"No, just run-of-the-mill lead," she said.

Mr. Bonfilio seemed confused. I cleared it up.

"She's a private eye, too, and she knows her way around. I've watched her work. You don't want to get on her bad side."

"Can I see?" inquired Mr. Bonfilio. Trixie smiled, took her little .25 caliber Star out of her purse, and placed the chrome automatic on the counter. Mr. Bonfilio picked it up, dropped the mag, and ejected the shell.

"A little gun for a little lady. Are you sure it's enough for you? I got a lot of choices here if you'd like to upgrade."

"I think I'm happy with what I've got. It's never failed me before."

"You should at least carry silver rounds," he advised. "I mean, if you're in the same business as Eddie Loud. If you're in the same room with Eddie Loud."

"The man has got a point," I conceded.

Trixie nodded, and Mr. Bonfilio bent down under the counter. He came up with another box—this time, twenty rounds of .25 caliber silver slugs, 50 grain, also from Western Cartridge.

"I wouldn't go hunting werewolves with it," he said. "But then again, even a .25 will provide some incentive if you aim properly."

"I always aim properly," Trixie told him, opening the box and examining the shells.

"You got some magazines?" I asked. Mr. Bonfilio nodded. He went back under the counter and came up with three metal magazines for the Star.

"These should fit," he said. He tested one out on Trixie's gun, and it did.

"I'll take it all," said Trixie. Mr. Bonfilio grinned and went to get another sheet for his clipboard. Trixie and I proceed to load her new magazines.

"Probably a good choice," I said. "I think we've got to be ready for anything."

"Yes," Trixie said. "That's the feeling I'm getting. And I always listen to my instincts. Unlike some others."

"I can't help it," I laughed. "It's that darn curse."

Mr. Bonfilio came back, and we completed the transaction. She signed her name at the bottom, a rich, flowing signature that looked like it should've been at the foot of the Declaration of Independence. Was that a heart she put over the final "I" in "Trixie?"

"I'll take care of all of this," I told Mr. Bonfilio before turning into Trixie. "Don't say I never bought you any precious metal." She smiled.

I handed over the cash—a lot of cash, but then again, I had never regretted spending my dough on ammo. I thought of it as an investment in keeping my carcass above ground.

"Always glad to see you, Eddie," Mr. Bonfilio said happily. "Until next time, unless you want something else?"

I was about to demur, but then an item up on the wall caught my eye. I pointed at it.

"Is that what I think it is?" I asked, not hiding my excitement. Mr. Bonfilio turned around, looked at the object of my attention and affection, and then looked back at me and smiled.

"Why, I do believe it is."

It was a Colt Model 1925 Machine Rifle, sometimes called an R80, but best known as the Colt Monitor. It was basically a Browning Automatic Rifle – a BAR – like the one I'd had back in the trenches, except they had added a grip and made some other improvements to the battle-tested light machine gun. It didn't sell very well in the civilian market, though the FBI had bought a few dozen of them, but it had shown its practicality in action. The guys who took down Bonnie and Clyde used one. Rumor has it they were firing silver shells. Bonnie and Clyde seemed so supernaturally impervious to bullets that their pursuers didn't want to take any chances. And they didn't take any chances. They put about a hundred holes in the desperados. If the pair had had any demi blood, it was filling the footwells of their Ford by the time those Texas Rangers finished blasting them apart.

"They aren't making these anymore for the commercial market. I just acquired this one," Mr. Bonfilio said, his eyes twinkling. "Do you want to hold it?"

Did I ever.

He got on a stepladder, reached out and took it off the wall, came back down, and handed it over to me. For a little guy, he handled that heavy piece of iron with ease.

I took it in my hands, and it felt solid, like I could use it as a battering ram. That's how I felt about the BAR back in France. It never let me down.

"Bring back some memories?" Mr. Bonfilio inquired.

"Yeah, good ones and bad ones."

"It's a pretty rare item," he said. "I'm lucky to have this one to sell you."

"Someday, it'll be illegal to walk into a store and buy a machine gun," Trixie said out of the blue. We both looked at her, incredulous. More crazy talk. What kind of country doesn't let a law-abiding citizen buy a machine gun?

I held up the weapon and sighted down the barrel at the wall. The .30-06 slugs this baby sprayed would probably take that wall down and the one behind it as well. That's why the FBI liked it. It could shoot through an engine block.

"I get myself in trouble, Mr. Bonfilio, but I've never been in Colt Monitor trouble."

"The guy I bought it from was a former werewolfer up in Montana."

"I guess he didn't like to take any chances."

"He said it did the job. He had to retire, though. One of the beasts came up from behind and took his arm before he put it down with his .45. No use for this item after that. It's hard enough to shoot a Monitor with two arms."

I sighed and placed the weapon down on the counter. It brought back a lot of memories, and I tried to pay attention only to the good ones.

"I guess your werewolf hunter was shooting silver slugs."

"That's right, said Mr. Bonfilio.

"I don't see how there would be much of a werewolf pelt left after a couple blasts from this gat."

Mr. Bonfilio smiled.

"He sold me the silver thirty-aught ammo that he had left over. I've got magazines, too. I'll make you a deal. I want to see her go to a good home."

"No, thank you, Mr. Bonfilio. This hand cannon under my shoulder is plenty. After all, I'm a private eye, not a soldier."

"I have a bad feeling that the way things are going around the world, a lot of Americans are going be soldiers again pretty soon."

"They will be," said Trixie. She sounded sad.

"Thanks a lot for everything and for the trip down memory range," I said. The proprietor smiled, took the heavy weapon, and got back on his stepladder to hang it on the wall. Then he came back down.

"I'm here if you need me, Eddie," he said.

"Well, maybe I'll be able to solve my current problems peacefully."

"You won't," Trixie declared. I followed her out the door.

It's pretty obvious where you need to go if you want to find communists. You go on the lot of one of the movie studios and find a writers' room. The Writer's Guild was lousy with Reds, but most of those Reds were pudgy, sweaty ones who talked a good game about the workers of the world uniting and such when they were trying to make it happen with some dizzy grade D starlet. But that was all they did – talk. They never got their soft hands dirty.

We were looking for a different kind of commie, the kind who did get his hands dirty, the kind who was serious rather than one of the posers. The Party was very active in this town, with lots of parlor Marxists and salon socialists holding little meetings while tasting *hors d'oeuvres* and sipping champagne. The Party cultivated the rich and the idle, and the people who wanted to be rich and idle, but that was only one side of the coin. On the other side were the ones doing the active measures at Uncle Joe's behest. Some of those active measures were just fine with me. Despite the Molotov–Ribbentrop Pact, where Moscow and Berlin had shaken hands and pretended to be friends, behind the scenes the commies and the Nazis hated each other with a burning passion. The party propaganda about German-Russian unity didn't fool anybody. Neither the Reds nor the Nazis was above leaving one of their opponents in a ditch with his throat slit.

But there were other active measures too, more worrisome ones like flat-out subversion, trying to undermine the loyalty to the US of A by sucking in the weak-minded and the foolish. We got a taste of that at UCLA with the frat boys from Tau Beta Stalin that we had left in a heap in the medical school building. Others were covert Reds, commies ordered to infiltrate the government or our defense industry up in Burbank and down the road near Hawthorne and El Segundo, where the defense industries were gearing up for the war everyone knew was coming. That's where we made our secret weapons, bombers, guns, and the like. They were always trying to organize covert communists to infiltrate those companies and, no doubt, feed anything they found back to Moscow.

I had a little bit of an understanding of how the Reds worked in Los Angeles, but I was no expert. Joe Dale Vance was the guy to talk to about all things pinko. He was head of the Red Squad in the Los Angeles Police Department. Those guys didn't play. The college boys of the FBI observed gentleman's rules in monitoring the local radicals, but the hard-bitten cops of the LAPD didn't. Their only rule was that there were no rules, except that the communists lose. I liked the way they thought. They spied on the Reds, tapped phones, bugged apartments, broke into offices, and hauled the occasional commie in off the street and down to a dark room for an in-depth discussion of what was going on in the Party.

I liked Joe Dale Vance a whole lot.

We met at the Frolic Room on Hollywood Boulevard for lunch and a martini. We were flat-foots together as rookies, and had worked a lot of cases over the years, and it wasn't clear which of us owed the other more favors. Sometimes, the world of demis spilled over into the world of politics, and that got everybody's attention. We cleared up any confusion with Marx-curious low-end demis but quick – stay out of human affairs or else. And for the most part, they listened.

The higher-end demis, the halfs and quarterbreeds, were not a problem – they rarely trifled with mortal affairs.

So, when I called Vance up and asked to meet, he didn't hesitate. We were there at the bar at noon on the dot, but he got there before us and had already finished his first martini as well as ordered himself another and a couple for us. Vance could sure put them away. He had kind of a baby face, but don't let that fool you. I've seen the guy put a pinko's mug through a glass door for looking at him wrong.

Like I said, I really liked Joe Dale Vance.

"I was happy to hear that you were bringing along Miss Trixie Gamble," Vance said. "Always a pleasure, Trixie."

"Hello, Joe," she replied. "How's tricks?"

"Any day I can throw a Red up against the wall is a good day. And I throw a Red against the wall practically every day."

"You guys know each other?" I asked.

"Know each other? She helped me out with a problem we had, a local commissar who liked little girls. The mom hired Trixie to find the kid. She tracked them down to a house with three pinkos, then she called me. My boys and I went in and got the little girl out the hard way. That is, hard on the Reds."

"Was the little girl okay?"

"They hadn't hurt her yet," said Trixie. "I got her home to her mom."

"How about the commies? San Quentin?"

"Last I saw them, they were digging holes out in the Mojave Desert. Last anyone saw them, in fact."

Yeah, I really liked Joe Dale Vance. The man knew how to take care of business.

"So, what's your problem?" Vance asked.

"We're looking for somebody, actually two people, and we think the communists have them."

"Another little girl?" I could see in Vance's eyes that he was ready to get his shovel and head out to Lancaster again.

"No, grown men. But one's the guy the client is looking for. We're kind of at a dead end. I figure you know the serious Reds, the ones who might be able to pull this off, not the clowns who type up scripts that are love letters to Stalin or college kids posing as Lenin. The real ones. The dangerous ones."

"Most of that action comes out of the Soviet consulate on Wilshire. Of course, we're watching it all the time, but they go in and out, and we can't see what's in the trunks of their cars. There are some serious hitters on their team, Eddie. Do they know who you are?"

"They do. They've already made a play. That didn't work out so good for them."

"Well, I'll give those Red bastards one thing. They're committed. They're not gonna give up. And I'd watch myself, because I got word that the Smirnoff Brothers are in town."

"The Smirnoff Brothers?"

"Yeah, Alexi and Ivan. They're twins. Couple of dead-eyed killers. You heard about somebody trying to machine gun Trotsky down in Mexico last month? Word is it was those guys, and that's unusual. They usually don't miss."

"Are they American?"

"No, they're real Russians, NKVD." That was the Russian acronym for the, *Narodnyy komissariat vnutrennikh del*, the People's Commissariat for Internal Affairs, except like most things with the communists, even the name was a lie. They didn't just do internal affairs. They did external affairs, too. Those are the killers Stalin would send out across the globe to whack his enemies wherever they were.

What were a couple of pro hitters from Moscow doing here in Los Angeles?

"There is something big going on," said Vance. "You know we listen in all their calls, but they're being more careful than usual. Really careful. They're not saying much of anything over the wires. Something's going on. I don't know why, but it's big."

"And you say the center of their active measures is the consulate?"

"Yeah, down on Wilshire east of the Miracle Mile. That's where whatever is going on now is going on. Usually, they'll go out to safe houses or the mansions of rich dummies who joined the Party to impress their girlfriends. But lately, for the last week or so, they've really tightened up. Do you think this is related to what's going on with you?"

"I don't know," I said. "Could be."

"So, what's going on with you?"

"Well, Joe, we think they've kidnapped a demigod, and our client wants him back."

"Why the hell would the communists kidnap a demigod? They *hate* demigods. Lenin called them 'parasites of the proletarian class.' They hunt them for sport in Siberia."

"Search me. If we knew why, we might have a better idea of what's going on."

"Look, I'll give you all the help I can. I'll let you know if I hear anything about a kidnapped demigod, but that doesn't sound like the Reds' standard operating procedures. They are usually trying to weasel somebody into a government job or spy on one of the airplane companies in the South Bay or take over a union, that sort of thing. I've never known them to be in the demigod business before. And I don't know why Moscow would care enough to send the Smirnoff Brothers to California. If that's why they're here, you got a real problem. Those guys are grade-A psychos."

"Well, that's just what we needed to hear," I said and finished my martini in one gulp.

Trixie downed hers, too.

11.

I was feeling a little lightheaded from that martini I had knocked back with Detective Vance, but my buzz faded away pretty quick. There was something going on back at the office.

I had called Gladys, and I could tell she was upset. Gladys was not the kind of girl to get upset unless there was something to get upset about. That's why I had her around – she was my voice of reason in the chaos. But whatever had happened, she was scared.

"Eddie, you need to get back to the office," she said. "Right away."

I asked her what was going on. She just repeated herself.

Back to the office, then.

We got in the car and made our way over. Trixie was worried. I asked her if she saw what was happening in her dreams or visions or whatever the hell they were.

"I don't know," she said. "I'm not seeing anything."

I did not like the sound of that.

I got to my office building, parked out front, and we went up the stairs. I got to the door with my name plastered across it and went inside.

The first thing I saw was the barrel of a chrome .45 automatic hovering in front of me with a smiling lunatic behind it. No wonder Gladys was upset.

She was sitting in the chair behind her desk, a Virginia Slims butt smoking in the ashtray. Her company had clearly been there a while and made themselves at home.

There were three of them in all. I had seen them around town. The boss was Mickey Cohen, who worked for Bugsy Seigel. One thing about Bugsy – don't call him Bugsy if you like breathing. He didn't like it. He might throw you off a roof.

And Mickey might hurt you too if you got on his bad side. He was a round-faced guy who could've been a butcher or a baker if he hadn't gotten bent, but he was a brawler. He used to prizefight back when he grew up in Boyle Heights before he started running with the mob. He was about thirty, and business was obviously good. His seersucker suit cost more than a working man's house. Though he was perfectly capable of doing his own dirty work, he had brought a couple of goons with him. There was a big one, of course. There's always a big one. Somebody's gotta break the legs. I knew him by reputation. His name was Tire Iron Marv. With a nickname like that, you really didn't need a last name.

It was the other guy who worried me, a slippery, thin little guy with his fedora pulled down over his forehead and his eyes darting around. He was the one holding the heater in my face, grinning, just looking for an excuse. I didn't know him, but I didn't like him, and it wasn't just because of his .45-caliber introduction.

"Come on in, Eddie Loud," he hissed. I complied. After all, I had a gun in my face, and discretion was sometimes the better part of not getting your head blown off. I was hoping Trixie would keep walking down the hall as if she didn't know me, but she didn't. She came in and closed the door behind her.

"Who's the dame?" the gunsel asked.

"Who's asking?" I asked.

"I got the gun, I get to ask the questions. But you're kind of offending me. You don't know who I am, and that bothers me. I got a reputation."

"Not with me."

"I'm Theodore Rizzoli," he told me proudly, like I should care. "You've heard that name, I'm sure."

"Nope. Not ringing a bell."

"They call me Teddy the Weasel. Do you know why they call me Teddy the Weasel?"

"Because you're a little weasel?"

I guess that hadn't occurred to him. I guess there was some story behind his nickname that he thought didn't make him look like a creep. I was under his skin, though. I thought for a second that he might actually squeeze that trigger and make a mess of my wall. Luckily for my face and my janitor, Mickey intervened.

"Okay, Teddy, lighten up. No need to make things unpleasant," Mickey said. "We're here on business. Can't do business with a stiff."

Teddy smiled in a skewed way that reaffirmed my initial assessment that I was dealing with a psychopath and lowered his shiny 1911A1. But not all the way. If I went for my magnum, he would plug me before I got my hand under my lapel. And even if I took care of him, there was Tire Iron Marv to deal with. No, I would have to talk my way out of this jam.

"So, why do I have the honor of hosting the infamous Mickey Cohen in my office?" I asked. "Do you want to hire me for my detective skills? Unfortunately, I'm all booked with clients at the moment."

"No, you got it all wrong, Eddie. I don't wanna hire you, but it is your detective skills that I'm interested in," he said. He looked at Trixie.

"Now, the lady here, I've seen her around. Ma'am, I'm Mickey Cohen. Glad to make your acquaintance. And you are?" He extended a paw, and she shook it.

"I'm Trixie Gamble, and I'm a private eye too."

Mickey seemed impressed.

"I've heard of you. You find people, little kids, women. That's a good thing. An honorable thing. That's a *mitzvah.*"

"I appreciate your commitment to law and order," Trixie said. Off in the corner, Tire Iron Marv stared at her, a little too much like King Kong stared at Faye Wray.

"I do what I do, and I don't make any excuses about it. I sell things to people that the law says they can't have. But little kids, women, that's all off-limits to me. Anybody who hurts them needs to take a swim in the Pacific with cement overshoes."

"A mobster with a code," I said.

"I said for women and children. Men, that's a different story, and you're a man. So, maybe you should watch your mouth, or I let Teddy here go to work on you with a knife and fork."

"That Weasel nickname have something to do with a knife and fork?" I asked Teddy. He didn't seem amused.

"Enough of this," Mickey announced. "I've got things to do. I'm a busy man. Let me make it really easy for you. Where is this Chuck Gaultier guy?"

"Never heard of him."

"Word on the street says different, and Gladys here confirmed it. You're looking for him and the doctor he's got with him. So are we. Where is he?"

"Now, Mickey, why is the mob interested in a demigod?"

"That's my business, Eddie. Your business should be keeping me from letting Teddy here tune you up. Answer my question."

"I don't know. If I knew where he was for sure, I'd have him."

"You know, that makes sense. I believe you."

"Well, the basis of any new friendship is trust," I said.

"Eddie, I want to be friends with you, and you sure as hell wanna be friends with me because my other friends here can be real unpleasant. Now, here's how this is gonna go down. You're gonna keep looking for this demigod, but when you find him and the guy who's with him, you're gonna call me. You got that?"

"Oh, I'm reading you loud and clear. But, you know, it might help if I knew why everybody in this town seems to want a piece of one particular half-demigod who doesn't seem to have an enemy in the world, or at least didn't."

"Like I said, it's business."

"Well, so far, this guy's been in the hands of the Nazis and the communists, but I think you probably knew that, and now you legitimate businessmen want him too. Everybody, including my client, wants this guy. And I can't figure out why."

Mickey walked up to me and gently tapped me on the cheek with his open palm, not hard, not insulting, but a little bit condescending.

"You're a good man, Eddie Loud," he said. "You two do this thing for me and you got my friendship, and that means something in this town."

"So do our reputations. What about our client?"

"She'll be fine," Mickey said. "Believe me."

He turned to his henchman.

"Let's go, boys," he told them. Tire Iron Marv moved like Frankenstein's monster out through the door that Mickey held open. Teddy the Weasel followed, slipping his .45 under his coat and staring me right in the face.

"I kinda hope you cross Mickey," he said. "I'd like a chance to get to know you better."

"Teddy, next time, you're not gonna get the drop on me," I told him. "And things will play out a lot differently."

Teddy didn't like that. He stopped, and his smile turned into a frown.

Mickey wasn't having it. He pushed the thug out the door and looked back at me.

"I want that demigod," he said. "And his doctor. Both of them. Unbroken. I'll be checking in."

He shut the door behind him and was gone.

"Even I couldn't have foreseen the mob showing up and sticking its beak into this case," Trixie said.

"Is there any bunch of bums in this town who isn't looking for Charles Gaulthier?" I asked rhetorically.

"Did you catch what Mickey said?"

"I got the gist. He wants us working for him."

"No, I mean about Constance Showers."

"I don't get it."

"Gladys, did you tell him who our client was?"

"No," Gladys said, putting her smoldering cigarette butt between her lips and inhaling. "He never asked."

"Then why did he know she was a woman? 'She'll be fine,' he said. *She.*"

I hadn't caught it, but that was a good point. How the hell did he know who hired me? How did he know about me at all?

"The more I find out about this case, the more confused I get," I said. I walked over to the bar tray and poured myself two fingers of Maker's Mark.

"Ladies, you want any?"

"Sure," said Trixie.

"I'm gonna need more fingers than that," Gladys said. "And so are you two."

I finished pouring their belts and looked over at her.

"What do you mean, Gladys?"

"I mean, before those bums showed up, you got a telegram. Western Union."

She took a page off the desk and held it up. I traded it for a hefty tumbler of whiskey. Gladys downed the whole thing in one gulp.

I exhaled loudly as I read the telegram. I didn't believe it, so I read it again. But there it was. There was no denying it. It was a twist that I did not see coming.

"So, who's it from and what's it say?" Trixie asked, irritated.

I still couldn't believe it, so I read it a third time. She tapped her stiletto heels impatiently.

"Well, Eddie?" Trixie asked. She was getting tired of waiting.

I looked up at them.

"It's from Apollo. And he's invited us to Elysium."

How do you dress to visit a demigod? I had never been to Elysium, though I knew people who had. They didn't say much –

they seemed vague about the experience, as if the memories were not fully formed in their minds – but I got a little out of them. You dressed well, but some people got there and changed into robes. I guess that made them more comfortable. Some put on trunks, or nothing, to swim.

I picked my finest ensemble, a blue suit nicely tailored by a little Chinese fellow downtown on Alvarado Street. He always sewed a little patch of cloth inside the left shoulder, where the hammer of my magnum would otherwise rub and wear a hole in the fabric. It was that kind of attention to sartorial detail that I appreciated.

I matched it with a handmade white pinstriped shirt and a flashy red tie. Earlier in the day I had gone down to Bob's barbershop and gotten a trim. All the young men getting their stylish haircuts amused me. War was coming, and pretty soon, they were going to say goodbye to fancy barbering for a while. I knew that from experience.

Back in my flat, I checked myself in my mirror. I looked all right, not embarrassing, which was probably the most I could hope for. I opened the chamber of my gun to make sure there were six silver slugs ready to go. I had my speed loaders in my pocket. My tailor cut the suit special so you could barely see the outline of my gun unless you knew where to look.

I picked Trixie up outside her place, and she had obviously taken the invitation seriously, too. Every night at Elysium was a party, and she was ready. She wore a white sequin gown with silver shoes. Her hair was done up under a fascinator that was pinned down to it. Her lipstick was ruby red, her eyes framed in black mascara and blue eye shadow. Of course, she was in stiletto heels – I had never seen a woman who could walk as well in them. It was like she was born to it.

I didn't want to ask where she was hiding her .25, but for the life of me, I couldn't figure it out.

I went around and opened her door for her, and she slid into the passenger seat. I got in, and we started driving.

"You look nice," I said.

"Oh, this old thing?"

Enough fluff. I got down to business.

"So, why does Apollo want to talk to us? I'm assuming this isn't just a random invitation to his nonstop bacchanalia up there in Elysium."

"Maybe he's curious about where his son is," Trixie suggested, not sounding very convinced. I didn't need to point out that Apollo had many, many sons, grandsons, and so on. He had been pretty active with the mortals back in the day. Not all of the half-demis inherited the immortality or the planet would be overrun with his brats. When you got to about 50, and you still looked like you were 20, then you figured you were one of the lucky ones, like Charles Gaultier. The unlucky ones who inherited their mother's mortality faded fast, as mortals do.

Of course, the demigods were not breeding like they used to. The coming of Christianity had turned them from religious figures into something else, something less but still similar to royalty – the kind of exiled European royalty that, without an actual throne, killed time burning through their looted money in Paris or London. It was sad, even pathetic.

Sure, rich families loved to be able to brag about a few drops of demigod blood from back in the dusty pages of their genealogies, but the Olympians of 1940 weren't what they used to be. It was said that the fact that they couldn't be openly worshiped anymore sapped their powers. I suspected what really kept them in line was the thought of Ares down at the bottom of the Black Sea somewhere, screaming into the darkness. Forever.

Count Vlad Tepes had changed the course of human history. He might be more of a hero for bringing the fear of mortals to the demigods if he hadn't also had the habit of impaling his enemies by the thousands. And, of course, there were rumors that he was a vampire. Kind of a mixed bag, that guy.

But in any case, the Olympians weren't what they used to be. Some interacted with humans, some never did – for example, no one had seen Poseidon in five hundred years. Most of them kept to themselves locked away in remote palaces in remote corners of the globe. But not Apollo. Apollo was right there, out in the open, at least sort of. Everybody could see Elysium from everywhere in Los Angeles. The lights never went out at night, and the music never stopped. The estate even outshone the Hollywoodland sign, especially after its owners stopped paying to illuminate it.

Apollo was the demigod of music, after all. And also of prophecy, not so incidentally. Of all the demigods, he needed to interact with mortals. But he only did it on his terms.

So, what were the terms to be that night?

"I guess we just play it by ear," I told Trixie. "You ever met a full demigod before?"

"I can't say I have," Trixie replied. "You?"

"I met Athena once when she came here on a tour," I said. I was a little kid, and my parents took me to see her. They were well off and part of polite society – plays, theater, the symphony, that sort of thing. Of course, I was a great disappointment to them – instead of becoming a doctor or a businessman or something else respectable, I became a soldier, then a cop, then a private eye.

Ma and Pa thought it was a great honor and an opportunity to meet a real Olympian. I guess it was. The demigoddess of wisdom was the other demigod who interacted with humans regularly, acting as a patron of the arts around the world. Maybe she was just trying to get on the mortals' good side in case they one day decided that Ares's fate was merely a good start.

I remember how she glowed. I had never seen anyone like her before or since. It was almost as if she wasn't real. And when she looked at you, it was like there was no one else in the universe but her and you, and she was looking inside your mind. I felt like

I couldn't hide anything from her, that she knew everything about my 12-year-old self.

Demis made a point of not using their supernatural abilities to their fullest so as not to provoke the mortals, but they were still beings of incredible power. They weren't human. They were more than human.

Athena was wise enough to control it, and Apollo was cunning enough. Maybe the others were in hiding because they couldn't control it. The one common theme among the Olympians and the tales of their doings before history truly began is their impulsiveness. It's hard to have self-control when you can do almost anything. Like I said, they were more than human, with all the human frailties magnified as well as the strengths.

Athena radiated kindness and warmth, but I knew my mythology. I knew what she had done to Medusa out of jealousy. I knew what she had done to others. That was the thing about the Olympians and the lesser demis. You couldn't let their beauty or their smarts make you forget that they could be very, very dangerous. After all, we're just mortals.

I shook Athena's hand like everyone else in the receiving line, and I've never felt a hand like that before or since. I could feel the energy in it. It flowed through me. And when she looked at me, for a moment, I had her full and undivided attention. Then she said, "My kind's fate is tied up with yours."

That was it. That was all. No explanation, onto the next hand to shake and introduction to make down the receiving line. My parents were absolutely baffled. I was speechless. It never occurred to me to say anything. What would I say? What could I say?

But maybe she was right. In the LAPD, I got put on the God Squad. I didn't ask for it. The job found me. And now I was the private detective you call when somebody with Olympic blood is involved. Of course, she was right. After all, she was Athena.

I told all this to Trixie as we drove up higher and higher into the Hollywood Hills. Then I asked her if she was excited to finally meet one of the Olympians.

"As you might imagine, my family and I aren't eager to have anything more to do with them."

"You know," I said. "Troy fell thousands of years ago. Your family is still not over it?"

"Eddie, have you ever known a woman to forget when you did her wrong?"

I acknowledged that she had a point.

Elysium took up acres upon acres of prime Hollywood Hills real estate. At the center of the massive compound was the main house, more of a palace really, where Apollo dwelled and where his party never ended. It was all of white marble, with columns and carvings, looking as if they'd been lifted from Athens and dropped into Los Angeles. It was said dozens of workers had died building it, and I had no doubt that was true. When he had moved to Los Angeles twenty years before, everybody who could swing a hammer or dig with a shovel tried to get a bit of his fantastic fortune. The result was a marvel that you could see but you couldn't touch without an invitation.

The grounds were surrounded by a red brick fence at least fifteen feet high and overgrown with ivy and other vines. Even the formidable exterior was beautiful. I had never been inside, though most of the who's who had. Few talked about their experience openly – maybe they were afraid of not being asked back, maybe for some other reason – but everybody in town knew the rumors about what it was like in Elysium. There were stories of gardens and pools, trees and meadows. Apollo was trying to make it like his old home, like Olympus. The consensus was that he succeeded.

"Do you think he really has satyr guards? And centaurs?" wondered Trixie.

"It would make sense," I said. "Humans will talk. They can't help it."

That was one of the many big rumors about Elysium and one of the more unsavory. The story went that Apollo's security were the half-men, half-goat creatures imported from the mountains of Greece. Supposedly they were aided by centaurs who patrolled the perimeter on horseback, so to speak. If you went on the grounds, the understanding was that you didn't talk about what you saw, though human beings always talk about it. No one outside ever saw the satyrs or centaurs Apollo had domesticated. You could still find them in the wild, but if they really were his personal praetorian guard, they were kept safely hidden inside those ivy-covered walls.

We approached the main driveway gate. There were guards, but they were human – impeccably dressed and impeccably armed. I could see the bulges under their suits. They carried clipboards and bad attitudes.

There was a taxi ahead of us holding a couple of bubbly doxies with blonde hair who had obviously been having a little champagne earlier in the evening. A bald one in a fedora went up to them, and I heard him through my open window.

"You ladies are barred," the sentry announced.

They protested, but he wasn't having it.

"You talked about what you saw here. You're never coming here again. Now turn this crate around and get out of here."

There was some wailing and gnashing of teeth, but the cabbie knew the score and turned around.

"How do you think he knew that pair was talking out of school," I wondered.

"He's Apollo," Trixie said.

I drove up to the line and braked to a stop. The bald one with the fedora stepped up to my window and asked me our names. I gave them to him, half expecting to be told to turn around, that we weren't on the list. But we were.

"Go inside the gate," the guard instructed. "You'll be met. Your car will be taken. And you'll be told your expectations while at Elysium."

Our expectations? What the hell did that mean?

I gently accelerated through the wrought iron gate into the darkness ahead. Behind us, the front gate clanged shut.

12.

There was a covered area, like a festival tent, where passengers disembarked from their vehicles. A wide, white sailcloth canopy flapped in the breeze above us, covering the space. Silent valets in blue uniforms opened our car doors and let us step out. One guided us off to the left and to the sidewalk, which itself was covered and ran like a snake up the hill under a white canopy.

"Marble," I whispered to Trixie, pointing to the ground. That sidewalk must have cost Apollo a fortune. We couldn't see where it ended.

Behind us, my car disappeared into the darkness.

"Miss Gamble, Mr. Loud," came a woman's voice. She stepped out of the darkness, clad in an expensive blue dress, her hair swept up and a clipboard and pen in her hands. "I am Miss Watson. Welcome to Elysium."

We walked over to where she was standing and were immediately interrupted by four other guests. Two men in tuxedos and two women in dresses were coming down the hill on the walk beneath the canopy. It had evidently been a delightful sojourn because they were laughing and smiling and almost, but not quite, staggering. They reached the landing where we stood, and another woman – this one in a white shift that made her look like a Greek slave – offered each guest a glass from a tray of drinks.

"Please," she said to them, insisting.

The quartet each took their glass of a dark golden beverage and toasted their evening. I knew what it was right away. Ambrosia. Illegal, especially for mortals, but there it was. Prohibition never worked for regular spirits, and they hadn't even tried to enforce it for Olympian ones. After all, it wasn't like Eliot Ness was going to come on the grounds of Elysium and take Apollo into custody.

"Ambrosia as a parting gift," Trixie said to Miss Watson. "That's interesting."

"Apollo prides himself on being the perfect host," the woman replied. Her voice was cold.

"Of course, when mortals drink ambrosia, they tend to forget the last few hours. Is that the intention or just a beneficial side effect?" Trixie asked innocently.

Miss Watson stared at her momentarily and then continued as if Trixie hadn't spoken at all.

"Might I ask if either of you have ever been to Elysium before?"

We responded in the negative. She went on.

"You must understand that this is a great honor. And this is particularly true for you. I see you were invited specifically. I've been here for three years, and I can tell you that that's quite rare."

"Do you know why he invited us?" I asked.

"His grace does not share his intentions with me," Miss Watson said. "Nor would I presume to ask him. If it is his will, he will share them with you. Or perhaps not. Perhaps you will spend a delightful and pleasant evening here at Elysium and nothing more."

"But not a memorable one," Trixie added. "Especially after the ambrosia."

"His grace prefers privacy in what he does here in his home. I'm sure you can understand his special situation. He is a demigod. There are those who are envious, those who are jealous, and those who are liars and defamers. His grace must take certain steps to protect himself and his reputation, which I'm sure you understand. After all, a visit to Elysium is a beautiful experience, one almost no mortals will ever have. All he asks in return is discretion."

"We're private eyes," I said, knowing full well she was already aware of exactly who we were. "Discretion is our business."

Miss Watson offered us a cold smile.

"Would you like to come up the hill?" she asked, turning without waiting for an answer and beginning to walk up the covered path.

"Guess who she reminds me of?" I whispered to Trixie as Miss Watson strode ahead.

"Miss Showers?" she answered. Of course, Trixie was right. The same haughtiness, the same coldness. "Did you notice her clothes? All brand new. Even her shoes. I suspect Apollo provides her an entirely new outfit every night."

"Nice gig to have. After you," I said, gesturing, and I followed along behind her.

To our rear, the four partygoers departing the grounds were shaking off the effects of their ambrosia. One of the women complained that she was foggy. Their car came out of the darkness and pulled up alongside them. The last thing I heard was one wondering why he was having trouble recalling the last few hours. I hope he was fit to drive.

It was about a minute-long walk up the hill, but once we reached the crest and emerged from under the canopy walkway, Elysium spread out before us. I had to admit, it was breathtaking.

"I will leave you to enjoy your visit," Miss Watson told us, and she departed without waiting for a response. We watched her walk to the house, stopping at each clump of guests she passed, addressing them each by name. That was her role, to liaison with the mortals, and to do that she had to know everyone.

For a full minute, we stood on the edge of the sprawling plaza in front of the massive main house, taking it all in. I had never seen anything like it, not even when I had visited Versailles on leave back in France. There were fountains and gardens, statues and singing birds. It was all laid out with exacting geometry, trimmed perfectly, and even the glorious flowers submitted to the discipline. One might think that a demigod like Apollo would be undisciplined, that it would be wild and chaotic to match his rumored personality, but that was not so. The lack of discipline was the mark of other Olympians, especially Dionysus. The demigod of wine, fertility, madness, and more wine had been kicked out of every decent country in the world. If I recalled correctly, he was currently living in a palace near Medellin, Columbia.

"Would you look at that?" Trixie said as she surveyed the tableau laid out before us. Apollo was one of the richest men – well, beings – in the world, and it was clear that he needed to be.

"No satyr or centaur guards in sight," I observed.

"I am a little disappointed," Trixie said mischievously. Satyrs and centaurs were both known for their ardent attention to attractive human women.

"Just keeping this up must take a battalion of gardeners and a platoon of craftsmen the entire day to prepare the grounds for the evening's festivities," I muttered.

"But what are those gardeners and craftsmen?" Trixie wondered.

Water flowed, and so did the wine, carried on brass trays by beautiful waiters and waitresses. It was obvious the human help was carefully curated, and the young men wore robes while the young women were adorned in cloth shifts as if they were servants in ancient Athens. Guests, in suits and dresses, delighted in the drinks and canapés, mixing and mingling, gawking and gaping at the fish in the ponds and the peacocks that strolled across the marble steps.

Music filled the space. There was a flawless classic trio, with a violin, a base, and a harp, playing at the top of the steps.

"I could get used to this," I said.

"But for how long?" Trixie asked. I was not sure why.

The guests, probably numbering seventy-five or so, were delighted to be there and engaged in animated conversations when they weren't simply staring at the miracles before them. About half the guests looked like well-to-do, but from the babble of languages, it was clear they came from around the globe. The other half of the guests were simply beautiful, men and women in their shining youth, arrayed in suits and dresses, most likely provided by their host since it was unlikely they could afford to dress themselves. They were part of the scenery, invited to wander among the guests as living decorations. After all, if there's anything that Apollo loved, it was youth and beauty. And that probably cost him ten bucks each a night.

It was Trixie, of course, who caught the subtlety.

"There's a velvet rope somewhere," she said. I didn't get it at first, and she saw that and explained. "These are the regular invitees who are just thrilled to be invited to Elysium at all. But you notice what's not here – movie stars and the host. There's got to be another section, the first-class section, the one for VIPs."

"Are we supposed to be there or here?" I asked.

"Maybe we're only supposed to be there if we can find our way in there. You know, like a test."

A passing young man carried a tray of drinks, and I liberated a couple flutes of champagne for us, handing one to Trixie. She sipped.

"Magnificent," was her judgment.

"And you think somewhere they've got the good stuff?" I asked.

"Why don't we go find it. I'm guessing it's in the house."

"You lead, I'll follow," I said, taking my own sip of the champagne. Bubbly wasn't my drink, but I could have gotten used to it.

We made our way through the crowds, admiring the statuary. It was mostly dedicated to celebrating the host – Apollo at rest, Apollo rampant, Apollo pulling back a bow, Apollo strumming a harp, Apollo just staring at you with eyes that followed you wherever you walked. You might think that he would have marble tributes to some of his relatives as well, but he didn't. Demigods were jealous demigods, and they enjoyed attention. They hoarded it. They weren't apt to share it, and it was common knowledge that their decline had been concurrent with the death of their worship after the rise of Christianity. The Church had declared their worship a mortal sin, idol worship, and the Inquisition sought to stamp it out. As part of their deal with the mortal world, the demis had forgone organized worship and handed over the keys to their temples to the mortal governments. Whether or not that had really sapped their strength was not clear, nor was whether their discretion in the use of their powers was fully their choice.

We wandered through the festivities, soothed by the trio's music. Of course, the music was first rate, as music was Apollo's forte, and it was probably a point of pride to only have the best musicians to serenade his guests. We reached the steps in front of the main house and looked up at them. No guests up there. I nodded to Trixie. She nodded back and followed me up the marble stairs.

At the top of the steps was a large marble landing lined with thick, high columns, and you could look back and down at the guests in the gardens out front. The windows of the second story above were blazing; there were no windows along the first floor. Only a black brass door and a huge man stood in front of it. He was dressed like a Greek hoplite, with a bronze breastplate, crested helmet, and long spear.

I figured I might get impaled, but I took my chances and walked up to him.

"May we go inside?" I asked.

He turned his head in our direction toward us, and I swear I heard a metallic creak. For a moment, he looked at us through the slits in his helmet but said nothing. Then he turned, with more creaking as if his joints needed to be oiled, took hold of a brass ring, and pulled one of the doors open. Light streamed out from the mansion, and so did music that put to shame the petty string-plucking of the trio outside that was serenading the pitiable folks riding in steerage. I had never heard anything like it, and as I inhaled, I smelled the incense from a dozen censors burning inside the house.

"Let's go," I told Trixie, and we stepped through the portal.

13.

Take what we had seen outside, in terms of beauty and sheer magnificence, and multiply it by a hundred to get some idea of what lay inside the door. There was music there too, but this was from flutes and lyres and made the noise generated by the trio outside seem like an idling Dodge honking its horn at an old lady taking too long to cross the street.

The interior was glistening white marble cut and polished to perfection. And when I say "perfection," that is what I mean. In even the finest buildings, the swankiest digs, you can look hard at the corners and the crevices and see specks of dirt, chips of paint, and the occasional dust bunny nesting under the sofa. Not here. The entire palace positively gleamed, from the floor to the impossibly high ceiling – oddly, it looked a couple stories higher inside than one would have thought looking at it from the outside. And the marble walls were smooth and flawless, not a chip, not a crack.

The people inside the exclusive redoubt were different, too. There were more young men and women in robes who were there as adornments, and they were stunning. Outside, the adornments had looked like the prettiest girls and most handsome men in their one-horse hometowns. But inside, it was Miss America-level and whatever the equivalent might be for men. They were radiant. And I knew that none of them were likely to remember much of anything in the morning. The money they found in their wallet or purse made up for the amnesia.

"What happens in Elysium stays in Elysium," Trixie whispered as she surveyed them. "That just came to me."

Likewise, the actual guests were mostly gorgeous, but some made up for what they lacked in physical beauty with power, riches, and influence. I saw an oil baron with his mistress – I had seen him before with his wife at a charity ball, and the filly he was squiring about tonight was definitely not her. I saw a senator with a woman who was his wife, shockingly, and I saw movie stars as well. Young Judy Garland was there, unstable both mentally and physically, accosting a server for another glass of what was clearly ambrosia.

The server was a nymph, lithe and beautiful. She allowed the shaky starlet to take a glass and moved on silently.

The satyrs were off to the side, with thick goat hair covering their goat legs down to their hooved feet. Their chests were muscular but human, dark-skinned, with thick arms that ended in human hands. Their faces were both human and goat, if that makes any sense, with piercing eyes and two horns protruding from the top front of their skulls.

For the sake of modesty, they wore something like loincloths made of leather and belted across their stomachs. Satyrs were known both for their endowment and their inability – or lack of desire to – control it. Their uniform solved this aesthetic challenge.

The ones stationed along the walls were guards. Each of them wore a leather harness with highly polished brass buckles and fixtures. Each held a scabbard with what appeared to be a thin scimitar on the right side and a dagger on the left. Affixed to the back of the harness was a leather quiver, the fletching of a dozen arrows protruding out of the top. The archers each had a compound bow hung around their back. There were maybe a dozen of these sentries spread around the room, silent, watching, probably lusting after the women. It must have been torture for them, knowing their reputation.

Not all of the satyrs were warriors. As we walked through the massive foyer and the musicians came into view, we noted that they were satyrs as well, blowing their pan flutes and strumming their lyres. Of course, they were skilled, even beyond skilled. They each had hundreds of years of practice.

The partygoers mixed, mingled, or listened to the music. Some danced to the piping as if in a trance. Others gambled at tables set up along the walls. As we passed, a satyr dealt a blackjack to John Wayne. Clarke Gable, sadly, busted after being dealt a king on his twelve showing. He shrugged, frankly not giving a damn.

No one noticed us as we walked through, and why would they? The atmosphere and refreshments were intoxicating, and it seemed to be a celebration of pure hedonism. But, apparently, things got even more intense beyond the entrance.

"Would you like to come swim in the Grotto?" a nymph asked me, ignoring Trixie. Her voice was like a cool breeze through a meadow. "We have a swimsuit for you to borrow, should you want one." I got the impression she was just asking me as a formality.

"Maybe later," Trixie answered on my behalf.

"There is a Grotto for ladies as well," the nymph replied, as if this was all perfectly normal. In Elysium, it probably was.

"We'll keep our powder dry," I told her.

"We have anything you desire," the nymph said. "You have only to ask."

"We have everything we desire at the moment," Trixie told her.

The nymph smiled wanly and walked off, her long white robe sweeping across the immaculate marble floor, making her look as if she were floating instead of walking.

"I can see why Apollo is so popular with the local swells," I said.

"He's smart. Make the rich and powerful his allies and they will ensure he is left in peace as long as he doesn't interfere in the doings of the mortals."

That made sense. Still, for all Elysium's beauty, there was also an air of decadence and decay, like at the tail end of a wild party that had dragged on for too long. The hedonism seemed almost rote, less scandalous than tired. But there was still some scandal. As it were, any decent vice cop would stroke out just walking in here. Of course, that assumed that there were any decent vice cops, which there were not.

Miss Watson appeared again, smiling with at least a little bit of warmth this time. She greeted several guests while walking over to us. She appeared to know everyone by name.

"Miss Gamble, Mr. Loud, so happy to see you in Apollo's private gathering. I mentioned that he was doing you a special honor, and I expect that you now understand what I meant."

"I've never seen anything quite like this," I admitted.

"There is nothing quite like this. And there is more. He wants to meet you."

"He?" Trixie said.

"He," Miss Watson assured her.

"And what does Apollo want with us?" I asked.

"As I said before, he does not feel obligated to explain himself. Would you please follow me?"

She did not wait for us to acknowledge her request. She simply did an about-face and walked toward the rear of the main room.

I looked at Trixie, and she looked at me. We were going to meet a demigod. That did not happen every day.

We followed, stepping out to catch up with our guide.

"Miss Watson, can I ask you something?" Trixie said. There was that honey voice again, the one with a dash of vinegar.

"Of course," Miss Watson replied, though I knew that Miss Watson would deflect or ignore any query that she did not want to answer.

"Do you know a Miss Constance Showers?"

Did Miss Watson nearly miss a step, or was I imagining it? It took her a moment to answer.

"Miss Showers was my predecessor," Miss Watson said tightly as if she was holding more back.

"And you have been here, what did you say? Three years?"

"That's right."

"This is such a prestigious position, majordomo to a demigod. I wonder why Miss Showers would have left it."

Miss Watson stopped and turned about, her smile forced.

"I am sure I have no insights into his grace's decisions about his staff." It was clear that the subject of Miss Showers was closed.

Trixie simply smiled innocently.

"Just making conversation."

Miss Watson maintained her strained smile and turned back around, continuing to walk. We were headed toward an elaborate bronze door against the rear wall. It was far, much farther than I would have estimated by looking at the outside of the mansion.

A pair of warrior satyrs, bearing long spears with bronze spearheads, stood to either side of the door. As we approached, they crossed their poles before the door to bar our way. Miss Watson stopped and turned to face us.

"This is his grace's inner sanctum," she said. "Please wait here."

She turned back to face the door, and the satyrs pulled back their spears. She went to the door, opened it a sliver, slid inside, and closed it behind her.

The satyrs dropped their spears to bar the way for us, should we seek to follow. We did not. We stood back, and they glowered at me. They seemed distinctly less hostile to Trixie.

"So, we are meeting Apollo," I whispered, keeping it down because I did not know if they spoke English. I knew meeting the demigod was a possibility when we got the invitation, but I never fully believed it would happen.

"The question is why Apollo wants to meet us?" Trixie said.

"Be on your toes. The part-blood demis can be tricky. I assume the full demis are another level of tricky."

"He wants something from us," Trixie stated.

"Maybe he's concerned about his son."

"Maybe," Trixie said, but it did not sound like she thought so.

The minutes dragged on, five, ten. All full and part-blood demis were on their own time schedule – they were notorious for their lack of punctuality. Maybe when your time frame stretched to eternity, you were not particularly concerned with a few minutes here and there. But with mortals, the sand was always draining down the hourglass. Time was money and life.

Then the door creaked, and the satyrs snapped back their spears. The portal opened. Miss Watson stepped through, yet while we could not see Apollo behind her, we felt him. There was a crackle in the air, an energy. The hairs on my arm stood at attention.

And then he came into view as he stepped into the room.

Apollo was well over six feet tall, his immaculately coiffed hair bearing a crown of laurel leaves. He wore a white robe of a fabric I could not identify, shimmering like silk but sturdy like cotton and of the purest white.

Apollo was the most beautiful man I had ever seen, though I was certainly no expert on male beauty. Yet, I instinctively felt his appearance was unnatural – he was somehow *too* perfect. He was perfectly proportioned, too perfectly, as if he had been designed too well. His forehead was perfect, his eyes – blue at the moment, though they seemed to change as you watched them – perfect, his jaw and chin perfect. His shave was perfect, too.

It was the same down to his feet, which were clad in leather sandals of impeccable quality – they might have been made of the skin of some exotic creature, in fact. They too were perfect.

The overall effect of his appearance was to overwhelm you. You understood that you were in the presence of something beautiful and deadly, unfathomably strong, and yet in the form of a human. It was disorienting; I had felt the same way when Athena took my hand back when I was twelve.

I doubt I could have spoken first, but Apollo made that moot.

"Miss Trixie Gamble, Mr. Eddie Loud," he said. The voice was like a drum; you could *feel* it as well as hear it. But it was not loud or thunderous, though it was well-known that it could be if a demi wished. Instead, it was strangely intimate and close, as if we were sharing something special inside a conversation that no one else could hear.

I felt honored that this brilliant and glorious creature was speaking to me. I felt the subtle urge to please him, serve him, and even fall on my knees in supplication. That passed in an instant, but it unnerved me. Eddie Loud kneels to no man, but then, this was not a man. His appearance notwithstanding, he was not human.

Next to me, Trixie was breathing shallowly, staring at the demigod before her. I could see that she was also trying to wrestle that primitive part of her brain into submission, the one the demis had taken advantage of when they appeared and made the cavemen bow down to them eons ago.

"Welcome to Elysium," he said. "I trust Miss Watson has ensured your visit has been a pleasant one."

I struggled to think of the proper response. My thoughts were cloudy, thick, and slow. Finally, I forced out a response.

"Yes," I managed to say.

"Good, good," said the demigod. He must have been accustomed to my rudimentary reaction because he appeared to take no notice of it. Thousands of years of mortals bewitched and transfixed by him had made him used to it.

"Your reputations have preceded you," he said. "Everyone tells me that there are no better detectives in Los Angeles."

"Thank you," Trixie managed to say.

"I was curious, though, about your progress."

"Progress?" I said.

"On locating my son."

That he was concerned with mortal matters, even one involving a putative immortal who happened to be his child, somehow shook me out of my awe. It lessened him in my eyes in a way, making him more human. I started to regain my self-control.

"I would have thought you could find him, being...," I began. "What you are."

He laughed, a laugh that sounded superficially deep and genuine but that struck me as mirthless and cold.

"The powers of my kind are somewhat overstated in mythology," he said. "What we can and cannot do is not perfectly defined, but rest assured, we are not omnipotent. We are not God."

My head cleared, and I felt the bitterness as Apollo said His name. The one true God, limitless in power, had displaced the false deities that were the demigods, and they held a grudge even when they appeared to pay homage to the true Lord.

"You cannot just ... find him?" Trixie asked.

"No," said Apollo, with another mirthless laugh. "My realm is different. I can play music that makes my satyr orchestra sound like a milk truck grinding its gears. I can foretell some things with great clarity. I am the greatest archer who ever lived. But I cannot simply know all or see all. That's why we have always relied on our mortal friends. Our power has limits, which is where you come in. What is mythology but stories of mortals doing things for us that we could not?"

"You are modest, Apollo," Trixie said. "Mythology is also about what the Olympians have done *to* mortals, what you have done."

He looked at her, and I felt a chill in my spine. It was a hard look, and beneath it I could sense a seething anger. But Trixie did not avert her eyes or shrink back. She stood there, waiting for him to speak.

Maybe he was not used to anything except abject submission, but it seemed to me that he hesitated a moment before speaking.

"I sense your lineage, Miss Gamble," he said. "Yes, I see it clearly. You are a daughter, a granddaughter by dozens of generations, but a daughter nonetheless, of Cassandra. I expect you have heard the tale of how I gave her the power of prophecy, and how she rejected me, and how I cursed her. A tale where I am the villain."

"I have heard it all my life from my mother," Trixie said.

"A tale that is three thousand years old," Apollo said. "Have you not considered that the truth could be twisted in a hundred retellings? What is that game you mortals have? Telephone? In fact, I loved Cassandra as I have loved many mortal women through the ages. I gave her a great gift, one of prophecy, a gift you yourself share."

"And when she rejected you, you cursed her that no man would believe her."

Apollo smiled.

"It was a cunning curse," he conceded. He seemed proud of himself. "But you do not know the whole story. You cannot, and I have no desire to share it tonight."

"So, you were the wronged party?"

"Do you think an Olympian cannot be wronged by a mortal, Miss Gamble? That we are alone to blame when love or ambition go wrong?"

Miss Watson, standing to the side, was becoming visibly uncomfortable. Apparently, mortals did not speak like that to Apollo, except mortals like Trixie did. I was on edge, too—whatever Apollo's purpose in bringing us here really was, this confrontation was likely taking us away from finding out.

"Great power brings great responsibility," Trixie uttered. Then she got that far-away look she got whenever something came to her.

Apollo laughed, and this time I sensed genuine amusement.

"There it is, your gift, Miss Gamble," he said. "That phrase, that hackneyed cliché, that will appear in the future, perhaps in a movie, and midwits will think it profound."

"I see a man in tights, a bug man," she whispered, sounding perplexed. "It's not clear."

"Yes, that's right. That's how it works. *Our* power of prophecy, because yours came from mine, is not like some film projected in our minds. It is flashes, phantoms, moments, images, particularly when the event is far off in the future. The near future is clearer, but it's never totally clear. For example, I can see a great war coming, massive armies clashing on land and sea and in the sky, and yet the outcome is a blur."

"I never see the whole, just pieces."

"Yes, that's how it happens. Perhaps I see more and bigger pieces, but you see more than you say, Miss Gamble, more than you share with Mr. Loud."

"Not clearly."

"You see horrors in the future we can barely imagine. Mass delusions, murder, the mutilation of children."

"Yes," Trixie said. "I see all of that."

"They call us Olympians monsters, and perhaps we have our flaws, but it's mortals who are truly dangerous. And it is exhausting."

He let the words hang in the air for a moment, then he brightened. He seemed to be intrigued by us, particularly Trixie. Maybe it was the novelty of meeting mortals who resisted the urge to fall gibbering at his feet.

"Walk with me."

He stepped forward, and I felt his presence in my bones as he passed by me. I shook it off and followed. Miss Watson trailed us.

"You do know that Mr. Loud was hired by Constance Showers?" Trixie asked. She looked hard at the demigod, trying to discern something from his expression. She was not rewarded with any indication of how he felt. With several thousand years of dealing with mortals under his toga, he was too experienced to let that happen.

"I was aware of that," he said. "She is the majordomo to my son, so that seems understandable."

"We understand that she was the same for you until a few years ago, before Miss Watson replaced her," I interjected.

"Yes, I remember her," Apollo replied, sounding bored. "You'll forgive me if she didn't make more of an impression. She was one of many hundreds of mortals who have assisted me through the ages."

"What I don't quite understand," Trixie said, that honey voice of hers in effect. "Is why she would leave the service of a demigod for, well, let's face it, a lesser principal. Unless, of course, you dismissed her."

Apollo stopped and looked Trixie full in the face. He wasn't quite hostile or angry, but he certainly wasn't happy. It was uncomfortable even for me, and I was not the one under his glare. That was a power they had over us mortals. You could feel it when they looked at you. Then he spoke.

"The performance of Miss Showers was satisfactory, I can assure you," Apollo said. "I did not dismiss her. She departed my service of her own accord."

"So, why would she leave you by choice?" Trixie wondered aloud. "After all, you are Apollo."

Maybe the implied flattery worked. When he spoke again, he seemed less perturbed.

"Miss Showers was always a striver," Apollo explained. "She always sought greater opportunities. Perhaps she felt she could be a larger fish if she swam in a smaller pond."

"I guess that Miss Watson was fortunate in that regard," I said. But the demigod ignored me and continued to walk as if this little exchange had never happened. The expression of Miss Watson, always one that appeared to be of mild annoyance, did not change.

The guests had all stopped what they were doing to stare at him. They smiled eagerly, seeking a glance and his favor. Some applauded, others shouted praises.

"Magnificent!" bellowed a bleary, craggy, Wallace Beery, a tumbler of ambrosia in his hand.

Apollo smiled, but I was learning they were as poor at hiding their emotions as mortals, if you knew what to look for. His smile was pasted on, his nods of acknowledgment were perfunctory, his "Good evenings" and "Welcome to Elysiums" all rote. He had done these empty rituals of greeting thousands of times. He would be doing them forever.

Trixie felt it, too.

"You're tired," she observed, sounding a little surprised at her words.

"An Olympian has great responsibilities," Apollo said bitterly. "To go along with our great power."

"How can you tire of this?" I asked, sweeping my arm across the glorious mansion. "This is the most beautiful place I have ever been."

"Yes. Isn't that the problem?" Apollo said, still walking through the room. It was odd—though other guests were standing nearby, it was like they could not hear our conversation. We were surrounded yet somehow alone. "What is there to look forward to when you are already at the pinnacle?"

"A lot of mortals would give their lives for the chance at living like this for a while," I observed.

"But they *can* give their lives. That is the difference," he said. He sounded worn out.

Apollo continued across the perfect marble floor. We followed, part of our little circle, surrounded by dozens yet utterly alone. As we walked, every face of every guest turned towards the demigod, and there were gasps, praises, and cheers. He accepted them with alacrity, nodding, waving, acknowledging, yet always moving past them. It appeared to me that he drank in the praise but, at the same time, was drained by it. It was strange to say about an eternal being, but he seemed to be carrying a giant weight upon those perfectly proportioned shoulders of his.

That he was devoting so much time to us seemed to me to be a great honor; the other guests were certainly jealous. I had the impression that Apollo was taken with us somehow, perhaps interested, perhaps merely amused. I couldn't quite put my finger on it, but we were different than the supplicants and lackeys who surrounded him at his endless parties. All of them wanted something from him, something for themselves, but what we wanted was cleaner and purer – some answers. And he wanted answers from us as well. We still hadn't answered his question about where his son, Charles Gaulthier, was.

"Allow me to show you something," he said. We followed Apollo over to one of the gaming tables that lined the walls. Clark Gable was gone, but John Wayne, the Duke himself, was there, along with Elisha Cook. It was quite a pair. They were playing blackjack, and the satyr dealer was silently passing them cards. Wayne busted, Cooke had nineteen showing. The satyr turned over a twenty. He took their chips.

The satyr prepared to deal again, but Apollo reached the table, and he stopped. The players' attention was on their host.

"Elisha, good to see you," Apollo said. "Marion, you're always welcome here." Only Apollo could call the Duke 'Marion.' His real name was Marion Morrison. He had changed it at the behest of a studio head to become a star.

"Well, I reckon I feel mighty welcome," the celluloid cowboy replied.

Apollo smiled coldly and looked at the satyr, who dealt him in.

The house had a pair of tens. Elisha Cook, a ten and nine, the Duke a soft seventeen.

Apollo had a blackjack.

The Duke hit, drew an eight, then a king, and busted. The satyr, his half-man half-goat, face expressionless, collected the house's winnings, and dealt again.

This time, the house was showing eighteen, Elisha Cook nineteen, and the Duke twenty.

Apollo had a blackjack.

He smiled thinly and turned back to us.

"You are on quite the winning streak," Trixie observed.

"Yes," Apollo acknowledged. "I've been on it for several thousand years."

"Maybe we can try roulette," I suggested. "I'll bankroll you."

He looked at me with grim amusement.

"I suppose you now understand why it's illegal for us to gamble and to participate in the stock market or other speculation," he said. And that was the law. Mortals, particularly the rich ones, insisted upon it. A demigod couldn't play the Dow Jones. In America and most civilized countries, they had to put their fortune into a blind trust to be managed by hordes of lawyers and accountants. Real estate was always a big part of their portfolios, hence Elysium.

Of course, the uncanny luck didn't necessarily pass to their descendants. By all accounts, Charles Gaultier got rich by being smart and savvy, rather than by way of being a spawn of Olympus.

"Is there anything you do badly?" Trixie asked.

Apollo laughed again, that same grim laugh. For a demigod of song and poetry, he was remarkably sad. Maybe that wasn't quite so strange after all.

"My choice of women is legendarily fraught," he said. Then he gestured to a trio of beauties staring at him from the wall. They were lovely Hollywood goddesses who Hollywood had not yet discovered, and they looked like they hoped to be real demigoddesses, or at least the consort of a demigod. They appeared hungry, even predatory. It was odd to see Apollo as prey, but there was no question to anyone who had ever been around Los Angeles who was the quarry and who was doing the stalking.

Apollo was unimpressed by them. In fact, they seemed to bore him.

"There was a time I could leave Olympus, transporting myself wherever I wished simply by wishing to, and find an enchanting mortal for an enchanting interlude. But by mortal law, I am no longer allowed to transport myself by wishing. And by mortal law, I can no longer breed. Not officially."

Of course, demis had violated both of those prohibitions over the centuries. Peripheral violations were typically ignored. An unauthorized journey, an unauthorized love child here and there, was no big thing. The main prohibition, the prime directive for demigods, was to stay out of the business of mortals, and with the thought of the suffering of Ares always at the forefront of their minds, for hundreds of years they had honored that iron diktat. They had focused on lives of idle pleasure, something Apollo seemed to now be taking quite for granted.

"Like I said," I observed. "A lot of mortals would give their life for a chance to live your life for just a little while."

"But how many would give their lives to live my life forever?" he asked. He paused, lost in thought, then strode purposefully toward the bronze portal that led out to the balcony overlooking the garden. The door opened by itself when he was a dozen steps from it, the bronze armored sentinel stepping aside as Apollo walked out to the veranda and the warm night air.

"Allow me to show you something," he said.

Leaning against one of the columns was a bow and a quiver of arrows. I hadn't seen them when we were coming through there the first time and, in fact, I hadn't seen them until he reached down for them at that moment. The bow was exquisite, bejeweled, and inlaid with gold and ivory. You could probably sell it and buy a small country. The quiver was also a masterwork, made of leather with fiery rubies and what had to be diamonds inlaid across it. There were probably a half-dozen arrows with the fletching sticking out; I wondered what priceless gems formed the arrowheads.

He picked up the bow and gracefully slipped the quiver over his shoulder and across his back.

"Watch," he said. And we did.

I will never forget the grace, the smoothness, and the precision of what happened next. He gripped the bow in his left hand and reached over his shoulder with his right to draw an arrow from the quiver. It was a seamless movement, utterly perfect, with no hesitation or error, bringing the projectile over his shoulder and down, nocking it, aiming it, and letting fly. The arrow shot across the lawn, its target a head. But the head was that of a statue, a statue of Apollo himself. The arrow struck precisely between the eyes at the bridge of the nose, and whatever the arrowhead was made of, it was enough to vaporize the stone. The statue looked like it had been guillotined.

He did it again and again, perfectly each time, seamless and fluid, firing arrows across the garden above the heads of the partygoers, striking five more of his own statues, each on the bridge of their nose. When he was done, the mesmerized guests looked at the six headless statues and then at their host standing above them on the edge of the veranda with his bow in hand and an empty quiver across his back, and then they clapped and cheered his display of mastery of archery.

Apollo smiled back coldly, placed the bow and the quiver where they had been, and then began walking back through the bronze doors.

"I would hate to be on your bad side," I said, imagining what he could do to flesh heads instead of marble ones if he decided to ignore mortal law.

"There was a time when humans feared us," Apollo answered fiercely. "When we could take their lives without hesitation or thought. But not anymore. We're both powerful and powerless all at the same time. And it will never change. It will go on and on and on until the stars burn out and then thereafter. Forever."

I had never heard anyone make eternal life sounds so bad. But then, I'd never discussed the subject with anybody for whom it wasn't a hypothetical.

"I asked you a question when we first met," Apollo said firmly. "What do you know about my son?"

"You must have dozens of sons," Trixie said.

"Hundreds from before we had to control ourselves," he responded.

"And why is Charles Gaulthier special among your sons?" Trixie pressed.

"Do you think we don't feel about our children the way you mortals do?" he asked her. His question sounded exquisitely sincere, yet I knew the answer, from mythology and my own experience, was "No."

There was silence for a moment, and then Apollo spoke again. This time, his voice had an undercurrent of impatience.

"Now, please answer me. And understand I'll know if you're lying."

"We think he's at the hands of a band of people, bad people," I said.

"The communists," Trixie clarified.

"A ridiculous cult fit only for fools, children, and degenerates," scoffed the demigod. "Mortals always gather themselves into cliques. Rarely are they so malignant as your communists."

Apollo studied Trixie's face and then mine, looking for something. Then he asked another question, almost offhandedly.

"Do you have an understanding of why these mangy malcontents have him?"

"We don't know why for sure," Trixie said. "But we know it's not just the communists who are interested in him. The Nazis, another of those ridiculous cults, kidnapped him. And then the mob wants him. And I suppose the Federal Bureau of Investigation does, too."

"What do you think is their motivation?"

Oddly, I felt like he had some ideas of his own. I inhaled, trying to find a way to put it that would not cause a reaction that might get out of hand if I was wrong, and he was truly concerned about his offspring. I decided to try something unusual for Los Angeles;

The truth.

"We believe it involves some sort of medical experiment. Something having to do with the secret of eternal life."

Apollo looked at me, and I *felt* him looking at me. And then a smile broke across his face, a real smile this time. He began to laugh, deep and genuine as if this was the funniest thing he had ever heard. And of all the things he did in our short time together, this was the first moment Apollo sent a chill down my spine.

"Thank you for coming tonight," he said, still smiling. "Goodbye."

He turned to go.

"Wait," I shouted, the private dick in me overcoming my sense of self-preservation. "We have some questions for *you.*"

He ignored us, walking off the way we had come after our introduction, but Miss Watson was there and two armed satyrs.

"Allow us to walk you to your car," she said. It wasn't a suggestion.

Down the long ballroom, the crowd swung in, and Apollo disappeared among the throng of his glamorous guests. We could not have followed the demigod even if we had wanted to. That was what the satyrs were there to prevent.

I looked at Trixie, and she looked at me. I did not see a lot of options.

"Ladies first," I said. And it was. Trixie and Miss Watson took the lead, I went second, and the two goat-men archers standing abreast went third.

We went outside once again through the bronze door, past the silent bronze sentry, and I noted that the magnificent bow and quiver were gone.

We moved down the marble stairs through the garden, passing several decapitated Apollo statues. The guests were giddy, having caught a glance of their elusive host demonstrating his archery skills. They were likewise thrilled at the sight of the satyrs escorting us. The gruff goat-men grimly stared at us, marching along on their hooves as they followed behind.

"He could've just asked us to leave," Trixie whispered to me over her shoulder.

"I've heard of an Irish goodbye, but I guess this is an Olympian goodbye," I replied. "Instead of us leaving without a word, the host eighty-sixed us without a word."

Miss Watson heard our exchange but ignored it. We were apparently unworthy of further consideration. Whatever Apollo had wanted from us, he had gotten. But, for me at least, it did not appear that he had given us much information at all.

We crossed through the garden and began to descend down the marble sidewalk that led to the parking attendants' station below. It was a warm and clear evening, and if you looked out past the canopy covering the walkway through the branches of the trees, you could see stars. Not as many as you could in the desert – the lights of Los Angeles were far too bright. But the city had its own wonders. The beams of searchlights at Grumman's Chinese Theater or some other movie palace down below us were dueling in the sky.

We reached the bottom of the marble walkway where it leveled out flat next to the driveway and where the parking attendants gathered by a desk. Without speaking to them, Miss Watson turned toward us. I got the impression she was glad to be rid of us.

"They are bringing your car around now," she told us. That was a nice trick. No one asked us for a ticket or anything else.

Apparently, they knew us by sight. Say what you will about Apollo, he ran a quality operation.

"Please thank our host for a lovely evening," Trixie said politely.

"Of course," replied Miss Watson, giving us the impression she had no intention of doing so. And it was clear to all of us that Apollo would've been completely indifferent to our gratitude if he had heard it. After all, we were mere mortals, just two more in the endless line of the hundreds of thousands or perhaps millions of mortals who he had interacted with over the eons. If you ever want to feel like you don't matter much, spend some time with a demigod.

We waited silently for a moment. Behind us, the two satyrs stood sullenly on their hooves at the edge of the walkway, watching and scowling. Then I heard my car engine and the crunch of gravel in the darkness up the road. One of the attendants pulled the car up alongside us.

"Before you go," Miss Watson said as she pivoted to her right. Behind her, a beautiful woman with a tray holding two flutes of what appeared to be ambrosia approached. I didn't see where she came from—it was like she materialized out of the darkness.

I looked over the Mickey Finns – ambrosia will do a number on any mortal, but Apollo's house blend seemed to be spiked with some additive that gave it an even higher octane – and glanced at Trixie. She was thinking the same thing I was.

"No thanks," Trixie said. "I don't drink and drive."

"I assume Mr. Loud will be behind the wheel, so please, drink up."

"I gave up alcohol for Lent," I said. Miss Watson was not finding our banter amusing.

"It is well past Easter, Mr. Loud."

"I have to keep it going longer than most. I've been a bad boy."

At that moment, the human valet stepped out of my door and walked around to open Miss Gamble's. We stood still for a moment, no one moving, no one speaking.

"Please indulge me," Miss Watson said. "It would be a pity to spoil this evening."

"It would be worse to forget it," Trixie replied.

"Apollo would be most displeased to hear that his guests have refused his hospitality," Miss Watson said, her impatience now coming through in her tone. "So, I must insist."

I heard the clop of hooves behind us, the two satyrs had taken a step forward, their paws upon the pommels of their scimitars.

"You gonna get the goat boys here to pour these down our throats?" I inquired. "Because that's the only way we're drinking them."

"Your choice, Mr. Loud. But you *are* drinking them."

"I don't do well with people telling me what I am and am not going to do," I said. "And neither does Miss Gamble."

"Mr. Loud is correct about that, Miss Watson. Nobody tells me what I'm going to do."

I saw Miss Watson nod at the satyrs and heard the metal scrape as they began to draw their blades. They were fast. But so was I.

My .357 was out, pointed at the closest one's heart, or at least where his heart should be. They both halted, blades half out of their scabbards, and looked to their mistress for guidance.

"I don't know if this pair speaks English," I told Miss Watson. "But they appear to speak fluent magnum. Now, tell them to back off."

She said nothing for a moment, so I decided to make it clear I wasn't messing around. My thumb pulled back the hammer, and the cylinder clicked over.

"I mean it."

"He really does mean it, Miss Watson. Take it from me. He shoots about half the people we meet."

At this point, the human parking attendant skedaddled. The young woman with the tray looked like she was about to step away, but Miss Watson saw her begin to move and barked out an order.

"Stay where you are!" she commanded. The terrified young lady complied, the flutes shaking a bit as their bearer shook.

There was another moment of hesitation. I wasn't looking Miss Watson in the face. I was too busy looking down the barrel at the front sight blade dancing across the goat-man's chest. But it was clear what Miss Watson was thinking. She didn't think it through.

"Take them!" She ordered, and the satyrs stepped forward as they pulled their curved blades from the scabbards. It was maybe three steps with those hooves, and I would be a shish kebab.

That wasn't in the cards.

I moved the sight blade just a bit and fired at the closest one's right shoulder. The round blew a hole out through the back, splattering its buddy with a gusher of scarlet. The force knocked the goat man on his goat rear, landing so hard that I heard the bow across his back crack. I pivoted to the other one, the barrel zeroing in on his heart. I wasn't going to shoot to wound the second time.

The two glasses of ambrosia that were the subject of the controversy shattered on the marble walkway. The woman holding them screamed and threw the tray up in the air before bolting back into the darkness.

"But how?" sputtered Apollo's majordomo. Apparently, she was under the impression the satyrs were somehow invulnerable.

"Silver slugs," I said. "Very useful in my line of work. Now, get in the car, Trixie." I could still hear the echo of the gunshot bouncing around the canyons.

"You have defiled Apollo's home!" Miss Watson shouted, finally displaying some actual emotion. For a moment, I worried that Apollo might appear to defend his homestead personally, but he didn't.

"Give your boss our regrets," I said. "Now, tell the one still on his hooves to toss his turkey carver into the bushes." She hesitated.

"Do it!" I demanded in that voice I used to use when my boys were reluctant to go over the top of the trenches in France.

She said something I didn't understand in a language I didn't know to the remaining goat-man. Reluctantly, he tossed the saber away into the spiny blue yucca plants just off the marble walkway.

I kept my gun on him as I walked around to my open door. Trixie slid into the passenger side and slammed her door shut. I ducked in, cranked the ignition, then put it in first gear, hitting the gas and pulling the door shut as I roared down the road. Behind me, through my rearview mirror, I could see the standing satyr pulling the bow off his shoulder, grabbing an arrow from his quiver, nocking it, and letting it fly.

"Duck!" I shouted to Trixie and pulled her down with me. The arrow shot through the rear window, punching a hole through it as if it were nothing, and lodging in the headrest of the driver seat with the point sticking a couple inches out.

I peered over the dashboard just enough to make a turn and then another, and I floored it toward the gate. The two sentries had their revolvers out, but I drove at them and they leapt out of the path of my careening Buick.

A moment later, we were through the compound's front gate and out of arrow range. Thankfully, the gate was open or the night would have ended very badly. I turned onto the street and sped away down the hill.

Safely away, we both sat up again, though it was uncomfortable with that arrow through my seat right where my head would have been.

"At least we got a souvenir," I said. "But not much else."

"Oh, I disagree," Trixie said. "We got some important information. Apollo knows much more than he's letting on. He's involved in this somehow. And so is your client Constance Showers."

14.

I punched the gas pedal hard as we barreled down the road, passing by the ivy-covered wall surrounding Elysium that loomed above us. I didn't know if some satyr up there was going to start firing off more missiles in our direction, but I didn't want to give him the chance. We needed to get the hell out of there.

"Black Ford ahead on the left," Trixie said, pointing to a parked sedan that was looking up the road we were coming down. It had a good view of the gate to Apollo's compound. Two guys sat in the front seats, both with the same suit and haircut.

"Feds," she announced, but she didn't need to.

"Connolly is going to be hearing from them that we were inside," I said. "I bet we'll be hearing from him soon."

"Not if I can help it. I like the feds about as much as I like the goat-men. That is, not at all."

We passed the parked FBI surveillance duo and both their heads swiveled towards us in unison as we passed.

"Do they have a cookie cutter that punches out these G-men?" Trixie wondered, and then she got that dreamy kind of look she gets. "You think they're bad now, but they're going to get a lot worse."

"I'm not sure I believe that's even possible," I told her, but then I remembered her exchange with Apollo about the future. Not exactly cheerful.

"They're going to jam up moms for trying to keep drag queens from pestering their kids," Trixie said from dreamland.

"Did you take a belt of that ambrosia when I was busy shooting at the satyrs?" I asked. The FBI was bad, but that was almost cartoonishly evil.

She did not answer. She just looked baffled.

We followed the various roads down the hill, eventually reaching Doheny. We kept heading south down past Sunset, preparing to turn onto Santa Monica Boulevard up ahead, but I parked to make a short stop so I could pull the satyr's arrow out of my driver seat.

"I can't believe our very pleasant visit devolved into gunfire," Trixie said as I tugged on the projectile.

"That happens to me more than you might think," I said, tugging on the missile. It was stuck in there but good.

"Remind me to call my life insurance broker and up my policy limits."

"When they see Eddie Loud coming, underwriters cry and undertakers smile," I replied.

I tugged again. The arrow gave way and came out with a puff of white batting. Now there was a hole through my seat, and there was a hole through the rear window, a little circular hole where it punched straight through. The arrow hadn't shattered the glass, so I could at least drive around without getting pulled over by some cop for not having a back windshield.

"You want this?" I asked Trixie, offering her the arrow. "A keepsake of our time together?"

"You hold onto it. After all, he was aiming it at your head."

True enough. I figured I could put it on the wall in my office if I lived long enough to ever see my office again. And a moment later, that became a real question as two big, shiny Buicks pulled over in front of and behind us, boxing us in.

A half-dozen men spilled out, and I saw Tommy guns. My hand went to my holster, but I thought better of it.

"We're not going to shoot our way out of this one, Trixie."

I relaxed.

There was a face at my window, the face of Teddy the Weasel. Mickey Cohen's pet rodent had his paws on an old-school Tommy gun with a wooden foregrip and drum magazine.

He knocked on the glass. I considered not answering, but he seemed so eager to chat that I felt it would be rude to ignore him. I rolled down the window.

"Told ya we'd meet again, gumshoe," he said, giddy. He was chewing gum, a big wad, loud and juicy.

"It's always a pleasure, Mr. Weasel. How can I help you?"

"You can go for that cannon under your shoulder. I'd like that."

"You know, Mr. Weasel, another dirty animal just bet he was faster than me, and he lost."

The psycho did not like that, not one bit. He stopped chewing his Wrigley's cud and was about to say something when his boss strolled over.

"Simmer down, you two," Mickey Cohen directed cheerfully, evidently amused by the standoff between me and his pet rodent. He looked his goon in the beady eyes.

"Get back in the car."

"Hey Weasel," I said. "You ever gonna tell me that story about how you got your nickname?"

The Weasel glared at me, and I smiled back, a big smile, lots of teeth.

I think if Mickey hadn't been there he would have tuned me up with that heater of his, but his boss was there and he yanked the leash hard.

"I said get back in the car," Cohen snarled. Reluctantly, the Weasel complied. I gave him a little wave which only seemed to make him madder.

The mobster turned back to me, shaking his head.

"You're like the guy who chain smokes in a dynamite factory, Loud."

"How can I help you, Mickey?"

"I'm here for an update. What happened at Apollo's place?"

"How do you know I was there?"

"How do you think? You're gonna make me a lot of money, Mr. Private Detective. And I'm gonna keep an eye on my investment."

Of course, he'd been following me or, rather, his goons had. Mickey Cohen was a suspicious guy, and I guess he wasn't going to rely on me keeping him informed of my activities. But I wasn't sure where the money part came in, and from the look on his face I didn't think asking him to explain it would be good for my health.

"We're still looking for Charles Gaulthier. He wasn't at Elysium."

"I know that," Mickey Cohen scoffed. "You think I'm simple? The commies probably have him on ice in the Russian consulate. Did your new friend Apollo tell you when he might be coming out?"

"He didn't mention that to us," Trixie said. "Why do you think he might know?"

"Miss Gamble, may I just say that you look like a vision of loveliness tonight?" Cohen said, seeming to notice her for the first time. "I figured he's a demigod. He knows stuff."

"If he knew, he didn't say," Trixie replied.

"So, what *did* Apollo say?"

"Not very much at all, to be honest. He just wanted to know where Gaulthier was," Trixie explained. "He did seem a little sad."

"About his boy? Not likely."

That was not what the demigod had seemed sad about, but neither of us felt the urge to elaborate.

"He asked us what we knew, which you know. That's all he said," I told the mobster, drumming my hands on the steering wheel.

"You sure that's all he said? I can understand if it's a little fuzzy. I've been up there, and they pour those drinks down your throat and everything gets blurry."

"We passed on the ones for the road," Trixie assured him. "We ended up getting this as a souvenir."

She held up the satyr's arrow. Mickey looked at it, considered it, and laughed.

"Just like Eddie Loud to go to a party and end up with the host trying to kill him."

"It doesn't happen *that* often," I protested, but the mobster ignored me.

"I still expect you two to find me my missing half-demigod. So, what's your next move, gumshoes?"

This was getting a little old. No matter what he thought, I was working for Constance Showers, not for him, but his six apes with heaters surrounding my car were a powerful argument against me taking that moment to clarify the precise nature of our relationship. However, my Irish was getting up, and I opened my mouth, ready to say something I was going to regret.

"If Charles Gaultier is inside the Soviet consulate, it seems like that's where we need to go," Trixie interjected before I could speak.

Mickey Cohen seemed taken aback. He considered for a moment and then laughed heartily.

"You want to get inside the embassy?"

"Consulate."

"Whatever it is. Do you think the commies are gonna let you just walk on in?"

"Mickey, are you doubting my abilities?" she asked.

"*You* I can see talking your way inside. *Him*, not so much."

"I'll keep him on a short leash."

"You better, and you better hurry. I got a feeling this whole thing is coming into a head, and when it does, I want Charles Gaultier in the trunk of my Buick. *Capiche?*"

"*Capiche*," she replied, smiling.

Mickey turned, and as he did, three more cars pulled up alongside us. I thought feds, but they weren't Fords. It was a Cadillac and a couple of Dodges, plus most of the guys spilling out of the doors were all blonde and blue-eyed and looked like they should be lounging around a swimming pool. Plus, there was another giveaway. They were each carrying that new German *Maschinenpistole* 40, the MP-40 Schmeisser.

"Nazis," I hissed, and my hand went to my .357's grip under my jacket. I immediately wished I'd remembered to replace that empty shell in the chamber.

"When in doubt, go over the top," I muttered.

I got out of my car.

Mickey Cohen's guys were standing ready, and their submachine guns were pointed back at the newcomers. It was a Mexican standoff, except none of us were Mexicans.

I did not see Merz, but then this was dirty work and he looked like the kind of guy who liked to keep his soft hands clean. But Major Strasser was there with his dueling scar, wearing a long leather coat that did a bad job of hiding the Walther P-38 on his belt.

I'll give him one thing; he was a cool customer. And so was Mickey Cohen. The Gestapo officer walked right up to us and looked over the mobster like he had crawled out from under a rock.

In my mind, I figured we were about a second or two from full-scale war.

"I am taking these two," Major Strasser announced. He meant me and Trixie.

"No can do, Major, it's past our bedtimes and we need our beauty sleep," I said.

"Be silent!" he shouted at me in the voice of a man used to having his orders followed. But I wasn't the kind of man used to following orders.

"I'm not some prisoner in one of your kraut dungeons," I said. "The next time you talk to me like that is the last time you ever talk."

The guns all came up, and now Trixie was out of the car and by my side. I didn't like that. I didn't want her in the crossfire, but every German who ever tried to give me grief in the past had ended up face down in the French mud, and I wasn't about to break my streak with this Prussian punk.

"We're not going anywhere with you," Trixie reiterated. Strasser glared.

"I am not asking!" he shouted.

"But I'm telling," Mickey Cohen said, his voice harder than I had ever heard it. "These two are working for me, so why don't you and your boyfriends get out of here before we clean the street with you?"

"You," Strasser said, scrutinizing the mobster's face. "You are that gangster, Cohen. That *Jewish* gangster."

I got ready to draw.

"Yeah, that's right, Fritzy. I'm Mickey Cohen. I work for Bugsy Siegel. And we're a couple of Jews you goose-stepping sissies can't push around."

I figured before the fusillade of bullets from their side cut me down, I could get my magnum out and remove that Nazi aristocrat's smug head. I didn't have any desire to die, but taking that bastard with me would at least mean it wasn't for nothing.

It turned out that my end wasn't to be there on North Doheny Drive that evening.

"You boys need to take a look at what's coming down the street," Trixie said. Then she pointed, and for some reason, they looked.

Five Fords, all identical, all driven by identical FBI agents.

"Now, I don't think anybody here wants to go to war out in the street in front of the feds," she declared.

I saw Major Strasser and Mickey Cohen think about it for a moment. To be honest, I wasn't sure which way they would go. Both of them nodded to their men and the submachine guns disappeared into their cars just before the convoy of Fords pulled up and Special Agent Connolly got out.

"What the hell is this?" he demanded.

"Special Agent Connolly, what a pleasure," Mickey Cohen said. "Why, I was just here with my friend soliciting a contribution to the B'nai B'rith. Unfortunately, he seems to have left his wallet at home."

"Get out of here," Connolly ordered. "Both of you. But not you two." He was pointing at me and Trixie.

"Yeah, I gotta get going. Mr. Loud, Miss Gamble, we'll talk soon."

Cohen walked casually to his car; Tire Iron Marv held the door open for him.

Strasser looked at me with a death glare.

"Loud, we will meet again."

"You keep saying that."

"Get out of here, you and all your kraut bums, before I haul the bunch of you in," Connolly said with evident disgust. The sullen Nazis slunk into their cars and drove off. Now Connolly could focus his full attention on us.

"What the hell were you doing at Apollo's house tonight?"

"Our job."

"I told you to stay the hell out of this. You have no idea what you're interfering with."

"Why don't you tell us then?"

"I'll tell you this. The next time I see you anywhere around anything having to do with this, I'm going to put you in a hole so deep they'll have to mail you sunlight first class. Now, get the hell out of here."

"Always a pleasure," Trixie said.

"Miss Gamble," Special Agent Connolly said, tapping the brim of his fedora.

She smiled back coyly, and we got back in my car. I turned on the ignition, hit the clutch, put it in first, and pulled away south on Doheny towards Santa Monica Boulevard once again. The feds watched us go.

"Why is it that every time I'm out with you, Eddie, I feel like I've cheated death."

"Probably because you have," I said as I drove. "Let's go find a bar, get a couple of highballs, and call Constance Showers."

15.

I realized that I was always calling Constance Showers from bars.

We were at Billy Berg's on North Vine just south of Hollywood Boulevard. The band was Toots Moroney and the Hep-Tones. They were on a break, which was fine with me because I wasn't much for jazz. I wasn't much for music you had to pay attention to.

With the phone booth door shut, most of the sounds of the hopping club could not get through. It was me, my burning Lucky Strike, and a tumbler of Maker's Mark. What I needed right then was a third hand for the phone. I doubted Apollo had this kind of problem.

I solved it by balancing the butt on the ashtray. Evidently, I was taking too long because Trixie shot me a deadly glance from our table. Some hefty clod was trying to put a move on her, holding himself up with a paw on the tabletop.

She could take care of herself. I gulped from my tumbler and made the call.

Miss Showers answered on one ring. Was she waiting for my call? Probably not. She did not sound particularly happy to hear from me. And it went downhill from there.

"You went to Elysium?" she shouted when I told her the story.

"When your old boss invites you, mortals RSVP," I replied. She did not take the bait about him being her former principal.

"This is not what I hired you for," she sputtered.

"No, it's exactly what you hired me for," I said. "My job is to get your boss back, preferably in one piece. While remaining in one piece – one of Apollo's goat-men guards nearly put an arrow through my skull."

That last revelation seemed of little interest to my client.

"I asked you to locate him. That was all. But you had to raid the Nazis and go up to Elysium," she said.

"I go where the case leads me," I said. "And it's leading me back to you. What is really going on, Miss Showers?"

"I am sure I have no idea. My employer was kidnapped from his home, by who and why I know nothing except what you have told me."

"Well, there's more. We visited the office of his doctor. Do you remember Dr. Hollister? Well, it looks like the doc had a sideline researching demis and immortality."

"That's a crime," she said.

"I'm aware. But it seems the research might have gone wrong because there was another high-blooded demi who went missing recently. And when the FBI found him, he was dead. I'm asking you again, Miss Showers. What is going on?"

"I told you, I don't know," she insisted. If she was lying, she was good at it, but then she was a woman in Los Angeles, so that was par for the course.

"Well," I continued. "That leaves us in a tough spot. Your old boss wanted to pump us for information. We didn't get much out of him except for your employment history. Why would you quit a sweet gig like that?"

"I left for other opportunities," she said. "It was on good terms." There was an undercurrent of defensiveness there not far beneath the surface.

"That's what he said. But that's about all he said. I didn't get much else. And we have another interested party who has involved himself in this affair. Mickey Cohen."

"The mobster?"

"Is there another Mickey Cohen out there running around with Tommy guns looking for a missing demi? I'm going to ask you straight and I want a straight answer. Was Charles Gaultier crooked? Did he owe the mob money? Was he in business with them?"

"No, as I told you, he was an honest man."

"When someone tells me somebody is an honest man, that's when I get suspicious. So far, we have the Nazis, the communists, the mob, and the FBI all trying to find your boss, as well as me and my associate Miss Gamble. You got a very popular employer, Miss Showers, for an honest man."

Again, she shifted instead of taking my bait.

"Do you know where he is now, Mr. Loud?"

"Know? No. Suspect? Yes."

"And?"

"And I think the Reds have him and Doc Hollister stashed in the Soviet Consulate."

"Why do you think they have him, Mr. Loud?"

"Maybe Comrade Stalin wants to live forever. And so does Hitler, Mickey Cohen, and maybe even J. Edgar Hoover."

She seemed pleased with that speculation. Then she got directive.

"Listen carefully, Mr. Loud. I am your employer, and I expect you to follow my instructions. I want you to ascertain for certain where Mr. Gaultier is being held and let me know the moment you believe he is being moved. Nothing more. No more heroics, no more raids, no more gunplay. Am I clear?"

"Crystal," I said, annoyed.

"Then good evening," she said and hung up.

I took a drink and a drag and returned to our table.

"Anchors aweigh, fat boy," I told the clod. My face said that this was not a debate but an order, and he obeyed with a few muttered curses as he waddled off.

I slipped into my empty seat.

"You're always making friends, Trixie," I said, sipping the rest of my bourbon. Our waiter was walking by, and I pointed to my empty glass. He nodded.

"You leave a lady alone in a joint like this, you're lucky if she's there when you come back," she said, exhaling the smoke of her Marlboro. "So, what news from Miss Showers?"

"She's not very happy," I replied. "And not very forthcoming. Even I can tell she knows more than she's letting on, and I don't have your feminine intuition."

"What's her angle, if not a loyal aide trying to rescue her beloved boss?"

"That I can't figure out," I said. "And I always think the worst of everyone."

"So, a trip to the consulate?"

"Miss Showers was insistent. No more going above and beyond. Just confirm our suspicions about where he is and let her know when the Reds try to move him."

"Why would she think they might move him if they are doing experiments on him?"

"Good point. Mickey was interested in that, too. Move him where? In any case, she was clear about the idea of rescuing him. Don't do it. And she's the client."

"Now, that's the thing, Eddie," Trixie said. "She's paying you pretty good money, right?"

"Yeah, even after I give you half."

"But she's not rich herself?"

"Nope. I don't get the impression the demis pay their minions much."

"Then, we're getting paid with Charles Gaultier's money."

"Yep."

"So, really, if you think about it, *he's* the client."

I nodded. It made sense to me. And I wanted it to.

"So, we need to do what's best for Charles Gaultier, our client, regardless of what Miss Constance Showers thinks," Trixie concluded.

"Your logic is impeccable, Trixie." The waiter came by and refilled my glass. I lifted it in the hand without the cigarette and gulped down a belt. Smooth.

"And I don't think our client wants to be experimented on in some Soviet dungeon any longer than he has to be."

"No, he would not want that," I replied after the Kentucky bourbon went down the hatch and settled in my belly.

"So, off to the Soviet consulate?" she asked.

"Let's go," I said, downing the remainder in a gulp. Still smooth. "And let's do it before the band starts up again."

I made another call, this one to Joe Dale Vance. I got through to one of his detectives on the Red Squad; Vance was out at the permanent stakeout overlooking the consulate. He asked if I knew where it was. Of course, I did. Everybody did, including the Russians.

It was on the fifth floor of an apartment building on Wilshire with three windows facing the street. The LAPD didn't pay the landlord rent. It just didn't ask the landlord any questions about what went on on the other eight floors and got the observation post for free.

Of course, it wasn't just an observation post. If you know anything about cops who get access to a ritzy apartment in a ritzy building, you know it's going to be their all-purpose home away from home. Think of a fraternity house with .38s and handcuffs.

So, when I banged on the door and it opened up a crack, the detective who answered – a thin-faced guy with a shoulder holster who I had seen around the station – looked me over and looked over Trixie twice.

"Lady coming in!" he bellowed over his shoulder after I explained who we were and who we were looking for. He didn't open the door any wider.

"Lady?" someone yelled from the back. "What the hell is a lady doing here?"

"The boys need to get themselves together," the detective assured us as we waited. Trixie smiled patiently.

It took about a minute to do whatever they were doing, and someone eventually yelled, "Okay." The cop opened the door wide and we walked in.

It obviously came furnished. Too bad it was cops in there and not decent folk. The landlord was going to be steamed, and the carpet, sofa, and drapes would definitely have to be once the police left. Cigarette smoke from a thousand butts hung in the air. Even I choked, and I wouldn't wear a gas mask back in the trenches. There were empty bottles of Lucky's Lager and low-end whiskey on every surface that wasn't already covered by overflowing ashtrays, empty boxes of Chinese takeout, and crumpled sandwich wrappers.

Below us, the traffic went back and forth on Wilshire Boulevard oblivious to the intrigue. About four or five buildings over to the east was the consulate, and you could see its front entrance and its driveway gate. It was an imposing structure, brutalist in the Soviet fashion, squatting there in the middle of our city like an ugly concrete tumor. Yet above it, far beyond in the hills, you could see the beauty of Elysium. It made for an interesting contrast.

The cops on surveillance duty had all tossed their jackets over the back of the sofa. There were four I could see, but the hall went off to the back where I assumed there were bedrooms. Joe Dale Vance was nowhere in sight.

A detective sat smoking on the couch with a bottle of Lucky's in his hand. Next to him, against the armrest, were a couple of Ithaca Model 37 shotguns. I was not sure what good they could do from the fifth floor, but that was hardly my concern.

Another detective sat near the window with some binoculars, and his partner sat at a table nearby with a notepad. The guy with the binos wasn't paying attention to us. He was looking out the window and calling out what he saw.

"Buick, plate one-Adam-one-two-David-John-Tom, departing, twenty-three fifteen hours," he called out. The cop phonetics always threw me – after all these years, I still thought in military phonetics: One-Alpha-one-two-Delta-Juliet-Kilo.

The guy with a notepad took it all down. There was a pile of notebooks next to him. They did this all day and all night, recording every car that went in and every car that went out.

"Back here," our host directed us, pointing toward the hallway. The place had three bedrooms, and he took us to the one in the rear and knocked on the door. Vance yelled for us to come along, and our detective guide left us to it.

I opened the door, and it was clear that Vance had moved into this room. He has a couple extra suits and shirts hanging in the closet, and I could see his toothbrush in the bathroom sink. He wasn't wearing his gun – that was lying on his night table next to a bottle of Seagram's and a dirty glass.

"I thought you were married, Joe," I said.

"I thought I was too," he replied, buttoning a shirt. "My wife and the milkman disagreed."

"Sorry to hear it," Trixie said. It sounded genuine and may well have been.

"Well, she used to tell me I was married to my job, and if I had been, that would've worked out fine because the LAPD wouldn't have taken my house in the divorce. But you guys didn't come up here to commiserate with me about my marital woes."

"We've got a problem," Trixie said. "And we need your help."

"Sure," he said. He looked around. "Where are my manners? Can I get you guys a drink?" He looked around for some additional glasses.

"We're good," Trixie assured him.

"Joe, we need to get into the consulate," I said.

"Inside the consulate?" he laughed, finding the idea genuinely amusing. "Eddie, it's the Soviet consulate. A diplomatic outpost. Do you two want to cause an international incident?"

"Definitely not," Trixie said. "We were hoping you could offer us a discrete way inside."

"You know you're with Eddie Loud, right? He's not exactly Mr. Discretion."

"Believe me, I am *very* aware," she replied. "But we really need your help."

Vance sat down at the edge of his bed near the table and picked up the bottle and the glass.

"Well, *I'm* having one," he said, pouring. "Let me think for a second." He drank and pondered for a moment, and then he smiled broadly.

"You have yourself an idea, don't you, Detective Vance?" Trixie said coyly.

"I do," the detective said, finishing his glass and putting it down. "But it's kind of crazy."

"I like crazy," Trixie said.

"Exactly how crazy?" I asked.

"Pretty damn crazy. They're having a reception tomorrow night. A couple hundred slobbering Soviet Union fifth columnists are showing up for a night of caviar and communism at seven sharp. We're going to triple our team here just to keep track of them all."

"But I assume they'll have a guest list," I said.

"Oh, they do, and we've got a copy." The Red Squad was probably leaning on some diplomatic clerk they caught in a compromising position to feed them information like that.

"Yet, somehow, I don't think we're on it," I said.

Vance just smiled and poured himself another slug. As usual, Trixie was ahead of me on the uptake.

"I think Detective Vance is proposing something a little different. I think he is suggesting we take the place of a couple already on the list."

"Bingo," Vance said. "And I've got an idea about who. Of course, we check out everybody whose name shows up on one of these, and I've got the perfect couple in mind. I just need you to look fancy. When these commies do parties, they dress for success."

"Don't worry," Trixie said. "Eddie cleans up nice."

"Okay, but I want something in return. I want to debrief you after you get out of there, and you can tell me everything that you saw. Oh, and if you get caught, you never heard of the Los Angeles Police Department, the Red Squad, or J.D. Vance."

Trixie got that vacant look again.

"I think everybody's going to hear of J.D. Vance someday," she said blankly. Vance furrowed his brow.

"Don't mind her. She's a little odd sometimes," I told Vance, who was still baffled. "It's a deal. If we get out alive, we'll tell you everything we saw, and if we don't, we never met you."

"Then be back here at 5:30 sharp tomorrow," he said.

"We'll be here," I said before I realized that I couldn't promise we'd be alive that long.

We were back at the apartment at 5:30 p.m. sharp the next day. I had dropped off Trixie, gone home, and slept until the crack of noon, then went out by myself and got a club sandwich. It felt good to be normal for a change. It was probably the first twelve hours in the last few days when nobody tried to put me on a slab.

I picked up Trixie, and she was dressed to kill, but I wasn't sure how. That is, I once again had no idea where she was hiding that little pistol of hers. Her handbag was way too small, and her dress didn't give any clues. But I was a gentleman and didn't inquire further.

She wore her hair put up in Greek demigoddess style, held in place with long hairpins. It would've made an impression on me if she wasn't my partner. It made an impression on Vance. He just stared at her and muttered something about us looking swell.

Detective Vance did not let us into the detectives' frat house again – he came out into the hall and led us downstairs. He had suggested that I park my ride around the corner, and I did. We took his unmarked Ford.

"Where are we headed?" Trixie inquired.

"Traffic stop," Vance replied.

There was a Cadillac parked up ahead on Santa Monica Boulevard hemmed in by two black-and-whites. A couple of young patrolmen were hooking up a moderately attractive, finely dressed lady and a toad of a man, though he was sporting a very expensive suit for an amphibian.

We pulled over. Vance told us to stay in the Ford, and we all waited. The windows were down, and we could hear them yelling about "fascist brutes" and "damn Nazis" as the cops stuffed them, not particularly gently, into the back of a patrol car. It drove off, and Vance got out. We followed.

"Bernard and Margot Rivenhaven," he said to us. "That was them. They're now you."

One of the uniforms came over and handed the detective two rectangular pieces of paper and a set of keys.

"Got him for drinking and driving," the cop told his superior. "And her for interfering with an arrest."

"Was he drinking and driving?" Trixie asked. The cop looked at her, confused.

"Everybody is always drinking and driving," the uniform said. "Hell, I had two Millers at lunch."

"Good man," Vance said before dismissing him. He turned to us, handing us the papers. They were Department of Motor Vehicles forms in the names of Bernard and Margot Rivenhaven.

"These are their driver's licenses. He's a big time lawyer from Bakersfield who represents commie union organizers out in the pistachio farms when he's not chasing ambulances. She's his wife. They don't run in the Red circles in LA and we've never seen them on a guest list before. Evidently, they thought this invitation was a big honor. Too bad those outfits are going to go to waste in the drunk tank. Should be the perfect cover for you two."

"Thanks, Joe."

"You can thank me by not getting caught and by forgetting me if you do." He handed over the keys. I turned to Trixie.

"So, tell me you have a good feeling about this."

"I don't have any feeling about it at all. Nothing good, but at least nothing bad."

"Then I guess we take our chances. Shall we go, Margot?"

"Off to the party, Bernard," she replied, smiling obliquely.

16.

I liked tooling around in Bernard Rivenhaven's Cadillac. It was stylish and drove like a cloud had dropped from the sky down onto Santa Monica Boulevard. We drew a lot of looks, and Trixie waved at a few slack-jawed folks at the bus stop who were no doubt thinking we were movie stars. Actually, they were probably thinking that she was a movie star. Me? I was just the chauffeur.

We pulled up in front of the Soviet consulate on Wilshire and a young man in a valet's uniform trotted around the hood to take my keys, while another valet opened the passenger side door for Trixie. She stepped out in her dress, towering in her heels, and every pinko eye in the vicinity turned to her.

We played off the attention with the casual disdain that only the truly rich and truly beautiful can exude. We were enjoying the Rivenhavens' high style right out in front of the Soviet Union's consulate. If you were one of the top-shelf communists, there is nothing like communism for living the good life.

We weren't alone, not by a long shot. This was a social event of the fellow traveler season. There were a lot of folks pulling in, unloading their cars, and marching up the steps into the consulate. This was a big to-do, but I still wasn't sure what it was actually about. Was it Lenin's birthday? Marx's anniversary? Regardless, they had assembled quite a crowd. They are young communists, old communists, rich communists, poor communists, and more than a few middle-class communists, all gathered together to celebrate the Revolution and to swill vodka on Joe Stalin's dime. Communists of the world unite, you have nothing to lose but your livers.

Inside the entryway were a couple of sullen apparatchiks standing at a large oak table holding clipboards. They were running through the names of the guests, confirming them, and checking them off. We got in the line, waiting our turn. After all, lines were something the Soviet Union excelled at. At the head of the queue was a well-dressed couple with more money than sense. They were babbling about the proletariat. The apparatchik did not blink. Behind the couple were a pair of guys in second-rate suits that were probably first-rate by the standards of their closets. They gave the Slavic maître d' their names, and he ran a thin finger down the list until he found them, checked them off, and nodded for them to proceed inside.

We got to the head of the line, and the first time he showed any emotion at all was when he beheld Trixie. She smiled at him, and his frowning lips became, if not a smile, at least a straight slit. I gave him our assumed names, he checked off "Bernard and Margot Rivenhaven," and then he actually spoke.

"Enjoy your evening of solidarity, comrades."

"Anything for the Revolution," Trixie assured him. We left him standing at his table.

The reception was being held in the large open foyer just beyond the front door. It took up much of the first floor and was the size of a ballroom – a grim ballroom. The consulate was quite a contrast to Elysium; this was Elysium with every bit of symmetry, beauty, and joy wrung out of it.

It was the height of pure utilitarianism, an ugly temple of socialism that was stripped of character, humanity, and individuality, much like socialism itself. The walls appeared to be built from gray cinderblock, and the floor was concrete. The ceiling had exposed ductwork and wiring. The only decorations on the wall, besides the red flag with the yellow hammer and sickle of the Union of Soviet Socialist Republics, were hanging portraits of the Party's perennial heroes – Lenin, Stalin, Marx, and Engels.

"Did you notice that Uncle Joe is the only one with a portrait who is still drawing breath?" Trixie observed in a low whisper.

"I don't think Stalin likes competition," I said. I noticed there were other places that could have held portraits and probably, at one point, did hold other portraits. But after the Moscow show trials, most of the USSR's former heroes were now designated villains. They got erased from photographs with an airbrush and from existence in the bowels of the Lubyanka with a Makarov pistol shot to the back of the neck. You needed a program to keep track of who was still in the good graces of the Communist Party, and who had gotten, or was about to get, the chop.

"Don't mention Trotsky," Trixie said mischievously. "I think that might out us."

But I wasn't laughing. We had a slight problem. I saw them across the room, past the multitude of communist guests who were drinking up their host's booze. Three or four young men, college-age, were gathered around and chatting with a few obvious Soviet types. A couple of them had black eyes and one had a bandage.

"Remember our friends from the medical school?" I whispered. Trixie looked over and saw them too. "They might or might not recognize me, but they sure as hell are going to recognize you. So, let's keep as many of these drunken Reds between them and us as we can until we figure out our plan."

We did not make a plan in the car coming over because there was no way to make a plan. We knew what we needed to do – we needed to get away from the reception and go looking for the missing Charles Gaultier and Dr. Hollister – but we had no idea how to do it. For one thing, we weren't quite sure *where* they might be. I was thinking they would be in the basement—the communists sure loved their dungeons—but they could be anywhere in the sprawling complex. We had to find them, free them, and get them out of there somehow. And I had no clue about how to pull off any of it.

"I need a drink," I told Trixie.

"What else is new?" Trixie asked. "It looks like there's a bar over there." We started walking over to where a short line stood in front of a man in an ill-fitting tuxedo mixing drinks. His inventory tilted heavily toward vodka. As in tilting all the way over.

"What would you like?" the bartender growled. Obviously, he was part of the consulate staff, an import from Moscow or its environs, impressed into service serving drinks to the local allies.

"A white Russian," Trixie replied, smiling her smile. "When in Rome, am I right?"

The bartender either didn't find it funny or didn't get it, and he next looked at me.

"Vodka, neat," I said. He set to mixing Trixie's drink and pouring mine. It was a pretty measly pour. I wouldn't have tipped him even if tipping wasn't already frowned upon as exploiting the working class.

We faded back into the crowd.

"How is it?" I asked as Trixie took a sip of hers.

"Just like you'd expect from a bartender who's probably in the NKVD," Trixie said. "You give a prisoner a couple of these and she's sure to talk, and not from the alcohol."

I took a sip of my vodka. It tasted oily, like it was distilled from tar instead of potatoes. But at least the price was right.

We moved through the crowd, maximizing the distance from our friends from UCLA. Around us, the fellow travelers mixed and mingled eagerly. There was a lot of talk about world-wide Revolution and the proletariat, but also about stock picks, summer vacations, and gross box office receipts. In Lost Angeles, you never let politics get in the way of turning a buck.

The guests seemed genuinely excited to be there in the belly of the beast, most of them American Reds who were delighted to be around real-life commies straight from the USSR. The Russian diplomats were getting it from all sides, being treated like royalty, and that seemed to scare them a little. Being royalty correlated with a short lifespan in Russia. Just ask the Czar and his family. Moreover, half of the staff was no doubt informing to the NKVD on the other half – and vice versa – and most of them probably understood that if they enjoyed all the attention too much, they would get sent home and then to Siberia.

But the American Marxists were clueless to that Soviet intrigue. Communism was a game, an affectation to them; to the Soviets, it was life and death – mostly death. The American Reds acted out with the same kind of giddy fandom you would see from the tourists hanging around outside the Brown Derby when Shirley Temple or some other star walked by. I was surprised no one was asking the Russkies for autographed headshots.

"Oh, what's it like to actually live in the worker's paradise?" cooed one overweight woman bursting out of her gown as she spoke to a bored military attaché wearing way too many medals for a country that hadn't been at war except with its own citizens in twenty years.

"It is good," the colonel responded unconvincingly. He took a giant sip of his oily vodka. The woman nodded eagerly, hoping he would elaborate. He just took another sip.

I scanned the reception hall, weighing our options and listening to the string quartet playing something classical from the balcony above. They were not terrible, but it was a far cry from the satyr orchestra up on the hill. We needed to get out of there and into the bowels of the consulate.

I focused on trying to find a way out of the reception hall. There were elevators, but they were blocked off with velvet ropes and guarded by a duo of hostile-looking consulate security thugs. There was also a large staircase in the center of the foyer that led upstairs to where the actual consulate offices were. That was blocked off with more velvet ropes and three more bullet-headed Ivans making sure nobody got lost and wandered upstairs.

Several hallways led back into darkness from the ground floor. I wasn't sure where those went, but none of them were blocked off with velvet ropes, at least as far as I could see. I was stumped.

"So, how do we slip out of here so we can look around?" I asked Trixie. I took another sip of my vodka, and it tasted like I could run it in my Buick.

"Just what I was wondering," she answered. Trixie was looking the place over, too, checking for angles, seeking opportunities. We didn't have much time to lose. I was no expert in the laws of probability, but at some point during this soirée we were gonna cross paths with those battered frat boys and then things were gonna get ugly fast. I had my .357, of course, but while it was a quality gun, the Russians had quantity on their side.

"Look at them," Trixie marveled, nodding to the stairway. My eyes followed the path of her nod.

Two big guys were descending the stairs, but it was the same guy. Twins. Identical. And they looked mean.

"They must be the Smirnoff brothers Vance told us about," Trixie said.

"I guess Moscow is taking this demigod stuff pretty seriously if it's deploying heavy artillery like those two mouth breathers," I said. The twins stopped at the bottom of the stairs, surveyed the crowd with their stone faces, and then disappeared among the guests. From the looks of them, they probably chewed nails for fun.

"Caviar?" asked an unsmiling, uniformed waiter holding a tray. He looked like a guy who should be picking beets, yet who was shanghaied into server duty and outfitted in a white suit that didn't quite fit. But that wasn't important – he had caviar, and that was. Things were finally looking up. I had gotten a taste for sturgeon roe in Europe, especially the good stuff from the

Volga. I examined his wares but was profoundly disappointed. The tray held a half-dozen Ritz crackers, each with two or three puny black eggs dropped on top. I expect the money that was supposed to go for high-end caviar for their American catspaws was probably going into the chargé d'affaires's pocket.

"Pass," I said, and the amateur waiter moved on.

"These communists don't seem very interested in impressing their guests," I observed.

"They don't have to be," Trixie replied. "These are all true believers. Look at them. They're just thrilled just to be here. But, of course, they *are* here and not in Leningrad. If they really thought the USSR was a workers' paradise, wouldn't they want to be frolicking in the revolutionary Garden of Eden?"

I shivered at the thought of this salty crowd frolicking. We had just been up in Elysium, where everyone was beautiful. Most of these clowns looked exactly like what most communists were – unattractive, irritating malcontents. If there was an opposite to Elysium, the Soviet consulate was it. Of course, Trixie was the exception, and she was getting attention, though not the kind we necessarily wanted.

"Well, hello comrade and comradette," purred a short, smug man in a brown suit clutching a tumbler of the same potato rotgut I was trying to force down my gullet. His smile was as oily as the liquor, and his gaze was fixed on Trixie. "Isn't it wonderful to be around fellow revolutionAres fighting for the future?"

"To the revolutionary future," I interjected without even bothering to fake enthusiasm. I raised my glass and drank, and he mirrored me. Then he turned back to Trixie and smiled.

"Now, where did you come from?" he asked.

"Bakersfield," Trixie told him, doing that thing she did where she looked at a man and made him feel like he and she were the only two people in the whole, wide world.

"Well, then, when the revolution comes, we're going to have to make sure that Bakersfield is tasked with the production of women because, in the Union of American Socialist States, they should all be as beautiful as you."

I about tossed my vodka back up, but Trixie giggled in delight, and the little man was gratified to see it.

"I had no idea the comrades here in Los Angeles were so charming," she told him, reaching to touch his arm. He reacted to her speaking to him as if he was a dog and she was patting him on the head. "I'm Margot."

"And I am Marvin Kinchloe," he said and then paused expectantly. The silence hung in the air for a moment. I took another sip.

"*The* Marvin Kinchloe," he reiterated, giving her a chance to correct her evident *faux pas* in not knowing who he was. She just smiled expectantly, waiting.

"Well, I suppose that Bakersfield is a little far from Hollywood, so you might not recognize me right away," he rationalized. "I am a writer. A *Hollywood* writer."

Of course, I've been around Tinseltown enough to know that Hollywood writers had all the status of the guy who switches out the salt cakes in the studio commissary's urinals. So had Trixie, but she didn't let it show.

"A writer," she gushed, allowing a little awe to slip into her voice. "And a *Hollywood* writer to boot."

"Guilty," admitted Marvin sheepishly.

"Have you written anything I might've seen, Marvin?" she asked, demonstrating interest. He beamed.

"There was *Mission to Moscow, The Song of the Workingman, Death of a Coal Miner*, and...," he paused. "Also, *Abbott & Costello Meet the Minotaur*. That last one I had to do for the studio, you see, so that they would allow me to make films that are meaningful, that support the Revolution. But not openly, of course. Subtly. We can't be too obvious about our agenda, you know. After all, the studios are bastions of capitalism. Obviously, when the Revolution comes, I'll be able to write whatever I want instead typing out the kind of garbage they film just to make a few grubby dollars."

"You'll get to be a writer after the Revolution?" I asked. "What if they want you to work in a factory?" These guys always expected to be the poets and artists in their commie utopia; none of them ever considered that they might be the ones digging ditches.

Marvin giggled nervously, then ignored me to continue his conversation with Trixie.

"I'm working on a project now called *Red Star Over Albuquerque*. It's an oater. For the lead, they are looking at Randolph Scott."

"Randolph Scott," she marveled.

"But it's subversive, you see. The cattle rustlers are actually the good guys, the guys fighting against the capitalists to seize the means of cattle production! You see, it's *very* subversive."

"You are so brave to be taking a stand," Trixie assured him. He swelled with pride.

"I must be modest. I'm not alone. Many of us among the literary folk in Hollywood are actually members of the Party. Obviously, we have to keep it a secret. It can be very dangerous. We take great risks being leftists in Hollywood."

"That won't always be true," Trixie assured him.

"We can certainly hope not! Still, the Party recognizes our contributions, my contributions. I've been to many of these parties. I've been inside the consulate for special briefings that I cannot discuss, even with you. I'm also good friends with many of the diplomats. Keep it on the QT, but we Hollywood Party members work *very* closely with our Soviet comrades to further the Revolution."

"That is so impressive, Marvin," Trixie told him. He beamed. "Say, it's very crowded out here and very loud. Do you know some quiet place we can go where we can talk more?"

Marvin smiled the smile of a man whose greatest wish had just come true, but then he looked at me uncertainly.

"I think I need to get another drink," I said.

"He's just a friend," Trixie assured the dubious Marvin.

"A friend who needs another drink," I said before turning away and walking toward the bar. I glanced back over my shoulder. The pair huddled together and giggled, and then Marvin took Trixie's arm and led her across the room toward one of those dark hallways.

I got to the bar and lifted an unopened bottle of the caustic Russian vodka while the stone-faced bartender was serving someone else, then followed the pair at a discreet distance. I wasn't worried about Marvin seeing me. He wasn't looking anywhere but at Trixie.

They disappeared into the hallway. I reached the corner and looked around it. There they were, still walking into the dark. For a moment, I thought that Marvin was leading her toward the men's room. That would've worked out badly for him. But instead, he was leading her toward one of the doors beyond the latrines.

The door was locked. From where I was, I could see that Marvin was getting desperate. Then Trixie stepped in, whispering something to him, and he stood back. She looked around, reached to her head, pulled out something, and then set to work on the lock. After about thirty seconds, no doubt the longest thirty seconds of Marvin's life, the door opened, and she pulled him inside.

I took a look around me. I saw the head of one of the Smirnoff twins bobbing above the mass of partygoers cavorting in the foyer. I took another look around to see if any of my fraternity punching bags were in sight, and none were. Satisfied the coast was clear, I went down the hallway, clutching the bottle of vodka that I had just liberated from the bar. I was just another Red having a good time.

I got to the door and listened for a moment. I heard Trixie inside.

"You got the wrong idea, Marvin." And then I heard a thump and a muffled groan. I went through the door.

It opened into a long hallway leading back into the recesses of the consulate, and there was Trixie, standing as if nothing had happened. Not so, Marvin. He was leaning against the wall, clutching his nether parts and sobbing quietly.

"Marvin tried to redistribute my means of production," Trixie explained. She didn't have to explain how she had launched the counterrevolution with her high heels right into his groin.

I walked up to Marvin and laid him out with a right cross. I needed him unconscious anyway, but there was no law saying I couldn't also deliver a little justice and enjoy it. He fell to the floor in a heap, and I unscrewed the cap to pour vodka all over him. When they found him tomorrow, he was going to be just another drunk communist partygoer trying to sleep it off.

"Let's start looking for our missing demigod and doctor," I suggested, though I had no idea what we would do if and when we found them.

We started walking down the hall, which was lined with offices. They were all empty, and we were at a disadvantage. We couldn't read what was on the doors, desks, or walls because it was all in Cyrillic.

"I'm not sure they'd be keeping them in an office suite anyway," Trixie opined. "I think we need to find our way downstairs."

She was right. Our objective wasn't going to be up here. If I knew anything about Russians, they'd have them underground somewhere.

At the end of the hall was another door. This one was locked, too. It had a red-lettered sign on it in Russian that I couldn't read, but I knew what it meant anyway: Unless you want to end up in Siberia, don't go through this door unless you have business behind it.

Well, we had business behind it.

"Okay, Trixie, work your magic," I said. "Let's see if you can go two for two tonight on picking Russian locks."

Trixie smiled and reached into her hair, pulling out a pair of long, sharp hairpins. Then she bent down and began fiddling with the lock. This one was a little more complicated. It took her a full sixty seconds to pick it.

"Ta-da," she said upon hearing the satisfying click of the lock. She inserted the hairpins back into her hairdo and pushed open the door. Beyond it was a staircase running up and down the building.

"You have a career as a jewel thief if you ever decide to go that way," I told her.

"A girl has to have options," she replied, holding open the door. "After you."

I wasn't going to take any chances. I brought out the .357 magnum; the vodka bottle was still in my left hand.

"You really need the booze?" Trixie asked. It was only about half-full after I had soaked the Red writer.

"You never know when a bottle of booze is going to come in handy."

Holding my fifth of rotgut and my pistol, I went through the door to the landing. The stairs went up flight after flight into the darkness. The building looked about seven or eight stories high from the outside. But the stairwell also went downward, down into the dark. I looked around for a light switch and found one. I flicked it on.

The stairs went down two more floors, for a total of ten floors. We didn't have time to search all ten; we had time to search maybe one.

There was a landing at each lower floor and another door, again with the same Russian take on a "KEEP OUT" sign. We got to the first subfloor, and I listened at the door for a moment. Nothing.

"If I'm going to have cells or prisoners, they're going to be down at the bottom," Trixie said. "That's where the dungeon always is."

She was right, of course. We went down to the bottom floor and up to the door. I listened. Nothing.

"Three for three?" I asked Trixie. She nodded and out came the hairpins again. She slid them into the lock and jiggled until we heard the quiet click. The hairpins disappeared back into her hair as she stood up. Her hand went to the doorknob and twisted, and I pushed it open slightly.

There were voices on the other side, two guys, Russian, and they knew we were coming.

My mind raced, my plan formed, and I slipped my pistol back in the holster even as I grabbed Trixie around the waist and pushed on through.

A pair of slabs of Russian beef stood there, wearing boxy suits and staring. They had been amusing themselves with a half-drank bottle of Russian rotgut. They were absolutely baffled at how two people had gotten through that door.

One said something to me in Russian, and I don't speak the language, but again, I could translate. It was something along the lines of "What the hell are you doing here?" except with slurring and a few choice Russian words that you don't use around ladies.

I laughed, laughed like a fellow drunk, and lifted up my half-empty bottle of vodka to salute my two new Russian friends. Trixie was on board already, and she giggled, swaying and stumbling. We were just a couple of amorous communists looking for a quiet place to do a little conspiring.

"Hiya, comrades!" I hailed them. "Want a swig to celebrate the Revolution?"

I guess our acting was good enough – at least as good as in Marvin's last Abbott & Costello flick – because they seemed more exasperated than angry. They started walking over, to no doubt escort us back upstairs to our shindig, hopefully without their boss finding out that we had found our way in through multiple doors that they were supposed to have locked.

I smiled in the face of the bigger guy because it's always my policy to take out the bigger guy first when you have a choice of who to take out first. I brought that bottle across the side of his head with enough force to shatter it and spray glass and oily vodka all over his buddy's face. The first guy went down, and the second guy was trying to get the debris out of his eyes when I slugged him twice in the head. He stopped doing anything but breathing as he lay there on the floor next to his inert buddy.

"Well, that was discreet," Trixie observed.

"What is this place?" I asked, looking around. Yeah, it was a dungeon, but it also looked like a laboratory. There were shelves on the wall with all sorts of ingredients, all in English, and there was a table with beakers, Bunsen burners, and the rest of the gear you'd expect to see in a scientist's lab.

"Just like the Nazis," Trixie said. "If the Reds have them, they're around here somewhere."

We split up and walked through the laboratory. There was an elevator door on the wall. Flanking it were a couple of refrigerators and some shiny chrome tanks of who knows what.

I was the first one to see the iron-bar cells, cages not for lab animals but for men. And there were men inside.

One was wearing a tattered lab coat and a smock covered with stains. He was unshaven and older. He had a bed and a pail for his necessities. He was waking up.

"Dr. Hollister, I presume?" I asked because I couldn't think of anything else to say.

17.

The broken man in the cage looked up at me, afraid. Somebody had worked him over but good. He had a busted lip, bruises on his face, that sort of thing. His eyes were pits of pain. Obviously, no one was asking him to do the work. They were telling him, and apparently, he hadn't listened closely enough.

"Please don't hurt me," Dr. Hollister moaned, struggling to rise from the filthy mattress he lay on. "I'll get to work. The work...."

"I'm not a Russian. We're not here to hurt you. We're here to help you."

He looked at me with his wounded, wet eyes, not quite comprehending.

"I found the doctor," I yelled over my shoulder.

Trixie came over, surveying the cages.

"And I think I found Charles Gaultier," she said ominously.

He was huddled in a dark corner of another cell, covered by a threadbare blanket. He was the shape of a man, but of a broken one. His noble face was lined and drawn. His skin was sallow, and his hair was largely gone. He was bound in chains.

Silver chains.

"Is he dying?" I gasped, astonished. I've never seen a demi in that condition. I didn't believe they could be in that condition.

"Oh, no," Dr. Hollister muttered. "Not dying. Sick. In pain. But not dying. Not yet."

The shape in the next cage groaned. His eyes were yellow and unfocused. What had they done to him?

Experiments of some nightmarish kind. They could hurt him, but not kill him.

I went over to the demi guinea pig and knelt.

"Mr. Gaultier, we're here to get you. Constance Showers sent us. Do you remember Constance Showers?"

"She...she's the one," he whispered.

"Yes, she's the one who sent us to find you."

Gaultier looked at me and tried to speak, but there were no more words. He shut his eyes and breathed labored breaths. Assuming we could get him out of these cages, we would have to carry him out of the consulate. I went back to the doctor.

"We need to get you out of here," I said to Dr. Hollister, but I had no idea how to make that happen. "Trixie, look around and see if you can find any keys to these cells."

She searched the two knuckleheads, then began shuffling through the papers and the shelves. I turned my attention back to the doctor.

"What were they making you do to him?" I asked. "All this for some sort of immortality potion?"

"I don't understand," Dr. Hollister managed to say. He looked baffled.

The bastards who did this were now officially on the Loud List of guys needing some payback.

"No keys," Trixie announced from behind me. "And that's not some office door lock designed to keep out honest men. That's a prison lock designed to keep dishonest men in. I can't pick it."

I told her to keep looking for the keys, and I tried the cage lock, shaking it and pulling on it, hoping for a miracle. No miracle. It was secure.

The scientist reached through the bars and put his hand on my wrist, grabbing it tighter than I would've thought he could.

"You have to stop them," Dr. Hollister said. "You have to stop them."

"Stop what? What am I stopping?"

"They only need one thing, only one more thing before they can make me make it."

"What are you talking about? What do they want you to make, Doctor Hollister."

"Medusa's serpent," he said. "They need another."

Every word was an effort for him as he pulled himself towards the bars to look in my face.

"They'll make me make it when they get another of Medusa's serpents. I have no choice! And then we will go...there."

He fell back, exhausted, and shut his eyes.

"Doctor, wake up!" I shouted, probably louder than I should have. Trixie knelt beside me.

"No keys, Eddie, but I found this." She handed me an ampule, and I read the label: "Amphetamine Sulfate."

"That's how they get him wide awake to work for them," Trixie explained.

"That and beating the hell out of him. So, what do we do now?"

Trixie didn't have a chance to answer. We heard noises, the sounds of feet on the stairs from where we had come.

"We have to go, Trixie, and we aren't going out the way we came."

"What about them?" Trixie asked. I shook my head. There was nothing we could do. Dying here – or worse – at the hands of the Russians wouldn't help anybody.

"Elevator," I said, rising up, running over, and pushing the call button. Before the doors opened, I grabbed the two Russians' half-empty vodka bottle and handed it to Trixie.

The door opened. The elevator was paneled in dark wood. The door slid shut, and I hit "L." I noted a keyhole that activated the car panel's button for "B2," where we were. You couldn't just drop into the basement lab.

We began to ascend to the lobby.

"Follow my lead," I said to Trixie. The dial above the doors swung to "L," and the elevator car came to a stop. The door slid open, revealing the party in full swing. Noise filled the car from the chattering guests and the classical quartet.

The only ones who seemed to notice the elevator had opened were the two guards stationed outside, and they were a bit confused. Their job was to keep people from going into the elevator, but apparently, no one had explained to them the possibility that someone might come out.

The first one stepped in front of the open doors, looking a bit baffled, and spat out something in Russian – before he got a good look at our clothes and at Trixie, he may have thought we were diplomatic staff.

That was all the time I needed. I pulled him inside the car with us, threw him against the wall, and hit him in the gut. He keeled over. The other guy entered the elevator car and came at me from the back, completely ignoring Trixie. Nobody should ever ignore Trixie. She closed the door and clobbered him on the back of the head with that vodka bottle. He crumbled like a cookie.

I took a couple more swings at the first Russian, connecting with his face, and knocking him loopy. To be honest, I probably hit him harder and more than I needed to, but after what I saw in the dungeon, he was lucky he was still breathing when I left him on the floor of the car next to his pal. I adjusted my suit, which had gotten a little rumpled in the ruckus, and nodded to Trixie. She pushed the button to open the door.

I let her through first, knowing that everyone would be looking at her instead of the mess we were leaving behind inside the elevator. I hit the "Close Door" button again – the control panel was in English – and slipped out before the doors slammed together.

A few eyes were admiring Trixie, but other than that, the guests sensed nothing unusual. I glanced over to the grand staircase, where a couple more meatheads were stationed before we went downstairs, and they seemed oblivious. I took

Trixie by the arm and began leading her through the crowd towards the front door.

We got about halfway before a kid of maybe twenty with a shiner the size of a softball on his left eye stepped in front of us.

"You!" he shouted, pointing. "CounterrevolutionAres!"

I gave him a shiner in the other eye and laid him flat out on the concrete floor.

"Come on!" I shouted to Trixie, but she was already moving.

The women and some of the men in the crowd started screaming and yelling. It was pandemonium as they went to and fro, most out of our way but some in it. Those guys in our path didn't last long. One little guy who could've passed for Marvin's first cousin got caught in my way. I grabbed him by his lapels and tossed him into a waiter. He, the waiter, and the tray of chintzy caviar sprawled across the floor.

The front door was up ahead, and I took the opportunity to look behind me.

There was one of the Smirnoffs, and he was coming after us with something that would've been a lot more intriguing to a gun aficionado like me if he wasn't trying to kill us with it.

Whichever Smirnoff it was, he was clutching a Pistolet-pulemyot Degtyaryova—a PPD-34/38. It was a submachine gun with a wooden stock that kind of looked like a short rifle with a shrouded barrel, except it had a big drum magazine like an old-style Tommy gun. It fired a 7.63×25mm Tokarev Russian pistol bullet and was issued to the NKVD for suppressing counterrevolutionAres like us.

I had never seen one before in the flesh, but now I saw one pointing in our direction. Smirnoff was not concerned with the partygoers surrounding us as we ran. He leveled the submachine gun and fired off a burst. By some miracle, only one person was hit, apparently a Soviet diplomat who caught three and spun like a top before falling into a bloody mess. That only made the women and many of the men scream louder.

I pulled Trixie along to that heavy oak table near the front door where they've been taking attendance. The guys with the clipboards were gone, but I didn't spend time looking for them. Instead, I flipped the table over on its side to give us some concealment, but it was not going to provide cover – the 7.63×25mm Tokarev rounds punched right through.

We dove behind it, and out came my magnum. Smirnoff sprayed again, and I could hear the rounds hitting the wood and breaking through, kicking up a storm of wood chips and splinters above us. We hugged the floor.

I kept waiting for him to stop shooting, but he kept walking and spraying as if there was no end to that drum. And they're almost wasn't an end to it – it held 71 bullets. But it fired fast, and after a few bursts of several seconds, the shooting stopped for a moment. I wheeled around the table with my wheel gun, and Smirnoff was busy slapping another drum into place. He raised his weapon to start again.

I was faster.

My silver hollow point caught him in the forehead, taking much of the back of his noggin off. That just made the now-very messy women and men behind him scream that much louder as the giant tottered and fell.

Beyond him, I could see more of the thugs on the staircase coming down with their own PPD-34/38s, at least a half-dozen of them led by the surviving Smirnoff.

We had gotten lucky once. We weren't going to get lucky seven more times in a row.

"Let's go!" I shouted, but Trixie was way ahead of me, heading to the front door. A Russian thug jumped into the threshold, his hand holding a Makarov pistol that he started to raise toward my companion.

Again, I was faster. I hit him in the gut with a bullet like I was wielding a sledgehammer, and he flew backward onto the sidewalk minus his spleen.

We spilled out the front door and passed the prostrate Russian, running into the street where guests were still leaving their cars. The valets were smart enough to clear out, but not the rich communists. There was a lovely Chrysler there, with an abandoned woman standing by its open passenger door and a man who looked like he walked off a monopoly board by the driver's side. I ran around to him.

"Keys," I demanded.

"Absolutely not!" the rich communist said.

"Keys," I repeated. This time, I put the barrel of the magnum in his face. He wisely consented to participate in our redistribution of his wealth.

On her side, Trixie simply gave a push to the stubborn woman, who fell on her tail in the gutter, screaming obscenities that would have made a sailor blush.

We got into the car, and I cranked it. I hit the gas just as the Russian spilled out the door. One of them opened fire, and I didn't have to tell Trixie to duck down with me. The bullets smashed through the rear windshield and out the front windshield as well.

"Vance's boys are going to have plenty to write about tonight," Trixie said as I accelerated down Wilshire Boulevard. It was almost 8 o'clock, but there was still traffic, and behind us, it looked like the Russians were nationalizing a few vehicles of their own.

I stepped on the gas and headed west, racing in and out and between the slower cars that didn't have a pack of communist killers on their tail. We could see three or four of our pursuers behind us, at least three to four hundred yards back. I got a couple laughs out of it when they sideswiped or clipped oncoming traffic or the vehicles they were trying to get around. I'm a pretty good driver, but then again, I'm from Los Angeles.

I think in Moscow they're still driving donkey carts.

"Reload me," I directed Trixie, handing her my magnum and a speed loader. "Keep the extras you dump!"

She did, but she also kept an eye on the Reds behind us.

"You're not losing them," Trixie observed. She was right about that. They still stuck to my tail, and I couldn't shake them. I came to La Brea and headed north. I figured it would be a lot harder to get them to engage in a blazing gun battle in the middle of a busy street than on some side street. But I was wrong.

I got caught behind a delivery truck and a bus near the intersection with Beverly, and the nearest Russians, in a Dodge, started making up the difference. I could see it was Smirnoff, the one with his skull still intact, leaning out the passenger side with his PDD – 34/38.

"Down again!" yelled Trixie, who had seen him, too. We crouched down and several shots punched out some of the remaining glass in the back window and went through the windshield. The back trunk was stitched right to left and left to right with bullet holes. The bus up ahead of us caught a few stray rounds, too, with one of the taillights getting smashed out. The delivery guy pulled left hard across oncoming traffic and slammed into a light pole.

"Where the hell are the cops when we need them?" wondered Trixie as I put a little distance between us and them. We sat back up.

"Out getting loaded, if I know anything about cops," I answered.

Trixie looked back as she handed back my loaded gun.

"They aren't backing off. They want us bad."

"I'm not sure whether it's because I whacked the Smirnoff twin or because we know their secret."

"Well," Trixie said. "It's not like anybody can do anything about it. It's a consulate, a diplomatic facility. It's Soviet Union territory. The FBI can't go in. The LAPD can't go in. Nobody can do anything about them having those two downstairs in their dungeon."

"Well, FDR could declare them persona non grata and boot them out of the country, but there are so many damn communists in his administration that's never gonna happen."

"Someday, a man's going to come and expose these Reds, but America is not going to listen," Trixie said in that far-away voice she got when she was prognosticating.

"Sounds like an American hero."

"He will be."

More bullets stitched along the side of the car and shattered the passenger's rear window. Smirnoff had gotten closer in his Dodge, and the two cars full of his NKVD buddies weren't that far behind.

Sunset Boulevard was up ahead. I swung around the traffic and made a hard right despite the red light.

"We need to take the initiative," I said. In France, I had found that the guy reacting was usually the guy dying, and we've been reacting far too much to these Red bastards.

I hit the brakes hard, and we skidded to a stop. A Chevy had slipped in behind me, blissfully unaware that there was a guy with a submachine gun behind him who wanted to shoot me. My tailgater hit his brakes and skidded to a stop about an inch from the rear of my bumper. It wouldn't have mattered much if he had slammed into it. The car's body looked like Swiss cheese.

Of course, it wasn't my car. If he ever got it back, its rich, communist owner could at least console himself with the fact that he was supporting the working class by paying them to repair it.

"What are you doing, Eddie?" Trixie asked. I always enjoyed it when she couldn't predict my next move.

I put on the parking brake, threw open the door, and rolled out, gun in hand. The Dodge appeared coming east, headlights on, moving fast. I took aim at the engine block and fired four times. Then I lifted the magnum and fired two slugs through the dark windshield right where the driver's face should have been. I hoped it would work. I was firing silver bullets down Sunset

Boulevard, not lead, and while I knew what silver did to supernatural beings, I had to hope for the best versus Detroit steel.

It did something. The Ford shimmied and lurched left in oncoming traffic, smashing hard into a beer truck making its way west. It was a solid impact, but not solid enough to take out the occupants. We might have a couple minutes while they shook it off to put some distance between us. I saw the remaining Smirnoff getting out of the car and flagging down one of the others.

And then I looked down at my driver side rear tire. The Goodyear whitewall was hissing out of a 7.62mm hole. One of Smirnoff's rounds had caught it and punched through. So much for distance. It would be a miracle if we had a half mile before that tire disintegrated and I was sparking down the street on steel rims.

I jumped back in and hit the gas.

"You get them, Eddie?"

"I bought us a couple minutes at best, but we're not going far. They blew a tire."

"Think, Eddie," I told myself. These Russians weren't giving up, and they didn't care how obvious they were being. Whatever all this was, it was worth a major diplomatic incident. And then I saw it – the Hotel Excelsior, the home away from home for Hollywood stars and starlets, often together, for robber barons, tourists, and rich businessmen whose wives had kicked them out for cavorting with their secretAres. I pulled over to the curb about half a block up.

"Let's go," I said.

We jumped out, and I grabbed her hand, and we ran down the sidewalk to the entrance.

"Checking in?" asked the confused bellman at the door. I answered in the affirmative, and he pointed me to the registration desk. It was a fine mahogany desk highlighted with brass. Behind the counter was a wall of slots, each with a room number, for mail, messages, and room keys for guests who were out on the town on the Strip.

We took a moment to compose ourselves and catch our breath. I heard one of the bellmen talking to another as we made ourselves presentable.

"I left a package for Lee in 651," he told his co-worker.

We stepped forward to the front desk, and saw a young man, earnest and clean-cut in his suit, at the desk speaking to a hirsute man and a woman.

"I have a reservation!" the man insisted. He had a harsh accent, Russian, Polish or the like.

"I'm sorry," the young man demurred. "We are simply not…equipped…to provide rooms for your kind." The young man pointed to a brass sign on the wall, posted per law for all to see:

"WE DO NOT SERVICE VAMPIRES, LYCANTHROPES, OR SIMILAR CREATURES IN THIS ESTABLISHMENT"

"Bigotry!" the hairy man shouted. He pulled a document from his pocket and displayed it. "I'm domesticated!"

But his federal domestication certificate carried no weight at the Hotel Excelsior.

"I'm sorry. Those are the house rules."

"It's past the full moon!"

The young man sadly shook his head.

"Come on," the woman said, taking her companion's arm. They turned to the door, and I could see the letter "V" branded on his forehead. The word for "wolf" in most Slavic languages was "*vuk*," or something like it.

In Eastern Europe, they dealt with lycanthropes harshly. This fellow was lucky he was not a rug in some castle. Of course, wolfmen often dealt with Balkan peasants harshly. Even a domesticated one could be dangerous. Though I felt for the man and the ugly discrimination he faced in finer establishments –

some more enlightened hotels would allow werewolves to take rooms after posting a hefty cleaning deposit – I was happy to have my silver slugs handy in case this got ugly.

The werewolf and his companion passed us gruffy, and left the lobby. We stepped forward.

The young man at the front desk greeted us, clearly hoping we would not be such a challenge.

"Welcome to the Hotel Excelsior. May I be a service?"

I said a quick prayer that there would be a key in Box 651, and it was answered. There it was.

"Key for Mr. Lee," I said.

"You're Mr. Lee?" The young man said, dubious.

"I am."

"Mr. Wen Ho Lee? From Shanghai?"

"Yes," I said firmly.

"And I am his wife," Trixie said.

"Mrs. Nha Fong Lee?"

"The same."

The young man paused for a moment, reached back, took the key from the box marked 651, and handed it over to me.

"Please let me know if I can be of further service," he said uncertainly.

"Why yes, you can," Trixie said, turning on that smile she had for when she wanted a man to do something for her. "We have some friends who may come looking for us. They want to cajole us into going back out on the Strip and celebrating, but we're very, very tired. They are foreigners and don't understand that Americans mostly like to get to bed at a reasonable hour. Can you be discreet if anyone comes looking?"

I opened my wallet, peeled off a $10 bill, and passed it over to him. It was a nice place, and he got nice tips, but this was a really nice tip. He may have been new, but he pocketed it like a pro."

"Of course. You can count on me, Mrs. Lee."

Trixie smiled, and we moved briskly into the elevator, whose door was open for a woman with a little black dachshund and a tubby little corgi. The door shut with the five of us inside. She introduced us to them. The black one snapped at me.

She was going up to eight. We were on the sixth-floor. The room was very nice, and the Lees were very neat. All of his suits and all of her dresses were hanging in the closet, and Mrs. Lee's vast shoe collection was on full display.

There were twin beds. Trixie sat on the edge of one. I went over to the phone to make a call. The operator got me through to Vance at the surveillance outpost apartment. He was not amused.

"What the hell did you do, Eddie? Do you know how much trouble you've caused?"

"Eddie, they've got a couple of American citizens down in their basement locked up. They're doing some weird medical experiments. I think they're trying to come up with an immortality potion. You can throw that on the list of felonies."

"List of felonies? Haven't you ever heard of diplomatic immunity? I know they were chasing you all through LA, firing machine guns at you, and you know what I can do about it? A great big nothing."

"Well, I'm not sure they're done looking for us. We're hiding out."

"For the love of Pete, don't tell me where you are! When the grand jury asks me, I wanna be able to tell them I had no idea where you two were holding up. You know you're a wanted man, and she's a wanted woman. I shouldn't even be talking to you."

"Look, you need to do something, J.D."

"There's nothing to do. That's Soviet Union territory, buddy. The USSR, smack dab in the middle of Los Angeles. They could be running around with bones through their noses, boiling human beings in a big cast-iron pot, and I couldn't do a thing about it. My hands are tied."

"This is something big. I don't know exactly what it is, but it's big."

"Yeah, it's too big, too big for the LAPD anyway – that's what the feds are saying. You need to watch yourself. Everybody's looking for you. You definitely better not go home."

"Hey, I'm no Albert Einstein but I'm not a dummy. Look, I know you've done me a bunch of favors, but I need one more."

"Damn it, Eddie, your account at the favor bank is way overdrawn."

"Look, when I call you back, I just need you to tell me if something happens at the embassy, like if they move out in a convoy or a bunch of cars. They've got to move these two guys, and soon."

"Where?"

"I don't know."

"Why?"

"I don't know that either."

"You know what you got, Eddie? A whole lot of nothing. Fine, you check in and I'll tell you if I've seen anything like that. Keep your heads down. Everybody out here is looking to chop them off."

I hung up.

"What the hell *do* we know, Trixie?"

"We know they're waiting for something to happen, maybe something about this Medusa serpent, and then they're going to take them somewhere for some reason."

"Vance was right. We don't know squat."

"I think we know it wasn't some immortality potion. When you said that, he looked at you like you were crazy."

"Then what's this all about?"

Trixie didn't have a chance to answer because there was a knock at the door. My gun was out and pointed at it. Another knock and the voice was the voice of the kid at the reception desk.

"Mr. Lee? Mr. Lee? Please open up. We need to talk."

"Are you alone?" I asked through the door.

"Yes," he said. "Your friends came by, and I have to say, they weren't very friendly. Please open the door."

"If you're not alone, kid, duck," I said as I turned the knob and pulled.

He was alone, and it was pretty clear by the way he was shaking in his shoes that he never had the barrel of a gun in his face before.

"I know you are not the Lees," he declared. "One of the bellman said you are Eddie Loud and that we should take care of you."

"You could be a private eye, too, kid," Trixie said as she joined me by the door.

"Well, your friends are down watching the lobby. If you don't want to run into them, you can't leave."

"We don't want to run into them," Trixie said.

"Look, you can't stay in this room, but I can give you another room on this floor. There's only one thing."

"What's that?" I asked.

"To share a room, you two have to be married."

"We're better than being married, kid," Trixie said. "We're partners."

The other room was nice, too. There were double beds, and we each took one. My magnum lay on the nightstand, but I figured we were safe. Who would want to bother Mr. and Mrs. John Doe?

We slept late, and at about 10 a.m., Trixie called down to the front desk to have them send up some coffee, some eggs, and a newspaper. I wish she had gotten a bottle of something brown, too.

"Eddie," Trixie said, sitting at the table with a slice of toast in one hand and the *Los Angeles Times* in the other. "Look at this."

"Did our little car chase through LA make the front page?" I asked.

"No, that was buried on page five. You need to look at this."

I walked over to her and followed to where her finger pointed.

"MUSEUM THEFT: SECOND MEDUSA HEAD SNAKE STOLEN IN A MONTH."

I took a sip of my coffee.

"They got the final ingredient for their recipe," I said. Trixie put down the paper and looked at me.

"Yeah, Eddie, but what are they cooking up?"

18.

Our new friend from the front desk, and after 6 a.m., the new kid who took the next reception shift, called us every hour or so to confirm that one or more of the Russians were still sitting in the lobby just in case we came down. I figured they would be watching the back door, too. With them down there and the cops out on the street, laying low for a while in the Excelsior was our best option.

I drew the curtains. It wouldn't do to have somebody's familiar peeking in on us if the Russians decided to hire a sorcerer to send his pet to look for us. I remember one demi had a crow belonging to some third-string wizard in Culver City keeping tabs on me after his official girlfriend hired me to catch him trysting with his unauthorized doxie. I finally pointed my pistol at it and told it if I saw it again, I was going to blow it into a cloud of feathers. Its master was watching through the crow's eyes and got the message. I never saw that big, black bird again.

It was no fun to be shut up inside that dark hotel room for most of the day, but we made the best of it. Trixie ordered some champagne and orange juice, and we made a couple of Buck's Fizzes. I didn't have a cleaning kit, so I wiped my gun with a dry wash cloth and ensured it was reloaded with six silver slugs. I didn't like killing time, but I knew it wasn't going to be long before something happened. Doc Hollister was pretty clear – they were only waiting for another batch of that Medusa snakehead and there was no way the thieves that stole it the previous night were anybody but Russians.

"It's going to happen soon," I told Trixie.

"We still don't know where or why," Trixie replied.

"I know somebody who does."

"Good old Constance Showers, the common denominator of our little equation."

I could've given her a call – I was calling out to check with Vance on what was happening at the embassy every hour or so – but the next time I talked to my client, I wanted to look her in the eye. And, more importantly, I wanted Trixie to look her in the eye. Trixie had a way of reading people, and we needed to read Miss Showers loud and clear.

A little after 5 p.m., they called from the front desk to tell us that the Russians had cleared out. One of them had come in, talked to the pair of watchers, and then the three of them had left. That seemed like a good omen.

"Time to go," I told Trixie. She concurred.

But first, I called Vance again. We were still wanted by the LAPD for questioning about the gunplay at the consulate and throughout the city streets, but the Russians weren't talking, so we weren't officially suspects. As for the comings and goings of the communists, nothing much was happening at the consulate. I told him I would check back later. He seemed happy to hang up. Then I called the Southern California Telephone Company operator and asked for the home address of Miss Constance Showers.

I had the kid at the front desk order us up a loaner car to be dropped off at the front of the hotel. Obviously, we weren't going anywhere with the car we borrowed after the party. We needed something clean. The cops would never know our loaner was driven by two fugitive private detectives.

I came out of the elevator with my hand on my revolver, just in case. The kid at the reception desk was as good as his word. No commies in the lobby. I went over and peeled off a few bills for him. He did good work and deserved to get a healthy reward. Who knows when I would need a favor again?

The kid outdid himself with the loaner car. It was a 1940 Buick Roadmaster convertible with bright white walls, deep green paint, and a khaki roof. I signed the form taking responsibility for it, though it occurred to me that, in my line of work, it might have been a bad financial move.

I put the top down, and off we went.

Constance Showers lived on the third floor of an apartment building on North Orchid in Hollywood, a couple blocks up from Franklin. She was maybe ten minutes away from Elysium, so it was at least convenient back when she worked for Apollo. It wasn't a slum, but it wasn't Bel-Air either.

"You would think that a couple of demigods would pay their employees a little more generously," Trixie said.

"Not really," I answered as I found a parking space and slid into it. "They tend to be a little tight with the old dollar. If they've got any wealth, it's usually wrapped up in real estate. But also, they don't really understand mortals and don't really think about them. It never really occurs to them how the mortals live, so it doesn't bother them not to pay them particularly well. There are usually so many mortals eager to work with demis that they can pay a cut-rate salary. It's glamorous, like Hollywood."

"From what you've told me about her, Constance Showers seems like a girl who would like the finer things."

"I got that impression, too," I said and opened the driver's door.

I chose to park a little down the street so if Miss Showers looked out a front window, she wouldn't see us milling about. I kept my head down as we walked down the sidewalk, turned on the walkway, and went up to the steps that took us to the front door. There was no buzzer; that would've been a little upscale. I opened the door, and we went in. There was no elevator either.

We walked up three flights of stairs, which had to be a pain for Trixie. She was still wearing that gown and those heels from the previous night. Her hair was still piled high and exquisite, pinned down without a dark strand out of place.

Miss Showers lived in Apartment 311. Trixie took the lead. She knocked on the door. We waited. It took a minute.

"What do you want?" Miss Showers asked from behind the closed door.

"Excuse the interruption," Trixie began. "I'm Rhonda from downstairs in 211. I got a letter addressed to you in 311 by accident. I thought I would bring it up because it looks like a check."

"I'm not expecting a check. Can you leave it out there and I'll get it later?"

"Honey, it looks to me like a check, and I'm not gonna just leave a check lying around for someone to grab. Now, if you want it, open the door and I'll give it to you. If not, I'm going to work."

There was a pause, and then the lock clicked, and the door cracked open.

That was enough.

I saw about half of my client's face and saw her one visible eye get very big before she tried to shut the door, but I'm a big guy, so I pushed through. Miss Showers stumbled backward, and I forced myself in. Trixie followed and shut the door behind us.

"Miss Showers, I would like to introduce my partner in this endeavor, Miss Trixie Gamble," I said.

"Pleasure to meet you," Trixie said pleasantly. The feeling was clearly not mutual.

As I looked around her modest apartment, I noted two suitcases and a leather satchel sitting on the floor. Miss Showers was wearing traveling clothes: a red sweater, a khaki skirt, and flats. A hat and her purse were on the kitchen table next to the sofa. Her outfit was nice and functional and also very stylish and, to my inexpert mind, a little pricier than you might expect to see in the cheap digs she lived in.

"Taking a trip, Miss Showers?" I asked.

"Just a few days. I need to get away. You can't imagine the anxiety all this has put on me." She walked back towards her kitchen. Trixie followed, but I hung back. Then Miss Showers turned.

"Mr. Loud, you have far exceeded and violated my instructions. I am afraid I'm going to have to terminate our relationship. I will see that you are paid the money you are owed."

"I think we are a little past that," I said. "It's time we cleared the air and had a heart-to-heart talk about exactly what's going on here."

"I told you what's going on. Someone – those Nazis, I guess – kidnapped my boss from his home. All I wanted from you is to know where he is."

"We know the answer to that last question," Trixie said. "We met him last night. He was locked in a cage in the basement of the Soviet consulate. Sadly, we were unable to bring him out with us."

"He has looked better," I said.

"I told you not to do anything, but tell me when he was being moved!"

"Yes, you certainly did."

"And his physician, Dr. Hollister, was in the cell right next door," Trixie said. "Does that surprise you?"

"What are you hinting at? Say it!"

"We think you know much more than you are telling us," Trixie said. "I can see it. So spill it, sister."

Miss Showers shook her head as she walked to her kitchen table. I stood back so I could look down the hallway towards the bedroom in case somebody came out of it unexpectedly. Trixie was closer, standing on a weathered rug in the tiny living room.

My client – my former client – reached for her purse, and her hand shot inside, pulling out a snub-nose .38. She turned and aimed it at us at gut level.

"Don't either of you move. I know how to use this thing."

"Miss Showers, you are pointing a gun at us. I've only been with Mr. Loud for a couple of days, but everybody who's pointed a gun at him has come to a bad end."

"Shut up, you tramp! If you hadn't gotten involved, none of this would've gone the way it has. All right, Mr. Loud, very, very slowly, take that gun out of your shoulder holster and throw it into the kitchen. No funny business, or I'll shoot you where you stand."

I've had people pointing guns at me lots of times. It had happened many times since Miss Showers hired me, but I hadn't expected Miss Showers to be the one standing behind a revolver. I guess I should have. Perhaps it was my trusting nature leading me to misfortune once again.

I complied, pulling the heavy gun out of my shoulder holster and tossing it away into the kitchen. It landed on the cheap linoleum with a heavy thud. Miss Showers turned her attention back to Trixie.

"Where is your gun, Miss Lady Detective?"

"I'm not carrying one. I prefer to use my head to defend myself."

"Throw that little purse of yours over into the kitchen anyway."

"If my perfume bottle cracks, I'm going to be very upset."

"You'll both be needing perfume when I'm done with you."

"That sounds like a threat, Miss Showers. Why ever would you want us dead?" Trixie asked.

"You had to go sticking your noses into it. You couldn't have just told me where he was. That's all I needed from you, and you couldn't even do that right!"

I could see from Trixie's face that things were becoming clear to her.

"You did not need to know who set Charles Gaulthier up to be kidnapped because it was you. You did it."

Miss Showers laughed, but the gun stayed on us.

"I was told you were great detectives, and you're just now figuring that out?"

"You sold him out to the Nazis," I said. "And then you hired me to find out where the Nazis were holding him. I told you, but the communists got there before we could get there. *You* told them too, didn't you?"

"Very astute, Mr. Loud."

"You sold him to the Nazis first, then the communists, and let me guess – then you sold him to Mickey Cohen and the mob."

"That's right. You almost messed up that last transaction, Mr. Loud. You were supposed to let me know when the Russians were taking him out so the mob could snatch him, but now I'm just going to tell Mickey to watch the road to Elysium. He'll take him from the communists on the way and pay me, too."

"I have some bad news, Miss Showers," I said. "Your mob buddies have double-crossed you. They came to me to get that information directly with no middleman or middlewoman. They're gonna cut you out of the loop."

Miss Showers frowned and swore – a lot. It was a bit disconcerting to hear the kind of language she was using to describe Mickey Cohen and his parentage coming from an attractive woman. If she hadn't had six .38 slugs aimed in my general direction, I might've washed her mouth out with soap.

"It doesn't matter," she rationalized. "It's a pittance compared to what Apollo is going to pay me. And then I disappear. Maybe South America. I hear Buenos Aires is gorgeous. Or Bali. I might have gone from capital to capital in Europe, drinking champagne and eating foie gras, but Apollo told me for years that he foresaw how war was coming."

"So, you sold out your new boss to your old boss?" Trixie observed. "Rather mercenary of you, dear."

"I don't owe either of them anything. I slaved for years for Apollo. He paid me nickels and dimes. Look around here. Every night, I worked at Elysium, and then I had to come back here. This was my world. A dingy, cheap world without a man, without any prospects. Oh, but I had the honor of working for a real live demigod. I was a nursemaid to a brat with near-magical powers. I had to listen to him whining and complaining about the burden of immortality. I even had to return the clothes he bought me for his parties. I finally left because I thought working for Charles Gaulthier might get me ahead, but it was the same. Long hours with just a little more money and no prospects for the future. He never saw me as a human being. None of them see mortals that way. To them, a mortal is there for a little while and then gone and they forget. I didn't matter to either of them. And after a while, they didn't matter to me."

"Why would Apollo be involved in this?"

"You know, a demigod can have practically anything he wants. He just has to want it, and it happens. But there's one thing an immortal can't have, something we mortals can."

"Death," Trixie said as it dawned on her. "They can't have death."

"So, that's the one thing they want."

"They are not forcing Dr. Hollister to make an immortality potion," Trixie said to me. "They are forcing him to make a potion to kill a demigod."

"Yes. It was my idea. I suggested it to Apollo, and he jumped at it. We agreed on a price; I made the side deals on my own. I made contact with the Nazis, and Berlin was thrilled to have the chance to set a demigod on its enemies in return for oblivion. I got them to kidnap Dr. Hollister because I knew he had already been doing illegal research. He knew what components to steal from the museums. But there was a problem. We needed proof that it would kill an immortal. The first batch of Doctor Hollister's formula they tested on a half-demi with immortality. He died, but the FBI confiscated his body. Apollo will never pay unless he sees it work, unless he sees it happen in front of him. Of course, that meant the death of his son, well, one of his sons. But demis are not known for being sentimental."

Now, it was clear to me, too.

"They are taking Charles Gaulthier up to Elysium tonight to show Apollo that their death potion, the one that has to have Medusa snake head essence in it, actually works."

"And whoever gives that to Apollo gets Apollo to do whatever he wants," added Trixie. "Apollo would be unleashed, with no fear of the Doom of Ares."

"You have put the pieces of the puzzle together," Miss Showers said, smiling cruelly. "Too bad no one will ever know that you figured it out."

There are a lot of ways that I did not want to die, and getting a bullet in the belly in a dingy Hollywood walk-up was near the top of that list. My gun was too far away to go for. If I charged her, she was going to shoot me a couple of times before I dropped dead at her feet. Trixie was closer to her, but I was in no position to whisper my plan of action to my partner. I had to rely on Trixie's ability to improvise.

There was the sofa between us. Maybe it could stop a bullet, maybe it couldn't. But I was all out of options.

I leaped down behind the sofa.

My sudden movement spooked Miss Showers, as I hoped it would, and she pulled the trigger. By that time, I was landing on my face on the floor, and the first slug went into the tacky painting of a dozen roses hanging on the wall. She fired again down at the sofa, and the bullet tore through the cheap material before planting itself in the linoleum in front of my face. It missed me by a couple inches.

I had hoped Trixie would take the opportunity to react, and I wasn't disappointed. But for a moment, I was confused because I didn't hear anything after the second shot.

"The coast is clear," Trixie said, and I stood up.

Miss Showers was standing there, still on her feet, her eyes wide, her mouth open, the gun in her hand quivering just a bit. Trixie was beside her, having taken a quick step forward, and her hand was against my former client's ear. I didn't understand for a moment until I looked at her other ear. A thin length of gray metal protruded from it, with a line of scarlet culminating in a drop of blood at its end. Trixie yanked, and the sharpened end of the hairpin came out of Miss Showers's skull. The woman dropped her revolver, swayed for a moment, and then collapsed in a pile on the floor.

Trixie wiped the hairpin off on the threadbare tablecloth and slid it back into her coif.

"You used your head, all right," I said.

Trixie knelt down by one of the leather satchels in the pile of luggage, pulling it open. Dollars, scores of them.

"Her blood money," Trixie observed. "A lot of it."

"But we haven't earned our fee yet," I said. "Our client – our real client – is still out there."

"Yes, so he is. Say, do you think she and I are about the same size?"

"I guess. Why?"

"Because I'm not about to go put a stop to all this up at Elysium dressed in a ball gown."

19.

We were going to Elysium, and the only question was when everything would jump off.

At some point, the Russians were going to haul their prize up to Apollo and sacrifice him to prove to the demigod that their death potion worked. Then they were going to ask him to do something for them, something that was probably going to change the world for the worse. The only question is whether they'd make it up there without being ambushed. The Nazis and the mob also wanted that potion and the test subject, too.

It could get pretty crowded up at Apollo's digs. And everybody in that crowd would want me and Trixie in our graves.

"This isn't the way to Elysium," Trixie observed. She was right. She was usually right.

"No, this is the way to the gun store."

When we walked into Bonfilio's, it was just closing down. The proprietor looked over. He had a smile a mile wide.

"Hi, Miss Gamble. Hi Eddie. You're lucky, as usual. I almost closed early today."

"Oh yeah?"

"I was completely bought out this afternoon," Mr. Bonfilio said. "I don't have a single silver .38, .45, or 9mm Luger slug left in the store." Those were exactly the rounds the Nazis and the mobsters would want. No doubt they bought them with fake documentation.

"How about 7.63 x 25mm Tokarev?" I asked.

"Isn't that some Russian caliber? No, I never had any of that."

This made sense. If the Russians at the consulate wanted silver bullets, they would have the boys back at the Lubyanka ship them to Los Angeles in a diplomatic pouch. A heavy diplomatic pouch.

There was one more crucial question. I asked it.

"You still got any of that silver .30-06?"

He smiled.

"I sure do. Does that mean what I think it means?"

"It sure does."

Grinning, Mr. Bonfilio turned to face the ladder, reached up to where the object of my attention hung on the wall, and retrieved the Colt Monitor.

"People are going to talk if they see me driving and you sitting in the passenger seat," Trixie told me. "They might question your manhood."

"They'll just think I drank too much."

"One day, people are going to have telephones in their pockets and they will call strangers up to drive them places in their own cars."

"Okay, we've discussed this before, Trixie. You've got to focus on the road and on what we've got to do. If you're having visions and such, you're not going to see them coming."

"I am already seeing them coming," she said.

Trixie was decked out in Constance Showers's traveling clothes. It turns out that they had been the same size, and my former client wasn't going to need them where she was going. Her hair was still up in that demigoddess style she favored, with those deadly hairpins of hers holding it so tightly that the wind blowing with the convertible top down could not muss it.

I had the Colt Monitor between my legs as I sat in the passenger seat, barrel pointed down to the floor mat. I pulled back on the action. Smooth as silk, but the gun was heavy as an anvil. It had to be if it was going to be blasting off those thirty-aught slugs.

I bought 100 of them. It cost a lot, but luckily I was flush with cash. We had taken Miss Showers's ill-gotten gains with us, and Trixie had handed the proprietor a stack of bills to pay for the machine gun and the silver bullets. There were five magazines; he threw in a cloth shoulder bag to carry them. I expect that after we left and he finally closed up, he went home, smoked a big cigar, and told his kids their college had just been paid for.

I saw a telephone booth and asked Trixie to pull over. I left the big gun in the car, got out, and shut the phone booth door behind me. Vance picked up on the second ring.

"What's the news?"

"Glad you called," he said. "Five minutes ago, every car at the consulate left."

"*Every* car?"

"Yeah, I mean *every* car. All going off in different directions, trying to confuse us. There's no way to follow all of them."

"It doesn't matter. I know where they're going."

"Are you gonna tell me?"

"Yeah, I guess I owe you that much, J.D. They're going up to Elysium."

"Elysium? What the hell are they doing? Kidnapping Apollo?"

"It's a long story and I don't have time to tell it to you, but all hell's about to break loose up at the local Parthenon."

"Well, I can't do anything up there. I'm on the Red Squad, and Apollo is the demigod of a lot of things, but as far as I know he's not the demigod of communist subversion. Even the God Squad can't do much up there without a warrant. A demigod's property doesn't have the same kind of diplomatic immunity as a consulate, but the LAPD can't go in there unless we've got a piece of paper signed by a judge."

"Probably better that you stay out of this," I said.

"Probably better that you and Trixie stay out of this."

"We're a long way past better. We have to finish what we started."

"Hey buddy, just be careful. Don't let this case finish you."

There were people flooding out of the gates of Elysium, not in cars, but on foot. There were the rich swells invited to the party, men in fine suits who had thrown away their hats, women in gowns who had thrown away their stiletto-heeled shoes, as well as the beautiful youths hired as flesh and blood objects of art, all running as fast as they could away from Apollo's estate.

"I guess we got here just in time," Trixie said.

We couldn't get the car inside the gate, so we just pulled alongside the road and stopped. Terrified guests kept running past us. The flood of them never seemed to slow. It must've been one hell of a party that night until all hell broke loose.

We got out and made our way towards the gate. I had the magazine bag around my shoulder and the machine gun in my arms, and nobody seemed to notice. It was just perfectly normal. A guy in a suit, a dame, and a Colt Monitor made their way upstream against the current, and nobody cared.

"*Raus, raus,*" someone was yelling from inside the gate near where they had once had their valet service.

I peeked around the corner, and through the mass of humanity that was running away, I could see a couple of brownshirts with Schmeissers urging the people to run, and not particularly gently. One older man fell, tearing the knees out of his slacks, and one of the Nazis kicked him. He's staggered on.

"The Reich is here already," I told Trixie. "Just two of them. I expect the rest of the bad guys have already gone up to the mansion. The only question is whether the Russians are here already."

"What do we do?"

I didn't pause to answer. This is one of those times when action beats words. I made my way forward against the flow of bodies, pivoting and zigging and zagging my way toward the two brown shirts. They were mostly looking up the hill towards the mansion and not paying much attention to the people they had driven past them. That gave me the edge I needed. By the time one of the Nazis turned and saw me, he didn't actually see me. He saw the butt of the Colt Monitor coming towards his face. Then he saw stars. His buddy saw him crash to the ground, his nose spurting, and he looked over at me just in time to get a nice butt stroke to the head. Fritz went down for the count as well.

"Come on, Trixie!"

We got a few steps, but we heard a commotion behind us. Passing all the terrified guests running away, we could see at least three cars making their way through the flow and not being particularly choosy about the occasional folks running into the radiator grills.

"Mickey Cohen," Trixie said.

"He didn't trust me to call. He was watching this place, just like the Nazis." I figured sometime I was going to have to deal with disappointing Mickey Cohen. Well, no better time than when I had a Colt Monitor slung around my neck.

We started making our way up the covered walk towards the house. There were still guests blowing downward, but fewer and fewer of them. I recognized Boris Karloff fleeing down the sidewalk and pointed out to Trixie that we had just passed Frankenstein.

"You mean Frankenstein's monster," she corrected me.

I wasn't sure what was going to be happening up ahead. I don't know if the Nazis had gotten there first or if the Russians were there already. Maybe the Soviets had made their sacrifice and got their wish granted and we were too late. But we didn't have any other choice but to press on.

It didn't help that there was a pack of mobsters coming up behind us. They didn't notice us among the retreating guests ahead of them on the path, but when they found us, they were probably going to be upset with us.

I glanced back to check their progress. They were in a mass behind us. And behind them, at the gate, another set of cars. Identical cars. And identical men.

"Connolly and the G-men are here, too," I told Trixie as we kept moving up the path, trying not to be knocked over by terrified partygoers.

"This is the social event of the season," observed Trixie. "And I am awfully underdressed."

We got to the edge of the plaza just below the mansion. I could now see several groups of people. One was clearly the Nazis. Major Strasser and Ulysses Merz were there; Strasser looked focused, Merz looked terrified.

The other was Russians, and it looked like they were carrying a couple prisoners along with them. And there were armed satyrs, too, plus at least a couple of centaurs as well. The cliques were all looking at each other, the Nazis with their German submachine guns, the Russians with their Russian ones, and Apollo's personal guards with their bows and arrows.

I didn't want to step out into the garden and become part of that, but I didn't have a lot of choice with Mickey Cohen and the gang coming along behind. Tire Iron Marv was there, and I could see Teddy the Weasel with his Tommy gun and a huge grin. So were another eight or nine mugs and gunsels. Right behind them were at least a dozen of J. Edgar's finest led by Special Agent John Connolly.

I stepped out onto the plaza with my Colt Monitor up, aiming back at the guns and bows aiming at us. With Trixie behind me, I moved towards a stone garden box that might provide cover. At worst, I figured I'd catch the first few shots. Maybe she could dodge while they were turning me into a pincushion, but probably not.

The band of about a dozen Russians was to my right. They were holding up Charles Gaultier, who looked like he was about to give up the ghost if giving up the ghost was something demigods could do without artificial intervention. He was wrapped with the silver chains, but in his condition they could have kept him tied up with silver thread. They had Dr. Hollister, too. Apparently, they had sparked him up with a dose of amphetamines because he was wide awake and straining at his steel handcuffs.

The surviving Smirnoff was there, standing next to a headless statue of Apollo with his PDD – 34/38 in one hand, glaring at me. If this all went to hell, I had a pretty good idea where his first burst was going be aimed.

Another dozen Nazis were on my left, with the glowering Major Strasser holding a Walther P-38 in his hand. Herr Merz was there as well, looking terrified. The rest of the Hitler youth had their MP-40 submachine guns.

Up near the stairs leading to the balcony in front of the mansion were another dozen satyrs and their half-horse cavalry. They had their bows out.

Trixie and I moved off the head of the path, with me pointing my machine gun alternately at the Reds, at the Nazis, and at the goat and horse-men of Apollo's personal Praetorian Guard.

Then the mob crested the hill. Mickey Cohen was in the lead with his .38, followed by his legion of Tommy gun-wielding thugs. They seemed a little bit surprised to see the situation and immediately became as deliberate and slow as everybody else as they moved to their slice of our little circle.

Everyone was watching, everyone was waiting, no one was making any sudden moves.

The last civilian guests filtered out of the plaza. It was just us participants in this mess now, or at least it was until a few seconds later when the clump of FBI agents topped the hill with their own Tommy guns and .38s. They seemed surprised to find themselves in that predicament. They stopped and aimed at the others while Special Agent Connolly thought about what to do.

It was yet another Mexican standoff, except no self-respecting Mexican would be dumb enough to get himself into that situation. Actually, with so many different contenders, it was more of a South American standoff.

"I'm seeing a man named Elvis and a very talkative, tiresome man who likes feet," Trixie whispered to me.

"Not now," I hissed as we all looked back and forth at each other, careful not to move too quickly and spook anyone else. I did a quick estimate and figured there were ten guns pointed at us alone.

"If someone gets stupid, we're all going to die," I whispered. "If we live through this, it'll be a miracle."

At that moment, Special Agent John Connolly stood up straight and began to speak.

"You asked for a miracle?" Trixie whispered. "I give you the FBI."

"We are federal agents of the Federal Bureau of Investigation!" Connolly bellowed as if anybody was unclear about that. He even took out his badge with his left hand, waving it around to show us. "And you are all under arrest!"

It didn't seem his men were expecting the others to surrender. They were pointing their guns just as intensely after he spoke as before.

"Hey, G-man, I don't think you understand the situation here. You boys are outgunned. In fact, all of you mugs are outgunned," Mickey Cohen shouted. "For every one of us up here, I got twenty more boys down the hill just waiting for me to whistle. So, why don't you play this smart? You Russians, give me the demi, the doc, and the potion, and I will call it even. You, Nazis, you get the same deal. You get to walk away in one piece. And you goat-boys, my deal is with your boss, so step aside. As for you, Loud and Gamble, I'll deal with you two later. So, just put down your iron and walk away, or else."

"Be silent, you two-bit Jewish hoodlum!" shouted Major Strasser. "Those men *und* that serum by rights belong to Adolf Hitler and the Third Reich!"

"*Nyet!*" Smirnoff yelled. "They are the property of the working class and its sole legitimate representative, the Communist Party of the Union of Soviet Socialist Republics!"

Then the biggest and ugliest of the satyrs yelled something that sounded like "Eeagh!"

They all looked at me now, expecting something. But I was getting tired of this, so I let them have a piece of my mind. After all, when in doubt, go over the top.

"Look, if we're going to have a shootout, somebody start it by pulling a trigger!"

No one took me up on it. They just stared at me.

There was a light from the balcony in the mansion. I could feel a presence, and I knew immediately what it was. I glanced up – everybody glanced up, ignoring their competitors who, a moment before, they had been drawing down upon.

It was Apollo, in a radiant white robe, looking at least seven feet tall though I knew he wasn't. He had his crown of laurel leaves around his perfectly formed head and hair, and he stepped casually to the end of the balcony to survey the combatants arrayed below him in the plaza garden. He waited for a long moment before speaking, ensuring every eye was upon him, every ear was open to him.

"Welcome to my home. How kind of you to join me here. We all know the reason you came. Who has what I seek?"

"We have brought you your prize, and you must fulfill the bargain!" Smirnoff shouted.

"The communists have the property. How ironic. But it appears that if you attempt to deliver it, your rivals will object."

"We will object!" shouted Major Strasser.

"Yeah, we'll lodge an objection, too," interjected Mickey Cohen.

"This is a national security matter for the federal government!" Connolly shouted irately. "You are subject to the United States of America, Apollo!"

"Yes, quite. I have been subject to the governments of impudent mortal men for far too long. But that ends tonight. It all ends tonight."

"Here, let us show you that the potion works!" shouted Smirnoff. "And when you perform our task, we will give it to you."

"And what task would you have me do for the chance to die like a mortal?"

"You must use your power to go kill the traitor Trotsky! You can vanish to his hideout in Mexico, slay him, wish yourself back, and then the potion is yours!"

"Uh, no, that's the waste of a chance to use your power," Mickey Cohen said. "The potion belongs to us, and we've got a real task for you, Apollo. But I don't think Special Agent Connolly's boss is gonna like it too much."

"Are you threatening Director Hoover?" shrieked the scandalized Connolly.

"I'll be sure to ask Apollo here not to get any blood on his dress," Cohen told the G-man, and I prepared for the silver to start flying. It did not, not yet.

Then the demigod looked in my direction, and I could feel it, his presence and his power.

"Miss Gamble and Mr. Loud, I am surprised to see you here. Do you have a request, too, should you give me the serum?"

"How can you do this to your own son?" Trixie shouted. The demigod frowned, and I could feel his anger.

"Miss Gamble, you too would sacrifice anything and anyone if you were facing the horror of eternal life."

"Enough! These running dog lackeys of the imperialists have no say in this matter!" Smirnoff shouted. "We communists have the serum. You must deal with us and us alone!"

"I could just take the serum from you," Apollo suggested.

"I will let the vial break, and then it will all be gone," Smirnoff said, taking a vial of a viscous black liquid out of a leather bag with his left hand. "And I will kill this doctor so no one can ever make any more."

He handed the precious vessel and bag to one of his minions so he could devote both hands to his submachine gun. The minion tucked the vial away in the bag for safekeeping.

"It appears then we have quite the quandary," Apollo observed. "I think the best course of action is to allow you all to decide among yourselves who will present me with the test subject and the serum. Of course, my own guards might end up with it themselves and save me the trouble of granting your petty requests. I will return when you make your decision, but don't take long. Every additional moment I am alive is agonizing."

He made a flawless about-face and walked back into the darkness of the balcony.

Once again, we were back to our standoff. I saw a Russian lick his lips nervously over his submachine gun. One of the Nazis was shaking. Teddy the Weasel was enjoying it, imagining who he would pump bullets into first. One of the FBI men wet himself.

In the end, it was probably inevitable that the first shot would come from Major Strasser. The Nazis had a knack for starting wars.

The Gestapo officer looked around at the other clumps of opponents and then decided to go for the head of the biggest snake. His arm extended and his Walther P-38 pointed at Smirnoff and squeezed the trigger.

Of course, he was about 40 yards away, and it was a 9mm round. He was apparently out of practice because the bullet missed Smirnoff, but hit the NKVD minion with the leather bag square in the forehead. The Russian dropped the bag, and everyone on the plaza held his breath. There was no sound of breaking glass.

The minion blinked and fell, and the battle commenced before his corpse hit the marble floor.

If I was going to shoot anybody in the world, it would be Germans. I don't know how many of these Nazis were German and how many were at least nominally American, but I figured it was no time to be picky. I heaved the Colt Monitor up to my shoulder and aimed center mass at the nearest one.

The thirty-aught six bullet is something you can use for deer or bear or elk or werewolves. It's a big bullet, and it hits hard. My shoulder felt it as I squeezed off a three-round burst. The Nazi I hit felt it as most of his sternum exited his back and the impact knocked him on his tailbone, sending his Schmeisser skittering across the marble.

By that time, everything was going off, with everybody squeezing off rounds. Trixie grabbed me and pulled me down. I fell, thank goodness. We are next to a marble garden bed, and the bullets aimed at us – there were a lot of bullets aimed at us – either sliced through the flowers and plowed into the dirt or slammed into the marble, spraying us with chips and dust.

"Stay here, stay down!" I ordered Trixie. Without a gun, she wasn't going to be much use in a firefight. Spraying wildly with my machine gun to try to suppress the guys trying to suppress me, I rushed away toward the corner of the garden box where there stood a statue of Apollo, whose head I had watched vanish a couple days before. Bullets were slamming off it now, coming from all directions. I looked up and saw on the steps up to the mansion, a satyr pulling back his bowstring as he aimed towards my face. All satyrs look the same to me, but I couldn't help but think this was the one that had just barely missed me when he planted his arrow through the seat of my car. I dove just as he let fly, and if I hadn't, I would've been a private investigator shish kebab.

But the guy tried to kill me, and I couldn't let that go. I flipped the Monitor up and rested it on the marble edge of the garden box. Ignoring the bullets whizzing over my head and kicking up dirt all over me, I took aim at my assailant and squeezed the trigger.

It took under two seconds to kick out the remaining rounds in that magazine. Mr. Bonfilio had kindly given me enough silver tracer rounds to load those magazines with one tracer for every four bullets. As the sun set, it helped me aim.

The Monitor was loud and its kick was heavy, bruising my shoulder and blowing out puffs of gas and hot brass as I watched orange fingers of fire reach out and touch the satyr archer. They touched him good and hard. He slammed back, with his bow and arrow flying and his body collapsing against the marble steps.

I looked over and Mickey Cohen was squeezing off shots from his revolver in the direction of the Russians while Teddy the Weasel was emptying a drum into a couple of G-man. The Germans were firing their machine pistols wildly, with one cutting a satyr almost in half before the satyr's friend stuck an arrow through where his heart would have been if he wasn't a Nazi.

A centaur was galloping across the marble garden, waving a scimitar which he used to take the head off one of the Russians. I saw Smirnoff firing his submachine gun in the direction of the horse-man, but it was only a flesh wound. It didn't stop his ride, and I could see the equine assassin was targeting Trixie. The centaur accelerated to a full gallop, waving his sword. Knowing centaurs, cutting her to ribbons probably wasn't all he had in mind.

I shouted for her to watch out, but she couldn't hear me with all the deafening gunfire. I finished my reload and pulled back the bolt just as he raised his scimitar to strike. He was fast but not fast enough. I pumped at least a half dozen rounds into his chest, and he broke down and collapsed in a heap, rolling over and over and ending up in a flower bed just above where Trixie was taking cover.

I pivoted and emptied the rest of the shots at the Russians. I couldn't see either Gaultier or the doctor anymore. I assumed they were on the ground taking cover. It looked like I got a hit or two on the communists. That made me feel good – either a communist or a Nazi notch on my stock was a win in my book.

The FBI agents were really taking it on the chin. I saw one hit by a barrage of Schmeisser slugs and fall dead into a koi pond. Soon, only a couple agents were still shooting back, and Connolly wasn't one of them. He was lying there on the marble, and I could see he was all done.

Among the mob guys, Teddy the Weasel was having a high time of it. He was blasting away at anything that moved with his Thompson. But most of his henchmen were finished, bleeding or bled out on the marble, a couple with arrows sticking out of them. As for Mickey Cohen, it appeared he had decided that discretion was the better part of valor and hit the bricks. He would have some explaining to do to Bugsy Siegel.

I moved back to where Trixie was, pausing to spray some more thirty-aught six shots in the direction of the satyrs. By this time, the centaur cavalry was gone – if you see a half-man, half-horse thing coming in your direction, you're naturally going to put all your bullets into it, and that's what everybody did.

"I'm fine," she told me.

I took out another Nazi with a blast to the belly, and I was so busy keeping their heads down that I didn't see Smirnoff running in my direction with that weird commie submachine gun of his. In an impersonal gunfight, I didn't count on him making it personal. Of course, I did smoke his brother.

I had left Trixie lying down under the cover of the marble flower bed wall while I went back to the other end of it where I could use the decapitated statue of Apollo for protection. Smirnoff came down and around behind me, taking the corner where Trixie lay with that gun of his ready to turn me into the Soviet version of Swiss cheese. I had just emptied a magazine and was reaching into the bag for a replacement. It was my second to last one. After that, I would be out, and the Colt Monitor would be just a big, heavy hunk of metal.

So, when I saw him, my gun was unloaded. I didn't have a chance. He was going to do to me what Apollo wanted to do to himself, and there was not a damn thing I could do about it as he ran towards me, raising his gun, seeing nothing but me with a target on my head.

But Trixie could do something about it, and she did something simple and elegant. She raised one of those gorgeous gams of hers and caught Smirnoff in the shin as he sprinted. The gigantic Russian's bulk and weight, once an asset when terrorizing prisoners, now became a liability. He stumbled and fell, the submachine gun skittering away from him across the marble, coming to rest a dozen feet from him.

I knew I had one chance and I pulled that last magazine out of the bag and slid it into my weapon even as he got to his feet and then dove for the PPD – 34/38.

He got his hands on it just as I pulled back the bolt, and as he brought the weapon to bear, over his sights, he could see that I already had a bead on him.

I pulled the trigger.

I'm not sure about the ballistics involved. I'm not a technician, just an amateur with a professional interest in how bullets do what they do. There's a lot of talk among guys in my line of work about whether silver bullets are as effective on mortals as they are on supernatural beings. But I'll tell you one thing. At twenty feet, when you're dumping a whole magazine of thirty-aught six slugs into somebody, it doesn't matter whether they're lead, silver, or aluminum.

Maybe Smirnoff wasn't much of a dancer in life – who knows? – but he sure was in death. Each one of the slugs hit him like a jackhammer, jolting him back and forth, up and down. I kept my finger on that trigger, and I kept spraying. I wasn't taking any chances with that slab of Bolshevik beef. I stitched him from stem to stern, and when I was done with him, he had a face only a mother could love, if that mother was Medusa.

The Colt Monitor finally ran dry. That's when Smirnoff dropped, and it took a few seconds for him to stop twitching. And then I heard it.

The silence.

20.

Maybe the gun battle was over. Maybe people were just taking a breather. Maybe people were taking a hike and getting the hell out of there. That would've been the common sense thing to do. But I wasn't doing it, so I expected most of my opponents probably weren't either.

I grabbed the last magazine for the Colt Monitor and changed out the empty. A few feet away, the messy corpse of Comrade Smirnoff was staring at me, one eye open. Of course, he only had one eye left. Trixie was behind him, and I saw that she had that chrome Star pistol of hers in her hand.

"Where the hell did that come from?" I asked.

"A lady never tells."

That little .25 probably wouldn't be much use if the gunfight kicked off again, but it had better range than one of her deadly hairpins.

I raised my head up above the chipped and jagged marble edge of the garden box. It had been chewed up by bullets flying in at us from all directions. There was also an arrow sticking into the dirt in front of me, courtesy of some satyr. I could now see that all of the goat-men were sprawled out on the mansion's steps, shot to pieces. One centaur was lying on his side, his rear hoof limply kicking.

From my vantage point, I could see Major Strasser and several of his Nazis, including Merz, moving across towards where the Russians were. There wasn't much movement over there, just a lot of shapes lying on the ground. Considering how I just shot their leader to pieces, I didn't expect much more fight out of the communists.

But then, I wasn't too thrilled that the Nazis looked like they were gaining the upper hand.

The brownshirts got to where the Russians were, and I lifted up the Colt to hose them down, but one of them picked up a crumpled shape from the ground. It was Doc Hollister. Another lifted up what I had to assume was Charles Gautier. He was a mess, too, but moving. Major Strasser himself rifled through the leather bag and then held the vial of serum aloft.

They started hustling the captives forward toward the bottom of the stairs that rose up to the mansion. I didn't dare shoot. Doc Hollister was mortal and who knows what a silver bullet was going to do to Charles Gaulthier in his condition.

Then I felt it, the presence of the returning demigod. Only it was weaker than before – definitely weaker, as if he'd been drained by something. Apollo stepped out of the darkness on the balcony and looked down on the tableau before him of dead bodies and dropped weapons. From where I was, I could almost see a smile. He was pleased, as if this was some sort of sacrifice to him. After centuries of being denied sacrifices, he was enjoying himself.

But yet there was that edge of exhaustion.

"It seems you have won the competition, Major Strasser," the demigod said, his voice booming across the garden.

"We have the test subject, we have the serum," Major Strasser announced. He and his men stopped at the foot of the stairs, looking up at the demigod before them.

"We need to make this quick," Apollo told him from on high. "There are many mortals trying to get into Elysium now, police, mobsters, and such, and I will not be able to hold them back for long."

I heard a crash in the distance behind me, and then another, and I looked over my shoulder down the hill and saw a car flying through the air, then another, and another. There was smoke and fire, shouts and screams. Apollo was unleashing his powers to keep everyone else at bay; that was why he was growing exhausted.

If I was going to do anything, I needed to be closer. I turned to Trixie at the other end of the garden box.

"Stay here," I said, and I ran forward, keeping low, heading towards a three-foot wall that gave me some cover from the demigod and the Nazis. I was about 50 feet away from them.

If Apollo saw me, he didn't react. I know the Nazis didn't see me because they didn't pump me full of bullets. They were focused on closing the deal.

I was lifting my Colt Monitor when Trixie knelt by my side. She had sprinted to me.

"You could've been killed," I snapped.

"It's not my time," she said, dismissing my concerns while watching what was going on in front of us.

"We must now consummate the bargain!" Major Strasser said, holding up the vial. His black leather trench coat swirled around him as he gestured for emphasis.

But a couple surviving mobsters objected to that. One was Tire Iron Marv, and the other was Teddy the Weasel. They both stood up and fired their Tommy guns at the four surviving Nazis. One of the them went down. One other pivoted and fired back wildly while Merz cowered. Ted sprinted in our direction, managing to dive behind cover, but Tire Iron Marv wasn't as lucky.

Apollo pointed at him with an outstretched finger, a perfect finger on a perfect arm attached to a perfect torso. A blue ray, crackling like lightning, extended out and down through the air toward the unfortunate mobster, who was still blazing away with his submachine gun. The ray touched him in the chest, and he promptly exploded. Tire Iron Marv simply detonated in a cloud of smoke and red goo.

Apollo retracted his finger, hand, and arm and then smiled. It had been a long time since he had been free to exercise his powers to their maximum, and it clearly felt delicious. He regarded the red stain on the marble with satisfaction. He must have felt like a true demigod again for the first time in centuries.

Major Strasser regarded the dead mobster without pity and similarly looked at the dying body of his acolyte. But there was one more casualty. Doctor Hollister fell to his knees, one of the .45 slugs having penetrated his back. He then toppled forward, dead.

It was of no consequence to either the Gestapo officer or the demigod. Hollister was no longer required and his expiration was, therefore, irrelevant.

"What bargain do you propose, mortal?" Apollo asked imperiously.

Strasser again held up the vial of serum.

"The Third Reich will give you the gift of death," he said. "When you give us our prize."

"Which is?"

"To earn it, you will use your powers to go to London and return with what *der Führer* seeks – the head of Winston Churchill!"

Apollo smiled.

"A gift that would mean victory in your mortal war. I salute your wisdom. Your competitors had no such great ambition. Comrade Stalin would have the head of one of his minor rivals, this ridiculous Trotsky fellow. The criminals would have the life of their foe at the FBI, the transvestite. I am unsure what the FBI agents would have wanted me to do for the government of the United States of America," Apollo said. Then he had a thought that amused him, maybe a prediction, and added: "Perhaps they would have locked me in a wooden crate and stored me away in the back corner of some gigantic government warehouse."

"Do you accept or not?" demanded Major Strasser. The Nazi officer was not much for small talk.

"I can get a clean shot," I whispered to Trixie as I peeked over the upper edge of the wall.

Before she could respond, I heard footsteps and, as I turned my head Teddy the Weasel slid in next to us below the wall, submachine gun in hand, all cracked smile and crazy eyes.

He came too fast for me to swing the Monitor around and take him out of the picture, but he wasn't gunning for me or Trixie. If he had been, that would've been that.

"Looks like we're allies now, Loud," he giggled as he settled in next to me, weapon at the ready, head below the edge of the wall. "We go together like peaches and cream."

"Don't do anything crazy," I told him. "Not yet."

He laughed the laugh of a man in a rubber room.

"But I like crazy." That was for certain. Anybody with a drop of sanity would have run the hell away when all his friends got iced and his boss went over the hill. But no one ever accused Teddy the Weasel of being sane.

"First, you must prove to me the serum works," Apollo declared.

Major Strasser either grunted or gave Merz an order in German—it was always hard for me to tell the difference. In any case, the Merz and the other surviving brownshirt each grabbed one of Charles Gaultier's shoulders and raised him to his feet.

"Time to feed them some lead," whispered a giddy Teddy the Weasel as he lifted his gun. "I mean silver."

The sociopathic mobster was right. It was time for action.

"Give him the serum!" Apollo ordered the Nazis. They forced the son of the demigod to his knees in front of Major Strasser. "If it works, and he dies, we have a deal."

"You're my father," moaned Charles Gaultier. "How can you do this to me, your own son?"

Apollo snorted in amusement.

"You don't understand your own family at all," he scoffed. "But, in fact, I'm doing you a great favor."

"Now!" Teddy the Weasel said urgently.

"When in doubt, go over the top," I muttered as I lifted up my heavy automatic rifle.

"No," said Trixie, grabbing my arm. "Don't do it."

I looked at her, offended and angered. Who was this woman to tell me what to do?

"You'll die if you do," she said plainly.

"Let's go!" the gangster urged.

As I looked into Trixie Gamble's eyes, every instinct told me to ignore her, not listen, and charge blindly into danger.

And a tiny voice inside me, almost imperceptible yet clear, told me, "She's right." It was a very small voice, dwarfed by the thunderous howling of the voices in my head that commanded me to defy her. I listened to it.

I paused.

"Yellow bastard!" spat Teddy the Weasel as he scrambled over the wall with his Tommy gun in hand.

"Not yet," Trixie cautioned me. She was waiting for something, a sign only she could detect. I trusted her instincts.

Ted the Weasel rushed forward through the garden box, firing from the hip at the Nazis fifty feet away. He put a burst in the chest of one of the Nazis who was holding up Charles Gaultier by the shoulder – again, Merz lucked out – but Ted the Weasel never had a chance to shoot the American traitor.

Apollo's arm came up, and his finger pointed. There was the blue lightning that streaked out from the tip of his digit, lightning that was less intense this time yet still effective enough. It struck Teddy the Weasel in the chest, and he detonated there in the flower garden. Pieces of his submachine gun, his suit, and himself exploded in all directions.

"Now, we'll never get to hear his origin story," mourned Trixie.

"His what?" I asked, but then I decided to focus on not getting blown into atoms by an angry demigod.

Apollo dropped his arm, breathing heavily. Major Strasser, the vial of serum in his hand, looked back at the red splotch that had once been the mob hitman and turned to Apollo's son.

"Hold him," he ordered Merz. The American brownshirt leader grabbed Charles Gaultier by both shoulders and held him unsteadily. Apollo stared, breathing heavily. In the distance, down the hill, there was more metal twisting and explosions. The demigod was depleting his power rapidly, and I could see his exertions were taking a toll on him.

"You handle Apollo," Trixie told me. I didn't know exactly what she was going to do, but I was going to back her play all the way.

Trixie and I stepped up so that our heads and shoulders were above the edge of the marble wall, and I took aim with my Colt Monitor. I put the front sight post on the middle of the demigod's toga and pulled the trigger.

The silver rounds tore from the barrel of my gun, one in four of them a bright orange streak. The barrage of silver headed straight for Apollo, whose head snapped in my direction even as I squeezed the trigger. He saw the slugs coming, and his hand flew up, his palm flat, stopping the ten bullets of my first burst in mid-air. They hung there, silver cylinders, spinning in the sky. They would not have killed him, of course, but they would have hurt him. They would have marred his face and body, the silver burning his flesh until they were removed and he healed.

But while Apollo was avoiding the fusillade from my automatic rifle, he was unable to stop Trixie. She took careful aim because she knew she would have only one shot, and it had to count. She waited until it *felt* right to fire. She wasn't shooting with her hand or even her eye, but with the power Apollo had laid upon her family. When she felt it was right, she squeezed the trigger, not a moment before or after.

The tiny .25 caliber bullet raced out of the barrel and across the fifty feet to just below the outstretched hand of the Gestapo major, the one that held the vial of serum. The bottle shattered, and shards of glass bit into his palm. The liquid splattered on the marble, dark smoke rising from it as it was exposed to the air.

Major Strasser looked in horror at the priceless potion spilled out on the marble, ignoring the blood on his hand.

Apollo shrieked, an alien and inhuman cry that burned our ears and seemed to shake the ground. He waved his palm, and the bullets caught in mid-air scattered away across the ground as he turned his full attention on Major Strasser.

Apollo's face, once the ideal of perfection, was now a terrifying rictus of horror and rage.

"It was not me!" the Nazi screamed as Apollo's full fury turned upon him. Major Strasser stood where he was as if he had been nailed into the marble itself. Merz dropped Charles Gaultier and fled. I mentally added the Nazi coward to the Loud List of guys needing some payback. His time would come.

Strasser's eyes grew wide with terror. It seemed as if the sky darkened and the estate lights faded as Apollo rose up to seemingly a dozen feet tall, stretching out his arm at the Nazi. But there would be none of the relative mercy of the blue lightning for Major Strasser.

This was a sickly yellow light that flowed down from Apollo's outstretched hand to encompass Major Strasser. The Nazi screamed and shook and then began to smoke. His face began to melt, first white and pink, then red as the flesh gave away to bone. His skull was a silent scream. It seemed to go on forever, though it was probably less than thirty seconds, but he melted there on the marble into a bubbling puddle of obscene liquid flesh. The only things solid left when it was over were his black hat, P-38, and leather coat.

Apollo lowered his hand and seemed to shrink back to his regular size. The light seemed to come back. He fell to one knee, but then he looked in our direction, his eyes meeting ours. That presence, that power, was still there but diminished.

"Loud, Gamble, we are not finished!" he bellowed.

I stood up with a Colt Monitor pointed straight at him. Demigod or no demigod, my patience was gone. My ten or so remaining silver bullets might not kill him, but the pain they would certainly cause him, especially in his weakened state, seemed to be the only bargaining chip I had.

"Now what?" I asked, walking forward with Trixie at my side.

"Now, I will give you what you both denied me," the demigod said. "I may be temporarily weakened, but I'm still strong enough to kill you both."

"And if we are not alive to provide you with an alibi, they will come for you," I said. "Do you think we wouldn't have prepared for this? Do you think that if you kill us, a full account of everything you've done won't go to the authorities? Do you think you'll somehow avoid spending the rest of eternity wrapped in a silver coffin at the bottom of the ocean?"

Apollo laughed, a bitter laugh that mocked the very concept of laughter.

"Foolish mortal," he said. "You're lying. You did not make any preparations to do that because you could never have predicted this would happen."

"But I could have," Trixie said. "And I did."

Apollo considered the situation for a moment and then shared an ironic smile.

"You are hard to read, but I think you're lying," he said.

"You *think*," Trixie said. "Are you willing to bet eternity on that?"

Apollo laughed his bitter laugh once again.

"I allow you to live, and whatever story we tell the authorities paints me as a hero instead of a villain," he offered. "Remember, I will regenerate my powers in the coming days, and I may not be able to take on the entire United States government, but I can find and kill you both before they exile me to the deep."

He didn't have to remind me of that. I was well aware of how dangerous someone was when he had nothing left to lose. But that couldn't be the whole deal. Trixie beat me to the next part of the bargain.

"You are the demigod of healing," she said. "You also need to heal your son."

Apollo looked down on the prostrate body of Charles Gaulthier, who was barely moving.

"I can heal him. Is that all?"

"One more thing," I added, remembering to cross Merz off the Loud List. "You know that bigmouth Nazi coward who just ran away after seeing everything that happened and who is probably halfway down the hill and running right into the arms of the LAPD God Squad? You need to do that thing where he explodes."

"Gladys told me this was probably where you would be," Trixie said as she walked across the sand towards me.

I was sitting on the beach, looking out at the Pacific Ocean, not far south of Malibu. Out in the water were a few young guys who rode boards in the waves. They called it "surfing." I had my own prediction. I predicted that the sport would be big someday.

"Want a drink?" I said, offering up the half-full fifth of Maker's Mark I had been nursing.

"It's 9 a.m.," Trixie said, sitting down beside me.

"I know. You want some?"

She took the bottle, knocked back a slug, and handed it to me.

"Charles Gaultier is back home and in good health again," she said. "But I doubt he'll be attending any family reunions."

"I don't think they bother celebrating Father's Day at Elysium," I said. "No one at the FBI or the LAPD believes a word of our story, but after the last eyewitness went poof and a demigod gave a statement backing us up, they are closing down the investigation. A bunch of Nazis and communists decided to shoot it out at Elysium. A bunch of mobsters happened to be there. And some FBI agents got caught in the middle. Case closed."

"I think it's to everybody's advantage that this case is closed," Trixie observed. That was the way of Lost Angeles. In this city, there were lies, truths, and inconvenient truths. This case involved a lot of inconvenient truths. No one was going to cry because they had to wave goodbye to it.

"I lost my client, but I think I did right in the end by helping you save yours," Trixie said. She hit the bottle again.

"You did."

"Why did you listen to me?" she asked. "That was my family's curse. No one listens to us."

"I didn't want to," I admitted. "Everything in my head told me to ignore you except one little voice. Maybe the curse was weakened because Apollo was weak. Maybe I'm not as dumb and stubborn as people say. Maybe, over the last few days, you earned my trust."

"I am very glad you didn't blow up into a million pieces," she said.

"That's one of the nicest things anybody's ever said to me," I replied. I wasn't kidding.

She smiled and took another sip.

"Apollo got away with it," she said.

"I don't think so," I said. "And I think he has infinity years to think about what he did. In the end, would you rather be him or you?"

"For the first couple thousand years, probably him. After that, not so much."

It was my turn to take a sip. I did, a big one.

"We need to talk about the money," I said.

"It's dirty," Trixie replied.

"Maybe we can clean it up."

"By laundering it?"

I guffawed.

"We should take our fair share, and I mean a pretty fair share. We almost got cacked more times than I can count, and we're not in the charity business."

"What about the rest?"

I had already thought of that. That dirty money would be pristine again if we gave it to Captain Holderman and the veterans home. I made the proposal, and Trixie was on board. In a couple of days, I would drive out and present my old commander with an attaché case containing a very pleasant surprise for his old warriors.

"So, what happens next?" I asked. "Any predictions coming into that head of yours as we sit out here on the beach?"

"Just nonsense words. 'Beach Blanket Bingo,' 'Cowabunga,' and 'Captain Geech and the Shrimp Shack Shooters'."

I took another swig. I needed it.

"Trixie, are you sure you weren't hitting the sauce before you got here?"

She ignored the question. We looked out at the water and the waves for a minute, and then she spoke again.

"Look, Eddie, I think we work together pretty well."

I nodded, and she went on.

"I just got another missing person case. No demigods this time, but it's got a werewolf angle. Vampires, too."

"Somebody's always missing in this town." I took another generous slug of Maker's Mark and stared back out over the ocean before continuing.

"That's why we call it Lost Angeles."

AUTHORS' NOTE

Inevitably, some folks will not dig this novel's vibe. This book may not be their cup of tea, or of bourbon if that's your thing. That's okay. We really enjoyed writing it for you.

Now, some people will be picky about our timeline and how we used mythology. Okay, it's a fantasy book. Calm down. We know that we've played around with the time continuum, but hey, it's fantasy!

We just hope you enjoyed it too, especially all the Easter eggs we dropped in. This is a conservative book even if it does not wear it on its head like a fedora. Sometimes, you have to go in a different direction, but we'll be revisiting Kelly Turnbull soon enough (including in the upcoming graphic novel *Blue Flame*!).

If enough of you enjoyed the adventures of Eddie Loud and Trixie Gamble, you will see them again. In the meantime, thanks for reading!

KAS + IM, April 2025

ABOUT THE AUTHORS

Kurt Schlichter

Kurt Schlichter is a senior columnist for *Townhall*. A Twitter activist (@KurtSchlichter) with over 575,000 followers, Kurt was personally recruited by Andrew Breitbart to write for the original Breitbart sites. Kurt serves as an on-screen commentator and guest host on TV and on nationally syndicated radio programs. Kurt was also a stand-up comic.

Kurt was a successful trial lawyer representing Fortune 500 companies and individuals in matters ranging from routine business cases to confidential political controversies.

Kurt served as an Army infantry officer on active duty and in the California Army National Guard, retiring at the rank of full colonel. He commanded the 1st Squadron, 18th Cavalry Regiment. A veteran of the Persian Gulf War, the Los Angeles Riots, and Kosovo, Kurt graduated from the United States Army War College with a master's degree in strategic studies.

He lives with his wife Irina and their monstrous dogs Bitey and Barkey in the Los Angeles area, and he enjoys sarcasm and red meat.

His favorite caliber is .45.

Irina Moises

Irina Moises was not born here but got here as quickly as she could and is damn grateful- Thank you, God and USA- lives on the sunny side of the world, has been to Europe, went to a school, worked a job or more and married the incredibly multitalented and sexy Kurt Schlichter.

The Kelly Turnbull Novels

People's Republic (2016)

Indian Country (2017)

Wildfire (2018)

Collapse (2019)

Crisis (2020)

The Split (2021)

Inferno (2022)

Overlord (2023)

Also By Kurt Schlichter

Conservative Insurgency: The Struggle to Take America Back 2013-2041 (Post Hill Press, 2014)

Militant Normals: How Regular Americans Are Rebelling Against the Elite to Reclaim Our Democracy (Center Street Books, 2018)

The 21 Biggest Lies About Donald Trump (and You) (Regnery, 2020)

We'll Be Back: The Fall and Rise of America (Regnery, 2022)

The Attack (Kindle, 2024)

NEW NOVELS AND MORE COMING IN 2025 FROM KURT SCHLICHTER

The new novel of America in conflict, *Apocalypse : The Second American Civil War*! Coming Summer 2025

The next *People's Republic* novel, *Panama Red*! Coming Late 2025

The first *People's Republic* graphic novel (with artist Sean Salter), *Blue Flame*! Coming Late 2025